WHEN THE NILE
RUNS RED

WHEN THE NILE
RUNS RED

A NOVEL

DIANN MILLS

MOODY PUBLISHERS

CHICAGO

Cover Design: Brand Navigation
Cover Image: istock Photo
Interior Design: Ragont Design
Editor: Michele Straubel

Library of Congress Cataloging-in-Publication Data

Mills, DiAnn.
When the Nile runs red / DiAnn Mills.
p. cm.
ISBN-13: 978-0-8024-9911-0
ISBN-10: 0-8024-9911-2
1. Sudan--Fiction. 2. Political fiction. I. Title.
PS3613.I567W49 2007
813'.6--dc22

2007016281

We hope you enjoy this book from Moody Publishers. Our goal is to provide high-quality, thought-provoking books and products that connect truth to your real needs and challenges. For more information on other books and products written and produced from a biblical perspective, go to www.moodypublishers.com or write to:

Moody Publishers
820 N. LaSalle Boulevard
Chicago, IL 60610

1 3 5 7 9 10 8 6 4 2

Printed in the United States of America

TO THE SUDANESE SCATTERED
ALL OVER THE WORLD.
GOD WILL BRING YOU HOME.

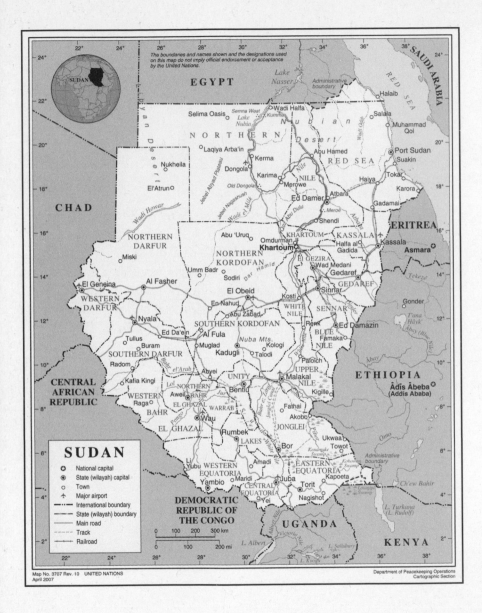

ACKNOWLEDGMENTS

Joseph Ayok, Jason Barrett, Tony Barrett, Frank Blackwood, Jack Casey, Beau Egert, Louise Gouge, Moses Haakim, Dennis Hensley, Mona Hodgson, Thomas Kedini, Rosemary Khamati, Dr. Harry Kraus, Dean Mills, Tom Morrisey, Abraham Nhial, James Solomon Okuk, Anthony Poggo, Rebecca Roberts, Charles Ramadhan, San-tino Swain, Peter Swann, my friends at Metropolitan Baptist Church, and Michele York.

A NOTE TO
THE READER

When the Nile Runs Red is set in Sudan in July 2005. The conflict in southern Sudan began when the northern government in Khartoum declared a jihad or holy war on southern Sudan in the early 80s, and the south responded by forming a rebel army to protect their land and people.

Some of the groups and terms you will encounter in the book are explained below.

Dinka
The largest ethnic tribe in southern Sudan; mainly an agricultural-pastoral people who inhabit the regions of Bahr el Ghazal, Jonglei, southern Kordufan, and the Upper Nile.

John Garang
A Dinka and a Christian, John was educated in the United States and Tanzania, and returned to Sudan to serve in the military. However, he chose to join the newly formed SPLM and became leader of the SPLA. After the peace treaty with the government of Sudan, he became vice president but was killed in July 2005 in a helicopter crash. For more information about him, visit http://en.wikipedia.org/wiki/John_Garang.

Government of Sudan (GOS)
The Muslim government with their capitol in Khartoum; launched a jihad against southern Sudan for over two decades.

Government of National Unity (GNU)
The new government of Sudan formed after the peace treaty in January 2005.

Janjaweed
Armed militia that gathers its fighters from Arab tribes, African Arabs. Notorious for racist activities, massacre, and rape, they are active in the fighting in Darfur (region in western Sudan) and oppose the SPLA as well as the Justice and Equality Movement, who are helping the persecuted people of Darfur. The Sudanese government (GNU) uses the *janjaweed* to handle the tribal disputes in Darfur. Several members of the international community have called their work "genocide."

Lord's Resistance Army
A rebel army originally formed in Uganda. These insurgents are brutal and often raid villages for child soldiers and sex slaves.

Sudan People's Liberation Army (SPLA)
The rebel army that fought for over two decades to defend southern Sudan.

Sudan People's Liberation Army/Movement (SPLA/M)
A collective term indicating a combination of the military and political leaders of southern Sudan.

Sudan People's Liberation Movement (SPLM)
The political wing of SPLA.

We always carry around in our body the death of Jesus, so that the life of Jesus may also be revealed in our body. For we who are alive are always being given over to death for Jesus' sake, so that his life may be revealed in our mortal body. So then, death is at work in us, but life is at work in you.

—2 CORINTHIANS 4:10–12

ONE

Sudan, July 2005
Rainy Season

lasted flying demons. Mosquitoes buzzed around Paul's head, into his ears, and on his lips. If they didn't carry a disease, they pestered a man to death.

"Tell me again about Jesus feeding five thousand men with two fish and five pieces of bread." The Dinka chief leaned in closer. "Sudan needs miracles like this."

Lines bore deep into the man's face, and his voice graveled with age. But his heart and mind reminded Paul of a child's, soaking up the words of Jesus in a way that encouraged his tribe to do the same. The two men sat outside the chief's *tukul* hut before the rains began for the day.

"Thousands of men, women, and children had gathered on a hillside to hear Jesus speak. As the hours—"

Rifle fire pierced the air. Then two more shots cracked. A woman screamed. Several more shots shattered the once-peaceful morning.

"Leave now, my friend." The chief stood and straightened to his nearly seven-foot height. "May God clear a path before you."

Wordlessly, Paul acknowledged the chief's instructions

and snatched up his backpack from inside the *tukul*. He stole behind the hut and saw the path ahead was littered with Government of Sudan soldiers and the fallen bodies of villagers. The GOS knew no gender or age. He touched the 9 mm strapped to his waist.

The chief clamped his hand on Paul's shoulder as if reading his thoughts. "Go. They'll kill us no matter if they find you or not."

The truth rang through Paul's mind. He'd be a prize for any of them. Men, women, and children fled in all directions. He raced toward the tall grass, but a GOS soldier must have spotted him. A bullet whistled to the right of his head.

He maneuvered through the rustling stalks, hunched over as far as possible without losing balance. The forest loomed ahead. Another shot sped past his right shoulder.

Close.

Too close.

Finally his steps sunk into the earthen floor of the forest, and he moved into the shadowed canopy, cool yet foreboding. A few moments later, he skirted around a few trees. He stopped to listen and observe any movement. When he felt certain no one had followed him, he cautiously retraced his steps into the tall grass.

Bent low, Paul peered through the brush to his left. The black-skinned soldiers hadn't moved on. They fired at anything moving. At least he was on foot . . . and alone. The pistol at his fingertips offered little protection with the odds against him. Why were the GOS in the area, unless they were in search of him?

He held his breath. A soldier stole past him. At first the battalion of soldiers spread out about one hundred meters outside the jungle in search of him, but when they didn't find Paul's position, they appeared to give up. Or so it seemed. Khartoum's fighting force oozed cleverness like sweat beaded on Paul's brow. Although a peace treaty had been signed, it didn't stop government soldiers in search of a man accused of treason. Neither did it stop his family from wanting him dead.

Paul maintained his crouched stance behind a pile of rocks and brush that offered a small ditch beneath it for him to hide. He refused to consider snakes. His knees ached, but that was of little consequence compared to what would happen if the soldiers discovered him.

Paul's thoughts lingered on the village he'd left behind, Xokabuc—"We Still Struggle"—where he'd delivered medicine and issued Larson's directives about how to administer it to those suffering from malaria.

He worried about the plight of those who'd survived the initial raid. They'd be questioned and most likely persecuted or killed if they refused to convert to the Muslim faith or provide information about Paul's whereabouts. Loyalty at a price. The sacrifice of these villagers, and others like them, more than bothered him. Many times he'd wondered if his death would lessen their suffering. Long ago he'd set his course to aid the persecuted Sudanese and spread the gospel of Jesus Christ. Nothing had changed, except his ideals rang nobler than the fear clanging through his soul.

Now, as always when he stood in the path of danger, his thoughts turned to his wife. *Lord, take care of Larson if I don't make it.*

His daring frightened her. But as a doctor, Larson often risked her life for the same cause. Together they made a good team—sort of like the Lone Ranger and Tonto.

"He's disappeared," a soldier called in Arabic. "Was it Farid?"

If the enemy soldier looked directly to the east, he'd discover Paul's position. His white T-shirt and khakis made it hard to blend in with the terrain.

"Maybe. We should have found him by now," the commander said. "He either fell into a pit or flew away."

The first soldier walked toward Paul's hiding place, his

attention focused on the ground. *Footprints.* Paul commanded his body not to move. The soldier pointed to spots of trodden grass.

"He headed for the jungle. Come nightfall, the lions will take care of him."

The commander joined him and bent to study the tracks. Paul thought he could hear the blood flow through their veins, smell the stench of their breath. If he was caught, would his wife and friends be safe? Nizam's letter lay in his backpack. Paul needed answers. More, he needed the truth.

"We could trail him, but I'm not so sure he's our man," the commander said.

"One of the villagers said he was Paul Farid just before I shot him."

The commander chuckled. "The infidel said that to save himself. He'd have claimed his mother was Farid."

The two laughed.

The commander stood and stared into the trees. Paul's heart pounded harder than the drums alerting nearby villages of the approaching enemy. The two soldiers scanned every plant and tree, often staring at Paul's rock and brush fortress.

"I saw Farid in Khartoum with the president's family some years ago. It looked like him running from the village. He resembles his brothers, especially Nizam."

My brother who may want me dead?

"Hard to say," the commander said. "Rumors are everywhere, but I'm itching to catch him. The reward would make me a rich man."

The soldier stared straight at the rock and brush where Paul hid. A grin spread across his face. He lifted his rifle and took aim.

❖ ❖ ❖

Larson Farid took a long drink of water and stepped into the sunlight. Home: the village of Warkou, the province of

16

Bahr al-Ghazal, the district of Aweil. The unforgettable Sudan. She had its location memorized as though she'd lifted the words from the pages of a travel brochure. Its hypnotic appeal never failed to draw her into its beauty. The lush, green earth with its abundance of waterfowl beside the Lol River, and the magnificent wildlife—from the tall giraffes to the graceful gazelles to the thick-skinned elephants—painted a pastoral setting. The soil, rich with nutrients, awaited plantings. But nature's cloak hid the turmoil.

Since dawn, patients had trailed toward her clinic, forming an endless line of despair. Weariness settled in her bones. Paul was right. She needed to rest more. Her back ached, and she craved hours of sleep. Queasiness spread through her stomach as though she'd taken a raft down the Nile's rapids. She didn't have time for such nonsense. People needed her.

Larson closed her eyes and willed the sensation to disappear. Why hadn't Paul come home?

He's encouraging and evangelizing, I'm sure. Paul never let an opportunity pass to talk about Jesus. Sometimes she wished he weren't so vocal; she wanted her husband alive.

Larson pressed her lips together. She had work to do. Lots of it. But the uneasiness marching across her mind, coupled with the sickness churning in her stomach, left her apprehensive.

Pushing away the sensation, she beckoned to a woman carrying a naked, sleeping infant—or maybe the baby was dead. A good many of her patients traveled for days to reach her. Too often, the ordeal killed them. She refused to dwell on those unfortunate Sudanese, but instead on those who recovered. They were the lucky ones, the ones who could go on living another day in hope of peace and a better tomorrow.

"Good morning," Larson said in Dinka. "Thank you for bringing your baby to me. I want to see if I can help him." Larson lifted the baby boy into her arms. She couldn't detect a pulse or a heartbeat. Her heart plummeted. The mother's emaciated body told the story.

The day wore on. Weariness wrapped its debilitating clutches around her, but she refused to give in. Perhaps she needed an antibiotic. But the thought of wasting precious medicine on herself didn't sit well. Rest. A few hours' sleep would wipe all this nonsense away.

"Larson," her assistant, Sarah, said, "you don't look so good. Are you sick?" The woman laid a wrinkled hand on Larson's arm.

"Just tired. I plan on going to bed early tonight. Paul will be back soon, and having him here always helps."

"Do you hurt somewhere?" Sarah tilted her face, shiny black from the many beads of perspiration.

Larson added the last stitch to a cut on a boy's forehead. Sarah took over with antiseptic. "I'm simply exhausted, Sarah. In fact, I'm so tired that my stomach is upset."

"How long have you felt like this?" Sarah kissed the young boy's cheek and complimented his bravery.

"A few weeks."

"And your monthly flow?"

Larson stiffened. *No.* She and Paul took precautions for that very reason.

"Children aren't for us. At least not until peace is set into place," he'd said. Combating multiple diseases wasn't the safest environment for a child either. "If you ever become pregnant, I'll insist you head to Nairobi, or better yet, the States," he'd continued. "Until my family is no longer after me, there can be no children."

"The pill will take care of that." The words echoed across her mind. She *had* taken her pills.

Larson paused before summoning another patient. Eight weeks late. She'd attributed the delay to stress and lack of sleep.

Sarah smiled, her face etched with lines of wisdom. "A woman knows no greater joy than to bear a child." She pointed upward. "It makes God's love and the love for your husband a complete circle."

Larson shivered. She should run a urine or blood test to be sure, but not knowing sounded better than learning the truth. She cringed at the thought of Paul's response to such a mess. *This is silly. A false alarm. I should be concentrating on my patients.* "I don't want to talk about this."

"Maybe God has a different plan."

"Not for me."

Sarah turned and tilted her head, as if she hadn't heard correctly.

"Having a baby is a ridiculous idea," Larson said.

The old woman chuckled. "We'll see what the future holds."

Hours later, Larson lay awake on the wooden-framed bed she typically shared with Paul. Despite her overwhelming urge to sleep, her thoughts rushed ahead. Pregnant? A baby would ruin her work—maybe her marriage. As she mulled Paul's declarations over in her mind, she knew he would want only the best for her and his child.

Sudan was not a toddler's playground.

The nagging thought persisted until she rose and made her way through to the clinic. She wouldn't get a moment's peace until she ran a test and found out for sure. As Sarah had said, maybe God's plans were different from theirs. Larson envisioned her husband's dark eyes and tanned skin . . . the shape of his mouth and his thick, nearly black hair. Dare she let her mind drift to thinking about a little girl or boy?

No, this couldn't be happening. More problems were brewing. Paul's brother Nizam had written another letter indicating a desire to see Paul. The thought frightened her. Her husband's Muslim family wanted him dead for converting to Christianity.

Larson completed the test and breathed a prayer for a negative result before taking a look.

Col. Ben Alier narrowed his gaze to concentrate on his orders from the Sudan People's Liberation Army headquarters. The print seemed small, or maybe his creeping over the forty-year mark had affected his eyesight. If it was the latter, that thought did nothing to ease his mind about any of the worries hammering in his head. In fact, hard-to-read print fell under the topic of a minor irritation. The signed peace treaty by the government and the struggling southern Sudanese was another matter.

Colonel Alier,

We are encouraged by the signing of the peace treaty uniting northern and southern Sudan. Khartoum promises to work with the South through the efforts of John Garang, as first vice president and advocate for the South. We are fortunate to be represented by our most highly respected leader. Only through arbitration can the people of southern Sudan be free from oppression and free to utilize our own resources. We have fought hard for self-rule and won. In six years we can vote to become an independent nation. Your presence is requested in Juba beginning 15 August. Our goal will be to focus on the immediate needs of the South and the best way to fulfill our responsibilities to the suffering and oppressed. We appreciate your commitment to the Sudan People's Liberation Army/Movement and your years of sacrificial service. Your contribution is of infinite value to the rebuilding of our country.

Ben lifted his head and closed his eyes just long enough to allow another thought to march across his mind. Incessant pain hammered against his spine and halted his musings. Too many years in the bush had weakened him physically, and now he paid the price. He stared at the letter in his fingertips.

How could the leaders of southern Sudan ever believe in

lasting peace? Khartoum had no reason to keep a cease-fire—other than pressure from the U.S. and the international community. For that matter, the U.S. now focused its attention on the war in Iraq. Sudan's affairs had little to do with U.S. endeavors.

Ben expelled a labored sigh. Every thought for as long as he could remember had centered on some facet of the civil war—the north/south conflict that had ground on for more than twenty years. He argued the points of war, planned strategic battles, or fought the GOS. The three-pointed sword of religion, politics, and oil occupied his waking and sleeping hours.

Shaking his head at the ludicrous thought of peace for a united Sudan, Ben crumpled the paper in his hands. He was proud to be a Dinka, even prouder to be a member of the largest tribe in Sudan, the ones who gave the government the most trouble. He had no intention of discontinuing the fight, any more than the lying GOS had.

"Arab devils. They should be boiled alive."

Commander Okuk entered the tent. After respectfully saluting Ben with his left and only arm, he relaxed. "The men are encouraged about the new peace."

Ben stiffened, and even that sent a surge of pain up his spine. "Good for them."

"Colonel Alier, is this not what we've been fighting for?" Hope rose in the man's voice. "I have known nothing but war since the day my mother gave me life. When my wife and children were killed, I joined and fought with the SPLA."

Ben fought the urge to lay a fist into Okuk's face. "Are you so stupid that you can't see? The last time we were near your village, the GOS had burned everything to the ground and killed the goats and cattle. What was left of your people had been herded into a displacement camp without food and medical help. And you trust a worthless piece of paper?"

The muscles in Okuk's face tightened.

21

"I'm a realist," Ben said. "Let the results speak for those who are committed to the peace process."

The tall, slender Okuk, barely thirty years old, maintained a controlled posture. He'd lost his right arm from a land mine, but that hadn't held him back from learning to shoot with his left. He had served his country three years with both arms and five with one. Ben read the pain in his eyes.

"And I dream of the free world pressing Khartoum to honor the end of bloodshed," Okuk said.

"I do too, but I have little faith in the word of a Muslim." Ben stood and towered over the man, the crumpled letter still in his fist. "I have seen nothing in the past that indicates willingness for the government to make concessions." He shrugged. "Who knows? Perhaps the U.S. has more information about Osama bin Laden's connections to Khartoum. Pressure from the free world to negotiate peace in exchange for monetary aid is another factor to consider."

Okuk nodded. "What are my orders?"

Ben felt the edges of the paper scratching his palm. "We'll move out in the morning as planned. If we encounter the GOS, then we'll find out if they're keeping a cease-fire."

The lines in Okuk's forehead deepened.

"You have a problem with my orders, Commander?"

"No, sir. I will alert the men."

Ben watched Okuk turn and leave. He'd rather die fighting than let the enemy deceive those who believed in southern Sudan. And what would he do in the event of permanent peace?

TWO

———————— ❧ ————————

*P*aul closed his eyes and prayed for Larson and for the work left undone in Sudan. He hoped the bullet pierced straight to his heart, ending any soldier's plan to escort him back to Khartoum. But they wanted him alive, or so he thought. Memories of the GOS's gruesome torture techniques gave him nightmares. The "ghost houses" flashed across his mind. He remembered the screams, the maimed bodies, the hangings, and the government's denial of the death chambers.

"Don't waste your ammo on a snake," the commander said. "The SPLA are certain to be ahead, and we want to surprise them."

From the corner of his eye, Paul saw a green mamba, not ten feet away. He inwardly moaned as it slithered toward him. If he moved, he'd give himself away, but the snake—one of the deadliest reptiles in Africa—had an aggressive reputation.

Several seconds passed while the two GOS soldiers said nothing. No doubt they were watching the mamba move over the brush and rocks.

No one escaped the reptile's fatal bite.

"Must have its eye on something," the commander said. "I'd like to watch."

Paul's pistol rested against his thigh, easy to pull out and fire. He needed to kill the mamba before it reached him. That also meant he'd have to eliminate the two soldiers. The sound of gunfire would bring down the rest of the battalion, still combing the area. To him, preaching "Love your enemies" meant not killing them—unless he had to.

The snake inched closer.

"Come on, soldier. We have kilometers to go, and I don't think the man's here."

"What about Farid?"

The commander shook his head. "Farid? Every scared villager and money-hungry man in the country has seen him. No one has time to chase down every rumor."

"Yes, sir." He paused. "But I did see a man fitting his description fleeing the village."

"As you stated before. But we have orders to overtake an SPLA compound."

Ben's there.

"Yes, sir."

The grass swished against the soldiers' pants, and Paul watched them tramp away. The commander shouted for his men to stop the search and move eastward.

The snake edged closer, squirming over brush and small branches. Its bright-green body extended over three meters in length. Paul had a knife in the side of his boot. If he missed, the mamba would strike. Two more seconds ticked by.

Paul reached for the knife and aimed at the snake, then released it with a snap of his wrist. The blade sunk into the mamba's head, pinning it to the ground. Adrenaline rushed through Paul's body. His ears rang, and he breathed in deeply to calm himself.

Thank You, Lord. He'd live another day. Suddenly the needlelike sensation in his knees became nearly unbearable. Unable to squat any longer, he eased his weight onto straightened legs, stooping over so as not to attract attention from any GOS soldier lagging behind.

After confirming the soldiers had left the area, Paul pulled his satellite phone from his backpack and flipped it open. He must warn Ben at the SPLA compound. The Rhino battalion had taken a three-day reprieve to rest up and gather supplies. Since the peace treaty, their work had officially ended—but that was a story for newspapers and international politicians, not the truth. How had the GOS found out about the compound's secret location?

Ben answered on the third ring.

"Hey, Ben, got a bit of news for you."

"If this has anything to do with Sudan's new government, spare me. I'm not in the mood."

Paul could have spent the next eight hours debating the value of peace, but he understood the deep-rooted problems his friend had with the fledging new government. "This is different, more your style."

"I'm listening. Are you in trouble? Larson okay?"

"Not us, you. I just encountered a whole battalion of GOS headed your way. They got wind of your location somehow."

Ben cursed. "A mole. Too much information has leaked out. And I think he lives in Yar. Commander Okuk says a cousin of his suspects a man living in that village. How far behind us?"

"About thirteen kilometers."

"We're ready," Ben said. "Thanks. I owe you one."

"Join us for dinner soon. It's been too long, and we miss you."

"Right. Real soon."

Paul disconnected the call, knowing how difficult it was for Ben to see Larson and him together. They'd been married for over two years, but Ben still carried the agony of a broken heart.

What a strange threesome they were, proof that war created unique relationships—or rather, God put people together for a purpose. Paul chose to dwell on the latter.

Thoughts of Larson pushed away all other issues raging inside his head. God had blessed him with her love. Her clear blue eyes and sandy-colored hair stayed fixed in his mind. She didn't look the part of a third world doctor. Neither did she complain about their primitive living conditions. He chuckled. Pity the man who ever got in her way or riled her.

He reached inside his backpack and pulled out the letter from his brother Nizam, the third in the last four weeks.

My brother,

I am disappointed that you will not come to Khartoum and meet with me at the Hilton. I want to see you, hear about your new life, and discuss your new faith. We have always been Muslim, and I'm sure this is simply an indiscretion on your part. I'm confused why you left your family when we have established ourselves as advisors to the new government.

I miss you. Let's be brothers again. I understand that you are fearful, and I can arrange secrecy. For now, let's meet near Kibum in Darfur. No one will suspect us there. You haven't answered my previous letters. Write me soon.
Nizam

Paul shook his head, stuffed the letter back into the envelope, and slapped it against his palm. Did his brother think he was a fool? He knew how his family believed: kill the infidel, and Allah will be pleased. But he'd agreed and mailed his reply. How could he refuse when he'd vowed to bring Christianity to all who would listen? Even if it meant his death. Perhaps he should have discussed it with Larson or Ben. This would affect their lives too. In fact, this decision had an impact on everyone he touched.

Unable to wait a moment longer to talk to her, he punched in the code for Larson's phone.

"Hey, gorgeous," he said. "How's the sexiest doctor on the continent?"

"Absolutely perfect. Missing her husband."

"Thanks. Missing you too. How's the clinic?"

"Busy. Some of today's patients have been walking for two weeks."

Paul envisioned the line of diseased and ill people. He should be in Warkou helping her. The patient load had to be staggering, whether she'd admit it or not. "I'll be home tomorrow, and I'll stick around until all those people are treated. Is Sarah holding up okay?"

"She's just fine." Larson laughed, and the sweet sound put him right there beside her—claiming a kiss, wrapping his arms around her waist.

"How about you? Mission accomplished?" Apprehension wove through her words.

"Of course. I delivered the medicine in Xokabuc and visited the chief. We had many converts before, but now everyone is praising Jesus."

"I'm glad." She paused. "Paul?"

"Yes."

"Are you playing Indiana Jones again?"

She's nailed me. "Whatever made you ask that?" He swallowed the ache in his heart for her. And the fear that had raced through him only moments before.

She sighed, and he knew the gesture was for his benefit. "Because you always call me after you've escaped some mess by the skin of your teeth."

"Can't a man call his wife to tell her he loves and misses her?"

"Sure. But your habit is to call early in the morning or late at night . . . or after your life just flashed before your eyes."

"Now, Larson."

"Are you all right?" Panic rose in her voice, and he imagined the tiny lines deepening around her eyes.

"I'm perfectly fine. A dead mamba is glaring at me. But what's a little snake?"

"Why don't I believe you're telling me the whole truth?"

"I have no idea." Paul took another breath and braved forward. "I talked to Ben, invited him to come by."

"He still feels slighted. Oh, I need to go. Call me later?"

Before he could reply, the phone disconnected. What was the rush?

❦ ❦ ❦

Larson hurried by Sarah, who stood in the doorway of the concrete building used as a medical clinic. She rushed past the line of patients while the contents of her stomach lunged to the top of her throat. Sweat soaked her shirt, and her body craved sleep. One o'clock in the afternoon. How would she make it until nightfall? Dizziness blurred her vision. In the next instant, she finished vomiting what little she'd eaten today.

Her thoughts clung to Paul. He'd experienced incredible danger, and his denial spoke fathoms. The source most likely didn't include a snake, unless it was a two-legged one. Larson wiped her mouth with the back of her hand. She felt as though a dreaded disease had attacked her, instead of a living, breathing little human.

A baby. The pregnancy test had already overwhelmed her, and now morning sickness raged through her body, long past the morning. She hoped this misery ended at the first trimester. Sarah sensed the truth already, but no one else must find out until Larson herself was ready to face up to unwelcome reality. What would she do with a baby? How would she balance her work with motherhood? Was it wrong to expect Paul to help?

As horrible as she felt this very minute, with her increasing need to rest and her empty stomach churning with bile, a thin balm of peace covered her heart. She was going to be a mother. Soon there would be three of them. Although the danger of bringing a baby into the world of Sudan distressed her, she had to trust that God had a better plan.

But none of it made any sense. *Pregnant on the pill, in the middle of Sudan's civil war.* Larson shook her head. No point in crying about it. For certain, her faith and her sense of humor would have to get her through.

Larson massaged her temples and straightened. Rats, her back ached. She needed to rinse her mouth, wash her hands, and get back to work. She must figure out how to hide this until she'd had more time to think. Paul couldn't find out yet. She had no intention of telling him until her stomach looked like she'd swallowed a basketball.

"Feeling better?" came a familiar voice.

Larson turned to see Sarah, who handed her a damp cloth. "Thanks, and yes, I'm better." She wiped her face and mouth. "What's a little upset stomach anyway?"

"You want to try eating the clay for the sickness?"

As much as Larson loved and appreciated Sarah, eating salty clay as many Sudanese women did during pregnancy didn't appeal to her. "No, thank you. I'll be fine."

Sarah looked away. "How are you going to keep this from your husband?"

Grateful for the dear woman's discretion, Larson forced a smile. "I'll find a way. Maybe this is the only time I'll be this sick. I can hide a queasy stomach."

"This is not the first time. I've watched you. What about your monthly flow?"

Larson shook her head. "Sarah, with as much time as Paul spends away, I doubt if he knows when my period is due."

"Paul Farid is a smart man."

Larson wrapped her arm around Sarah's shoulders. "I don't want his work or mine interrupted. Neither do I want to leave Sudan."

"I wouldn't want you to leave, but we don't think like God."

"I can't imagine Him ever wanting us to abandon the people we love."

Sarah gazed into Larson's face. "I believe Paul will be very happy."

"I hope so." Larson peered up into the clear afternoon sky, blue and pure.

The two plodded back to the clinic. Larson didn't want to talk about the baby anymore, especially when she didn't have any answers.

"Come on, Sarah. After seeing those two cases of Guinea worm this morning, we need to talk to these people about the filthy water. If we're not diligent, we'll have more cases of malaria and cholera too."

"I'll call the people together." Sarah shook her head. "We'll make them understand the danger."

❖ ❖ ❖

Ben stared at the sea of dead enemies. The blood of lifeless enemy soldiers painted the lush grasses crimson. Arms and legs lay over brush, and empty eyes stared back in shock. He'd seen it all before, so many, many times. No cries of loved ones. No moans for help. Silence ruled the terrain, except for a swarm of flies and mosquitoes. Vultures flew overhead, circling and gliding on widespread wings as though completing a ritual before the feast. The smell of blood whispered a message to lions and hyenas. Although some of Sudan's wildlife had been destroyed, the predators always sought out the prey.

Ben shifted his weight, trying to ignore the throbbing in his right forearm. A stray bullet had pierced the arm straight through to the bone and out the other side. But at least none of Ben's men had perished today. Other firefights had not left his men so fortunate. The element of surprise had given the SPLA the advantage needed to strike without warning. Ben watched the looting. His soldiers deserved whatever they found to use or barter. Someday the South might compensate these men, but that would be in the months or possibly years to come.

A moan from a nearby body caught Ben's attention. A GOS soldier lay in a pool of blood and mangled flesh. Half of his left side had been blown away. Standing above the man, Ben listened to him mumble a prayer to Allah.

"There's nothing ahead for you but hell." Ben spat the words in Arabic.

The soldier didn't respond. Ben turned and walked away. How many Sudanese civilians had the dying man murdered and maimed? How many brave SPLA fighters had died to free the South from Khartoum's tyranny? The ravages of war continued, with or without a so-called peace treaty. He'd never believe the government cared for all of the people. Even now Khartoum's focus had shifted to genocide in Darfur, Sudan's westernmost province and the home of black African Muslims who had displeased the Arab government. Ben intended to fight until every GOS soldier left his country.

He needed to contemplate the next few hours. Nothing could slow him down, not even the recurring nuisance that often attacked his back. Plans had changed. Despite their victory, the immediate future didn't offer any rest for his men. And there was his own injury to think about. Blood covered his torn and ragged limb and dripped onto his pants and the ground. The pain grew worse by the minute, but it was the fear of permanent damage that terrorized him.

"What now, Colonel?" Commander Okuk bound Ben's arm with a soiled shirt.

"Warkou." Ben reached into his pants pocket with his left hand and pulled out his satellite phone. He clenched his left fist a few times before he attempted to punch in Larson's code.

"Ben, what's wrong?" she asked without greeting him.

"I'm hungry. Are you cooking tonight? Some smoked fish sounds good."

"What's wrong?" she repeated.

"I thought I'd pay a visit."

"How badly are you hurt?"

Her concern brought back memories, memories he'd rather forget.

"A scratch." Pain tore through him like an enemy attacking from every direction. "Bullet went through my arm. I think I need you to take a look at it."

"How soon can you get here?"

"Near midnight with the truck."

"I'll be waiting."

Ben dropped the phone back into his pants pocket. He attempted to stand, but the pain caused him to sway. He tasted the acid of too many firefights and untended wounds. Closing his eyes, he concentrated on maintaining control.

"Colonel?" Okuk asked. "Are you ready?"

Bracing himself against the agony in his arm, he pulled out his phone again. They'd pick up Paul along the way.

THREE

Paul and Ben bounced along the narrow road toward Warkou in Ben's rusted and dirt-corroded truck. Commander Okuk had walked back to the battalion, leaving Paul to drive Ben to Warkou. The bald tires threatened to explode at any moment. The windows had long since been shattered, and their absence invited in the calmness of night sounds and a brief respite from the heat. Unfortunately, it also brought mosquitoes and other insects. Exhaustion seemed to seep from the pores of Paul's skin, a common occurrence after a stare down with death. He just wanted to sleep for about fourteen hours. But first he needed to get Ben to Larson. How selfish to think of himself when Ben's right arm lay limp at his side. Paul hoped she could help him. If she couldn't, they'd be calling for help from Nairobi.

Paul didn't claim to be a medical expert, but he'd taken a long look at Ben's arm when they'd stopped to change the bandage. The gaping hole looked like it needed more than antiseptic and stitches. Larson often performed surgery in her clinic, but this wound looked like it needed a plastic surgeon. Ben's whole life revolved around leading his men in warfare. What would he do if his arm were rendered useless?

"How are you doing?" Paul switched on the overhead

light and saw the blood oozing through the bandage and trickling down Ben's arm.

"My arm would feel better if I hacked it off." Ben's voice drifted weakly.

"Can't do that, partner. That's your shooting arm."

"You've spent too much time in the States. A real hero can use either arm, like Okuk."

At least Ben hadn't lost his wit.

"What did you take for the pain?" Paul asked.

Ben chuckled. "Nothing. One of my men might need it."

Paul wanted to stop the truck and shake him. "Sudan doesn't pass out medals to its soldiers."

"Yeah, but now I have the prettiest doctor in Sudan to patch me up." Ben moaned, then gave Paul a sideways grin. "Sorry. That wasn't necessary."

"No problem. I understand." Not that Paul liked the comment.

"You want to blow a hole through my other arm?"

"Maybe." Paul laughed. "At least we can joke about it."

"Not sure I'd handle it as well." Ben shifted in the seat. "What's going on with you?"

Paul figured he might as well talk about Nizam. "My brother has written me three times. Says he wants to meet with me and learn more about my faith."

"I hope you're not stupid enough to fall for that."

"I'm not. But it bothers me that they might target Larson. They know where I'm living, and the only reason they haven't arrived at our front door is the fact that your battalion is close by."

Ben chuckled—a forced one. "They're afraid of me. Be careful. I don't trust any Arab—except you." He laid his head back on the seat. "I have a son."

Paul wondered what caused Ben to reveal that information. Unless . . . "When did you find out?"

"Almost thirteen years ago. I've never seen him. Doubt if

he knows I'm his father. But lately I've been thinking about him."

The truck hit a bump and Ben sucked in a breath.

"Sorry. Are you thinking about contacting him?"

"Not sure." Ben's words grew fainter. "Too many things to think about. I haven't talked to his mother since I learned she was pregnant. But sometimes I wonder what he looks like, who he looks like."

"Larson and I decided not to have children. Too dangerous here."

"Smart . . . move."

❖ ❖ ❖

Larson fought the urge to sleep while she waited for Paul and Ben. Uneasiness needled her. What if Ben needed surgery beyond her capabilities? Paul said the wound looked bad, but she needed more information. What a shame that a cease-fire had been signed, with a new government in operation, and still Ben had managed to step into the path of a bullet. Sure said a lot for the GOS's commitment to peace, and seemed to validate Ben's cynicism about the possibility of a united Sudan.

Worry for him continued to torment her mind. Ben used to talk to her about everything—even the things she didn't want to hear. But since she and Paul had married, he'd stayed away. Hurting Ben had never been her intent. Under his crusty exterior was a man who loved his country and those who served under him. She'd seen him carry wounded men, women, and children to her after a firefight, often putting himself in more danger. Duty and honor aligned with his every breath.

Memories of the past washed over her . . . patching up his men, arguing about the war, seeing the longing in his eyes, avoiding being alone with him, and the decision to send his teenage sister to California for her safety and education. Larson knew he still loved her, which made seeing him and Paul together all the more awkward. Perhaps, in time, Ben's feelings would mellow.

Headlights flashed into the window of the clinic, followed by the rumble of a truck engine. Snatching up a rifle, she peered into the darkness to make sure the truck held her husband and Ben, not GOS or raiders. Peace might be on the tongues of most Sudanese, but she couldn't trust the government and its so-called commitment to peace. After all, she now had a baby to think about.

"Hold your fire, Larson," Paul called.

She propped the rifle against the wall and hurried out to see how badly Ben had been hurt. Already Paul stood on the passenger side with the door open. He reached inside the cab to assist Ben.

"Need any help?" she asked.

"No. I'm not dead yet." Ben attempted to stand with Paul's aid, but he slumped against the truck door and nearly fell.

"I've got him," Paul said. "He's lost a lot of blood."

The familiar ring of his voice, English words spoken in an Arabic accent, brought comfort—and a gnawing fear about the pregnancy. She'd deal with that later. Right now, Ben needed her.

She inhaled a quick breath and grabbed Ben's waist. He cursed, the sound echoing across the sleepy village. Larson saw a guard step from behind a *tukul*. She nodded, and he disappeared. This was the Ben she knew and could deal with.

Once inside, beneath a few strung lightbulbs lit by a diesel-powered generator, Larson examined Ben's arm. She inwardly winced at the mass of mangled flesh. He needed a good surgeon. She caught Paul's gaze. They hadn't spoken or touched yet. From the grim look on his face, he'd guessed the truth about their friend.

"How much fuel in the Hummer?" she asked.

"Less than half a tank. But there's more in the back."

Ben opened his eyes. "We're not going anywhere in your vehicle or mine. Patch me up, Larson. Do what you gotta do."

She shook her head. "Unless a good surgeon stitches your arm back together, you'll never be able to use it again. Probably needs a plate and a few pins."

"I've seen you operate before."

"You've seen a lot of people die too. This isn't a hospital for your kind of injury. I'm a doc-in-a-box gal."

"Get the instruments out and do it." The agony in Ben's eyes spoke volumes about the pain.

"Do you want to know the odds of whether you could contract an infection or not? Or how about ever using that arm again?"

"I'll take my chances."

Larson turned to Paul. "Don't listen to a word he says." She gathered supplies to clean and bandage Ben's wound.

"I need to get back—" Ben's face tightened.

"Shut up, Ben. You're not worth anything to your men like this," Larson said.

"You need to teach your wife some compassion." Ben glared at Paul.

"Listen to her. Then she'll give you compassion."

She laughed, anything to ease the tension flaring around them like lightning striking dried grass. Ben needed to be airlifted to Nairobi. "Do you think a pilot from Africa Inland Mission could pick him up? See if there's a medically trained person to ride along. I'll start an IV."

"Whiskey would help." Ben tried to pull himself up from the cot, but the loss of blood had weakened him.

"Hey, I'll get you a whole bottle of Johnnie Walker Gold once you're taken care of in Nairobi."

"Where's your plane?" Ben asked.

"I lent it to another pilot for Feed the World," Paul said. "Won't have it back for another week. Sorry." He pulled his phone from his backpack and punched in the numbers.

"Paul Farid here. How soon can I have an AIM plane to Warkou? Col. Ben Alier has been shot." He tossed an anxious look at Larson. "Not till near sunrise. All right. We'll be waiting. A nurse would help. He's lost a lot of blood. . . Yes, he's conscious. Thanks." Paul laid the phone aside.

"You may need to hold him while I clean this." She wrapped her fingers around the bottle of antiseptic.

Paul bent over Ben's side. The moment she attempted to clean the wound, Ben jerked and swore. When she touched the wound again, his body went limp.

"Good thing," she said. "Don't know how he's stood it this long." She glanced up at her husband. "I'm so glad you're here." She hesitated. "Was it really a mamba, or a member of your family?"

❖   ❖   ❖

At 3 a.m. Paul made coffee. Without caffeine, he couldn't stay awake any longer. Larson had given Ben something to take the edge off his pain, and now he slept.

"Can you get a little rest?" Paul asked her. She sat on the concrete floor beside Ben's cot.

"Don't think so. I'm afraid he'll wake up and need something."

"I wish you'd try. You look exhausted."

She wiggled her nose at him. "Thanks. Haven't seen my husband for over a week, and he has nothing but good things to say about me."

"You always look beautiful to me." He bent down and kissed her. "If I don't watch, some Dinka chief is going to want you for his own."

His hand touched her cheek, and she kissed it. "Talk to me about what's going on in Xokabuc."

He eased down beside her with his cup of coffee. "I was

able to get food and supplies into the other villages too. The chief in Xokabuc thanked you for the medicine."

"Any new cases of malaria?"

"A few."

"What happened, Paul? You might as well tell me."

"It's not important."

"Right. This is your wife. The one who knows you better than anyone else."

He pondered lying.

"The truth."

"All right. The GOS attacked Xokabuc. I went back later and helped with the dead and wounded. Ben picked me up there, but I need to get back."

"I'll go with you." She patted his chest. "Once the plane arrives for Ben, I can leave."

"I figured so. Another reason for you to get some rest."

"What about you?"

"I have other things on my mind. Some of which will have to wait until later."

She kissed his whiskered cheek. "You already know our lack of privacy."

"Never stopped us before."

"Which of the other millions of things that keep you awake are you thinking about now?" Anxiousness capped her words. Not her usual way of handling their hectic life.

"My family." He shrugged. "The genocide in Darfur. The Janjaweed militias are murdering those people right and left, and we both know the government is behind it all. The fate of Sudan with this flimsy new government. My wife, whom I leave alone much too often."

"Oh, honey, must you bear it all? God is bigger than all of this."

He slid his arm around her shoulder and pulled her to him. "I have to do my part. He's saved my wretched hide, and now it's my turn."

"Okay," she whispered. "Let's take one matter at a time. What have you heard from your family?"

"Nothing new. Nizam's letters still have me concerned. I'd like to believe he's interested in Christianity, but I don't want to walk into a trap. His last letter said nothing about my suggestion to read a Bible." He would not mention the proposed meeting.

She gasped. "Please, Paul. You're not thinking of a trip to Khartoum."

"Not today."

"Not ever. Promise me. It'll be a trap."

"We'll talk later. I'm thinking of going to Darfur. Every time I drop food and supplies, the Janjaweed or one of the fighting tribes snatches them up."

"Another dangerous trip."

"Are you upset about something?"

"No. But if you're going, I am too. We're a team, remember? And we've been there before."

"We'll go together after I make this next trip. And there's nothing to discuss about the new government. John Garang is the best man for the job."

"I hope he's been assigned more than one bodyguard."

"I'm sure he has the biggest, meanest-looking bodyguards around. He's been defending the rights of the southern Sudanese for over twenty years. He knows how to take care of himself."

"Your confidence makes me feel better. Any word on the international community stepping in to force Khartoum to honor their promises?"

"Not yet." He kissed the top of her head. "Get some sleep, *habibi*. I'll keep an eye on Ben. My guess is that the pilot from AIM will be here at the crack of dawn."

She relaxed against him, and he continued to sip coffee. He was fully awake now, and his mind sped with all the things he needed to do. But there weren't enough hours in a day. Plus, he had a gorgeous wife who needed him. She was upset about something; perhaps one of her patients wasn't doing well.

Nizam. He'd love to see his brother. They'd been close as boys. But that was before Paul's family wanted him dead. Since he and Nizam planned to meet outside of the refugee camp in Darfur, Larson must stay behind . . . just in case something happened. Used to be, he didn't care what reckless things he did in the name of Jesus Christ. Things changed when he and Larson married. His beloved wife softened his resolve to do whatever it took to feed the hungry of Sudan and tell them about Jesus. Now he wondered if he'd let God down by running from the village today.

Ben groaned. Paul studied the rugged man's face, but his eyes were closed. Coming here had to be hard on him. His wound. Seeing Larson. The ring on her finger. War brought strange people together—united enemies and tore apart families. *Heal him, Father. So many people killed and maimed. Sudan desperately needs lasting peace. When will this end?*

FOUR

———————— ❧ ————————

*B*en clawed his way through a pain-filled stupor. He had to be alert. His men needed him. A thick fog held him in the midst of a surreal world that threatened his hold on reality. The firefight played before him, and he remembered the moment when the bullet pierced his arm. Through his muddied senses, he heard voices and the hum of a plane engine. Had the GOS found him? Would they finally be able to take him out in a slow torture that would rival the horrors of the ghost houses?

A singular voice called his name, sweetly, urgently, as in his most private dreams. If he concentrated on her voice, he'd not feel the white-hot fire in his arm or speculate on what the enemy planned to do to him.

"Ben, can you hear me?"

He fought through the maze that held him captive. Moving toward her voice, he struggled for consciousness. The GOS must have her too. He needed strength to protect her. He blinked and attempted to focus on Larson's face.

"Ben, the plane is here to take you to a Nairobi hospital."

He licked dry lips and attempted to push away what the sound of her voice did to him. She stirred him still, and he despised the weakness. Then the details of the past several hours unfolded, and he remembered his wounded arm and the long ride to the clinic. "Thirsty."

Larson gave him a sip of water. "A nurse is here to care for you while you're on the way." She touched his uninjured arm. "Don't try to move. I've inserted an IV. It will make you sleep and take away the pain."

He nodded. Anything he said at this moment might give away his emotions.

"We're praying for you, so let God and the medical team fix your arm," Paul said.

Yes, Paul was there too. Now he remembered more. "Thanks. I . . . need it."

"Don't try to talk." Paul adjusted a loose sheet over him. "Rest and hurry back. We're going to lift you onto a gurney and into the plane."

Ben closed his eyes. Good friends. That's all he had left, except for his commitment to the people of southern Sudan. Larson touched his cheek, and he held his breath. Her touch meant more than a double shot of morphine.

He took a ragged breath. "Tell the chief at Xokabuc. I took revenge . . . on what the GOS did to his village. Tell him I'll be back."

"Of course you will." Larson stroked his cheek. "We all need you. Besides, who will Paul and I argue with? Who will I tell my stories to?"

"I'm ready for new ones," he whispered.

"I'll work on that while you're gone."

"The Rhino Battalion. I—"

"I've already contacted Commander Okuk," Paul said. "Larson and I will stop there en route to Xokabuc and return your truck."

"That man isn't ready to lead my soldiers." Ben gritted his teeth as the pilot and Paul moved and shuffled him about. Gradually the pain diminished, and a gnawing fear took its place. A recurring nightmare threatened to strangle his very purpose, and he wondered if it was an omen.

He feared he'd never lead his men again, and he'd never know his son.

❖ ❖ ❖

Larson watched until the plane disappeared across the star-studded sky, and its midpitch whine faded in the distance. A number of the villagers had watched the goings-on from a distance. She knew the terror of planes filled with GOS soldiers. The enemy raids had affected all of them, sending them racing into snake-filled bunkers. The horror of the bloodbath never became any easier to bear.

Tonight she'd seen a vulnerability in Ben not evident in all the years she'd known him. And he'd uttered two words: *Larson* and *David.* At the time, she'd cringed, thinking how Paul must feel.

"Who is David?"

"I have no idea," Paul said. "He mentioned to me on the way here that he has a son. Maybe that's his name."

"I'm sorry he called out for me." She bit back the tears. Hormones must be kicking into gear.

"*Habibi,* beloved, you can't control his emotions." He took her hand. "Love isn't something you turn off because it didn't work out. Ben will be okay. Time is a big healer."

"I know, but it makes me feel guilty for loving you so much."

"No need at all. I'm glad he called us to help him. Once he's feeling better, he'll be his old self, arguing over everything from politics to fighting tactics."

She managed a soft laugh. "I couldn't think of a single story to tell him."

"Have you exhausted every one from your farm days in Ohio?"

"Probably." Weariness tugged at her entire body. "I

should clean up the clinic. There's blood everywhere."

"I'll help you after we get some sleep."

"I love you, Paul. I can't help but worry about you."

"We're here together right now. God gave us today, and He'll take care of us tomorrow."

She sniffed. *I don't ever cry. If I'm not careful, he'll find out about the baby.* "I'm glad we're going to Xokabuc. It's lonely when you're gone. How many died in the raid?"

"We buried nine men, women, and children. Too many wounded. I was in a hurry and didn't count. They took two of the girls."

"Animals." She remembered when Ben's younger sister had been abducted and how difficult it had been to find her. Praise God she was now safe in California, along with a fifteen-year-old boy who had lived with Larson after his parents died. "You'll do what you can?"

He squeezed her hand. "I already sent a runner to the slave traders. We'll get the girls back. Money sings a strong song."

She leaned against his shoulder. "Sometimes I wonder if what you and I do really makes a difference."

"You're tired, upset about Ben and our friends in Xokabuc."

"I'm not complaining as much as I'm simply stating how I feel. To make matters worse, your family still wants you dead."

He pulled her close and kissed her. "One day, true peace will come to southern Sudan. Until then I must do all I can to help these people. I can't let fear stop me, any more than you can stop risking your life to give them medical attention."

"My Indiana Jones," she whispered. Would he avoid the danger if he knew about the baby? She shivered. A distraction might cause him to not take the necessary precautions and make mistakes. She couldn't tell him until she had a plan of sorts.

How would a baby change their lives? Would Paul be angry? Resentful? Send them both away? Larson wished she knew, and the unknown bore into her soul like a parasite.

Neither of them could deny their calling. Paul's dangerous flights with Feed the World led him into remote areas of Sudan where neither the United Nations nor the Red Cross dared fly. The mere thought filled her with dread and pride. God had protected both of them so far, and she must pray that He continue. Yet she was afraid for Paul . . . afraid of losing him.

❖ ❖ ❖

Paul woke with urgency in his spirit. It always happened when he had more things to do than time allotted. While Larson slept, he cleaned and disinfected the clinic. She didn't need to awaken to the blood-coated instruments and rags. He glanced up at the pipe leading to the roof. A rooftop reservoir caught rainwater for Larson to wash up before procedures. Primitive, but they had no choice. Many times, patients watched her perform surgery while they waited their turn. He finished the preparations for the day by spraying for mosquitoes.

His mind sped on to other things for which he had no solution: Ben's injury, Commander Okuk's inexperience leading soldiers, the horror in Xokabuc, Larson's obvious weariness, his desire to share Christ with his Muslim brothers, and the tremendous amount of work for them to do today. No wonder he couldn't sleep.

Am I a poor husband, allowing my wife to live and work in these conditions?

He carried the medicinal supplies and Larson's sterilized instruments to the Hummer, making sure he'd included plenty of bandages, sutures, Betadine, and lidocaine. Then he snatched up a bottle of Tylenol and added extra antibiotics for the always-flaring malaria. Before their marriage, Larson had needed to ration her supplies. At least that was one thing he could do for her—that, and purchase the armored Hummer HUT Lux and build the clinic. When he'd barely escaped Khartoum with his life, he'd managed to transfer his wealth to the States. His dream was to one day build Larson a hospital equipped with everything she could ever need, but not until peace arrived. The GOS would destroy it simply because she was his wife. *Love thy neighbor, while soldiers kill them . . .*

He gathered up the soiled rags and towels that had been soaking in a bleach solution and washed them in a bucket of well water. Once rinsed, he hung them up in hopes they'd dry before the rains began. A menial task, one Sarah would scold him for doing, but his mind sped too fast for him to sit idle. Usually Larson was up by now. She must have worked around the clock in his absence.

Paul took the familiar path to the river where Sarah and a few other women washed clothes and children played. The happy sounds were a grand diversion from yesterday—and from what lay ahead. Praise God the villagers didn't drink from the river. Living Water, an aid organization from the States, had dug them a good well about two years ago. And Larson had taught the women health and hygiene. Since then, disease in Warkou had been cut in half.

Paul waved and greeted the women and children.

Knee-deep in water, Sarah straightened. "What is Larson doing this morning?"

"She's sleeping, and I wanted her to get all the rest she could after last night. We're heading to Xokabuc later this morning."

"People sick?"

He shook his head. "GOS attack."

Grief and sadness swept over her ebony face. "And Colonel Alier wounded too?" She climbed to the riverbank.

"Keep that to yourself. The GOS will speed up their efforts if they learn he's been shot."

"I understand. How badly?"

"Through his right arm. He needed more than what Larson could do. That was the plane you heard early this morning."

"I'll pray, even if I don't like him much. And I still believe that John Garang will help our people. He'll make sure the fighting stops."

"I pray so, Sarah. If anyone can get the job done, he's the man." Paul didn't mention how long true peace might take, especially after what had happened yesterday.

He sat on the bank to watch the splashing children, and she joined him. From deep inside him came a rise of indignation. These children deserved to grow up without fear of government soldiers and disease. They had a right to a good education.

"My nephew Santino Deng serves with Colonel Alier, but he plans to leave soon," Sarah said.

"Had enough of fighting?"

"With the peace treaty, he wants to attend the University of Nairobi and study government and politics."

Paul smiled and nodded. "Good. Sudan needs strong leaders."

"First he plans to spend a little time with me." She clasped her hands, much like an excited little girl.

He studied Sarah, a little uncertain about how to voice his concerns. "Larson looks pale to me. Has she been working a lot?"

"Not any more than usual."

"Would you make sure she eats and rests when I'm gone?"

"I always do." Her voice took on an edge.

"I'm sorry. I know you do. It's just that she works so hard."

Sarah smiled. "Dr. Larson is like a daughter to me. I take care of her."

"Has she complained of not feeling well?"

Sarah laughed. "Not any more than most women." She pointed behind him. "She looks fine to me."

"Good morning. Is everyone up but me?" Larson's damp hair hung about her shoulders, and her blue eyes sent him a silent message. One that made him glad to be her husband. *She's only tired, nothing else.* He could erase this worry from his ever-mounting list.

"While you were keeping the ladies company, I showered and made our breakfast." Her eyes sparkled. "Sarah, was my husband giving you problems?"

"Not yet. But he was thinking about it." Sarah chuckled. "I was ready to throw him into the middle of the river."

"Am I outnumbered here? All I wanted to do was help my lovely wife."

"And you did." Larson sobered and made her way to his side. "Thank you for cleaning and washing while I slept. I should have brought you a cup of coffee. I'm sorry."

He planted a kiss on his wife's cheek. "Are you sure you want to leave today? We could wait until tomorrow."

"No. I can only imagine the number of wounded who need me. Another day could be the difference between life and death. "

"I'll look after the clinic," Sarah said.

"Thank you. A few patients need changes of dressings, and I made a list of those who need medicine. We should be back in two or three days." Larson gave Paul a questioning glance.

Paul nodded. "Three days sounds good. I still plan to take food and provisions into Darfur after we return."

Larson frowned, but then Sarah began asking questions about patients, and he listened to their exchange. If they'd been anywhere other than war-torn Sudan, their quiet conversation amidst this tropical paradise would have been peaceful. The centuries-old trees seemed to lift their branches to protect them, like a mother hen sheltering her young. His gaze swept over the other women and children and on to the opposite riverbank. With the rainy season swelling the river, anything could be lurking in the waters.

"Out of the water!" he shouted in Dinka. What he'd thought was a log had bulging eyes. But his revolver lay under the driver's seat of the Hummer, and his rifle leaned against the wall of the clinic beside Larson's weapon.

A woman struggled to the bank through waist-deep water, holding the hand of one child and carrying a baby. Moments before, they'd been laughing and splashing. Paul rushed in after her, measuring the distance between the crocodile and the woman. Blood flowed through his veins like a swift current. Another woman screamed. He didn't have his knife, but he had to try to snatch the three from the croc's jaws.

The woman stumbled. Paul reached her in time to right her, but the croc had already opened its massive mouth. He stepped between the woman and the hideous reptile.

A shot rang out. Or was that an alarm going off in his head? The croc dipped under the water. Another shot. The water around him tinted red. In the next instant, the reptile floated away.

Blowing out a ragged breath, his attention flew to Larson, who still had a rifle resting on her shoulder. Her pale face forced a smile, and she slowly lowered the weapon.

"Sarah always brings a rifle to the river," she said.

FIVE

---✦---

"If I don't get out of this hospital soon, I'm going to yank out this IV." Ben scowled at the plump, matronly nurse. "I want my pants and my weapons. This is nothing but a . . . hole of gloom." He'd started to call it a hell-hole, but he knew from experience what that felt like. Everything here smelled of disinfectant and sick people. And he wasn't sick, just mending from his surgery to clean up the damage from the GOS bullet. He could do that with his men. Besides, he could shoot with his left hand.

The nurse planted her hands on her ample hips. "I believe it's time for you to take a walk, Colonel Alier. Shall I help you with a robe?"

"Those aren't robes." Ben narrowed his eyes. "Those are gowns worn backward to cover my black—"

"Now, now, now." She wagged a finger at him as though he were four years old. "I understand that lying in this bed has made you grumpy, but after a walk you'll feel much better."

"I despise this place. And I'd feel better if a twenty-year-old nurse helped me."

She reached inside a drawer beside his bed and pulled out a blue and white striped gown. "Think of me as three eighteen-year-olds, and you'll do just fine." She smiled wide, revealing a few missing teeth. "Besides, at the moment you couldn't handle any woman."

He wanted to wipe that smirk off her face.

"Don't frown at me. From the looks of your chart, your arm shouldn't have been around that woman. Did a jealous husband catch up with you?"

Oh, he'd met his match with this one. But he was on the north wing, the high-security area for VIPs. "Don't be so sure of yourself. You don't know anything about me."

"You're right, and I don't want to know what happened. Except you look like trouble to me."

"When am I getting out of here?"

"I have no idea. Don't be in such a hurry. You're only heading back into Sudan to do the same thing again."

"At least the women there give me a little respect."

"As if they had a choice."

Ben had the perfect words to shut her up, but his doctor appeared in the doorway, a fairly young man who spoke English like the queen's prize subject. Whatever happened to young nurses and gray-haired doctors? He'd much rather have been in Warkou with Larson tending to him. But with his luck, she'd have assigned the wrinkled, formidable Sarah as his nurse. To think that one of his soldiers planned to live with her before leaving for the university in Nairobi. Ben would be afraid she'd kill him in his sleep.

Ben glanced at the doctor's name tag. *Dr. Phillip Khamati.* He'd forgotten it again.

"I see you're feeling better." The doctor glanced at his chart. "You're not asking for as much pain medication as I anticipated." Dr. Khamati paused a moment more. "I have your test results."

"Good. I'm ready to get out of here."

The doctor nodded at the nurse. "Give us a few minutes, please. Would you shut the door?"

She nodded and left them alone.

"This must be wonderful news." Ben's words didn't match the alarm ringing in his head. "All I want to know is when I can go home and when this arm will heal."

The doctor dragged a chair to his bedside. "I'll release you tomorrow after I run a few more tests. Your arm is healing nicely. No infection."

"Then what's the problem?"

Dr. Khamati lifted a sheet on his clipboard. *Too young. Entirely too young.* A moment later, the doctor pasted on a smile. Not a good sign. Not good at all.

"Are you going to tell me about the test results, or practice your bedside manners?" Ben asked.

"All right. Have you had much back pain?"

"Not any more than any other man who's fought in the wild for the last twenty-five years."

"We've found a problem. Looks like skeletal metastases."

"Give it to me in words I can understand." Ben should ask for the doctor's supervisor, or better yet, lay a fist across his clean-shaven jaw.

"Cancer of the spine. I imagine it gets worse after strenuous activity."

A pounding in Ben's head threatened to destroy his composure. "Since that's my life, I don't have a comparison."

"Other symptoms are that the pain worsens at night and doesn't get better with rest."

The increasing ache in his back for the past several months now made sense. *Cancer?*

"How far advanced?"

"I want to run a few more tests."

Ben cursed, reached for the plastic water pitcher, and threw it across the room. It barely missed the doctor and slammed against the wall.

Dr. Khamati didn't budge, but water dripped from his head. "That doesn't change the diagnosis."

"Makes me feel better. So how far advanced is this thing?"

"Indications are, it's spreading rapidly."

"How long do I have?"

"I don't like to give time. Statistics prove this often depresses a patient. But we need to schedule radiation, chemotherapy, and orthotic stabilization of the spine."

"I'm not wasting my days being poked and prodded like a stuck pig. I have things to do, and I'd like to schedule them in the time I have left."

Dr. Khamati sighed. "At the most . . . six months."

"Thank you. Now release me so I can get out of here."

"I can do that tomorrow. I'll give you a prescription for the pain. Taken on a regular basis, it will help manage the discomfort. Are you heading back to Sudan?"

"Absolutely. That's my life."

The doctor shook his head. "I'm sorry. I wish I could have brought better news."

"So do I, but I'll deal with it."

"If you're thinking about a second opinion, the test results have already been seen by a team of doctors."

How good of the doctor to consult others about his life. "I said I'll deal with it. I have a request."

"I'll do whatever I can for you."

"No one, including Dr. Larson Farid or her husband, Paul, is to find out about this. Neither do I want them to know when I'm released. In fact, I want my chart destroyed."

"I'll keep your condition confidential, but we don't destroy records." The doctor glanced back at the water-sprayed wall behind him. "Dr. Farid has called the hospital requesting information."

Ben propped himself up on one elbow. "Make up something to tell her. No one is to know about this. Do you understand?"

"Yes, Colonel. But reconsider what you're saying. Your friends and family will want to be with you, to help you."

"I'll be the judge of that. Now get out of here and leave me alone."

Once the door shut, Ben leaned over and grabbed the gown that the nurse-nightmare had called his "robe." He had things to do, and his days were numbered.

※　※　※

For hours Paul and Larson made their way toward Xoka-buc. The Hummer eased through water and mud-filled ruts in areas where Paul fought to see any kind of a path. Tree branches and brush swiped against the vehicle, making the way slow. Twice, when the road ahead looked like it had washed out, he considered turning around. If the engine flooded, he and Larson would be in trouble. The torrential rainfall had nearly destroyed what was left of the road. The return trip would be even more difficult.

The windshield wipers clicked rhythmically back and forth, as if to remind them they were in a land lost in time and steeped with danger.

"If they didn't need us, I'd suggest heading back," Larson said.

He glanced at her and nodded. "The apostle Paul would scold us for not having faith."

"I wonder if he battled Muslim soldiers, disease, wild animals, heat, and rising water?" She glanced out the window.

This wasn't his optimistic, take-'em-by-storm wife. The renowned Dr. Larson Kerr Farid fought the odds of a third world country entangled in the trenches of civil war to treat its people. Her sense of humor and relentless energy kept him on his toes. He studied her face. Pale. And she had refused to eat this morning and at noon.

"*Habibi,* what's wrong?"

She sat up straighter and took a deep breath. "Nothing. I'm angry with the international community for not forcing

Khartoum to abide by the peace treaty. Then again, the SPLA haven't slowed much either. The people of Darfur have lost their dignity in the middle of genocide. They need so much, and I really would like to initiate an educational program for the women and children. And here we are, once again, racing to a poor village to put Band-Aids on wounds that need hospital attention. Why did the GOS attack anyway? Do we have any idea?"

He formed his words so as not to frighten her. Better that she learn the truth from him rather than one of the villagers in Xokabuc. "From what I overheard while hiding from the soldiers, they received a report about my being in the area. In any event, I was the target. And someone had told them where the Rhino Battalion was camped. Guess you could say the attack was my fault."

"Oh, Paul, I'm so sorry. Here you are carrying a mountain of guilt, and I'm whining." She reached over and rubbed his shoulder. "I'm so selfish. Please forgive me."

"Nothing to forgive. You're human, and the mess here doesn't change."

Images of the war-torn village bathed in the blood of the innocent marched across his mind. Why hadn't he found the guts to give himself up? Had he turned into a coward? What kind of man allowed others to die to save his own neck? Disgust and revulsion with himself filled his mind. It didn't matter that the chief had urged him to escape.

"Paul, talk to me. You scare me when you keep things inside, and I don't like the look on your face."

"I'm feeling pretty lousy. I should have stayed and defended the village."

"Do you think your death would stop what is happening all over southern Sudan?" She shook her head. "The GOS would take that as a sign from Allah to continue the killing. Possibly destroy the fragile peace."

"You make me sound much more important than I really

58

am." For a moment the swishing windshield wipers held him in a hypnotic trance.

"I despise the free world's sitting on the sidelines and watching—like spectators in some gruesome game," she said. "As we suspected, the peace treaty isn't worth the paper it's written on. I want the fighting stopped and these poor people given a chance at life. We pray and pray, and still it seems God isn't listening. I mean, does He hear the cries of those who have lost loved ones? The men who watch their families do without food and medical attention?" Sweat dripped from her brow.

"In God's divine providence, He has a plan."

She nodded, and a tear slipped down her cheek. So unlike his Larson. A slow rise of panic took hold of his senses. Had she contracted some disease?

"I pray for God's plan, Paul. It seems like we're struggling against an enemy that no one can stop. You, me, all of the people we love are trapped in something over which we have no control. Every time you and I say good-bye, I'm afraid I'll never see you again."

"But you will."

Another tear ran down her cheek. "Waiting until heaven to see you when I'm living in an earthly hell is not reassuring."

"Don't you think I fear the same about you?"

"I'm never in the danger you are. Besides, you're much braver and stronger."

"No, I'm not. I just hide my feelings better. Just think of all the times you've picked up a rifle and used it. Look at all the times you were the first one out of a bunker to treat the wounded. What about all the times you've walked through water deeper than this—full of snakes and crocs—to take malaria and yellow fever medicine to a disease-ridden village? You're the one *Time* magazine interviewed and Oprah wanted on her show, not me."

She laughed. "I need you with me all the time to keep my morale up. I feel like our faith is tested on an hourly basis, and I'm tired of it."

Suddenly Paul realized what was really bothering her. "Larson, Ben will be just fine."

She shook her head. "It's not just Ben. It's everything. Sudan needs help."

"What are you suggesting? For the free world to drop bombs on Khartoum?" He sent a sad smile her way. "Innocent people would be killed and nothing solved. The whole Arab world would be sitting on the free world's doorstep."

Larson leaned back in the seat. "Of course not, Paul. I think I'm going to sleep a little before we get to the village."

His stalwart wife was sick. He knew it, and he didn't need a medical degree to diagnose it. Had her body been attacked by some parasite? He reached over to touch her forehead. The moment his hand felt her cool skin, she smiled.

"Sweetheart, I'm only tired. No need to worry. I'll be running circles around you once we get to Xokabuc."

His hand slipped to hers. He held it firmly until her body relaxed and the sound of her even breathing met his ears. She worked much too hard, often 24/7, all in the name of healing the sick and injured. He didn't deserve her. Never had. Especially with his family's death threats lurking in the shadows. But other Muslims had converted to Christianity and faced similar dangers. Why should he be any different?

Hours later, the Hummer rumbled into the village. Naked children greeted them, laughing and banging on the side of the vehicle. Larson quickly roused from her deep sleep. She waved at them, and for a moment, neither her face nor the children's revealed the pain of disease or death. That's what she did for him too.

For the next few days, his beloved wife would attempt to heal the villagers' bodies while he attempted to bring them spiritual healing. They made quite a team. Up ahead, some of the *tukuls* had been burned. These people barely survived anyway, and now they'd lost their homes. Fury swirled through him again—a common sensation of late. To think he'd once been among those who persecuted the South.

SIX

Three days ago, Larson had treated a little girl who had cut her leg fleeing the GOS raid in Xokabuc. The injury should have had sutures, but by the time Larson had arrived with Paul to the village, too much time had elapsed. This morning, the leg looked better: the swelling had decreased, and the angry red color of the wound had improved. Larson applied antiseptic to the leg and blew on it to cool the stinging. Each time the little girl screamed, her mother held her tighter and spoke soothing words of comfort.

Larson set aside the antiseptic and gauze to take the mother's hand. "Your daughter's leg is much better. You have been a big help to me today." A twinge of something unfamiliar gripped Larson's senses: a sense of protectiveness toward her unborn child. What if her own baby became ill or hurt? Would she be able to give her baby proper medical care?

Larson's abdomen threatened to convulse, and she laid her hand across it. In the past, she'd quickly tossed aside any concerns about the precarious life she and Paul lived. She no longer had that luxury. As long as she remained in Sudan, she could not ignore the prevalence of infant mortality. And who would raise their child if something happened to her and Paul?

Too many decisions to make.

"What must I do?" the little girl's mother asked, as though echoing Larson's dilemma.

"I'll leave medicine for her injury." Larson kissed the child's forehead and brushed away the tears that streamed down her tiny face. This little girl was Sudan's future.

Her back aching, Larson straightened and glanced at the line of patients who stood in the pouring rain outside the *tukul* that housed her temporary clinic. The rain hammered the thatched roof and splattered onto the ground, intensifying her awareness that her bladder was about to burst. Famine had spread throughout Bahr al-Ghazal province, and the rain was a blessing—even if it did make the wait to see her miserable. She'd urged as many people as possible to crowd inside. All were filled with hope that she possessed healing powers for them or for someone they loved.

She had no magic cure for those who desperately needed medical care beyond her ability, nor did she have an answer to the problem of her unexpected pregnancy. God had given her and Paul a child for a reason. If only He'd tell her why.

She pushed aside all the worrisome thoughts as the urgency inside her increased. She'd see one more patient and then excuse herself.

A middle-aged man stepped forward, the back of his left ear and neck swollen to the size of a grapefruit. *Untreated ear infection.* Larson wondered how he managed the pain.

"Good morning, sir," she said in Dinka. "What is the extent of your pain?"

The man stared at her.

"Sir, it would help me if I knew how badly you hurt."

The man took a deep breath.

Larson clapped her hands next to the ear that was not swollen. Nothing. She might be able to cure the infection raging through his ear, but she could not restore his hearing.

Frustration ushered in tearful emotion. Before her pregnancy, she had masked the serious conditions of her patients with a kind word and professionalism. Now she wept. Larson blinked and breathed in deeply. If she'd been able to treat this man sooner, he might still have his hearing. The little she did for these people often left her wondering why she continued to work so hard. But for those she could help, her efforts made a difference. Other international medical teams who made personal sacrifices to bring assistance to Sudan surely felt the same way.

A familiar arm slipped around her waist. "How are you?"

Pregnant and worried. "Good. I need a potty break as soon as I finish with this patient."

Paul grinned. "You must be getting old. I've seen you go eight hours without so much as a wiggle. And here you are needing one in less than half that time."

She slid him a frown. "I'm still younger than you and easily riled. You'd better mind your manners since I have all these tools of torture at my fingertips."

He laughed.

"How's your morning?" she asked.

"Better than expected. I feared the chief and the villagers would be disillusioned about their faith after the attack, but instead they believe Jesus is the only answer to their problems."

"Good. So good. I know you feared they'd blame God or you."

"They might not blame me, but I—"

"Paul—"

"You'd better take your break so I can get back to work. The GOS dumped dirt into the village's well again, and I need to help pull up the pipe and clean it out. I asked the chief if you could meet with the women tonight. I told him you wanted to teach them how to fight the sickness in the water."

"Thanks." She picked up a clean rag and wiped the perspiration from her forehead. How could her dark-haired husband always look so unaffected by the heat? The temperature had to be near 120 degrees. "I love you." She planted a kiss on his lips. "No man should look as handsome as you do out here in the middle of nowhere."

"Even with all these naked men around us?"

"Absolutely."

"Just wait till I get you back to Warkou."

❖ ❖ ❖

Four days had passed since Larson and Paul had returned to Warkou, and neither Ben nor his doctor had called back. She'd left messages repeatedly for both of them, with no results.

"Colonel Alier is resting."

"The doctor is not available at this time. Please check back later."

"I'm ready to go to Nairobi." Larson paced the dirt floor of their *tukul*. "I treated Ben first, and he hasn't the decency to call and say 'hello' or 'I survived.'"

Paul glanced up from his list of what to take to Darfur. Ammunition lay piled on the ground beside him. "Do you want me to try to find out what's going on?"

She shook her head. "If his doctor won't return my calls and Ben refuses to talk to me, I doubt if there's anything you can do. My guess is he's mad about being there and blaming me for not patching him up at the clinic."

"He lives for his men and for the next firefight. His priorities and methods are often difficult for me to understand."

"It's Ben—the invincible, stubborn Colonel Alier, who believes he has to single-handedly lead southern Sudan in its fight against the injustices of the government. No matter that there's a signed peace treaty."

He touched her arm. "He'll show up here one day and be his old self."

"I suppose so. Can you imagine the trouble he's giving those doctors and nurses?"

Paul laughed. "He reminds me of an old lion."

"Better yet, he reminds me of a bull my granddaddy used to have on his farm."

"Have I heard this story?"

"Probably, but you can listen again. Granddaddy had this bull that wouldn't bother anyone unless you got within fifty feet of him. I mean, this bull must have mapped out a circle fifty feet wide, and if you stepped over the line, you'd better hope you could outrun him."

"Did you?"

Her eyes widened. "You know the little scar on the inside of my right leg? That was from crawling under a barbed-wire fence trying to get away."

"So Ben is as mean as that bull?"

"Not mean, just territorial. He has this boundary line around him that no one had better cross."

"I did a few times, and I paid for it."

She frowned. "I remember. Who would have ever thought the three of us might one day be friends—or you and I married?" For a moment, she allowed her mind to drift back to the day Paul had first landed outside Warkou with a plane full of food and medical supplies from FTW.

She hadn't trusted the famed Arab Christian, despite the free world's claims of his benevolence. He'd been a part of a wealthy family in Khartoum who took pride in torturing and killing "infidels." When Paul's father had sent him to kill an old man who refused to convert to Islam, Paul couldn't do it. Something in the old man's eyes had reached deep within Paul's soul. After a few more visits, he'd become a Christian and freed the old man. Shortly thereafter, Paul had transferred his wealth to the States and fled the country. His family had been after him ever since.

Relentless.

"What are you thinking?" Paul grinned.

"You and me in the beginning."

"Yeah, I didn't know who was going to shoot me first—you or Ben."

He paused, and she realized he was remembering the GOS attack shortly after he'd landed. The soldiers had nearly killed him in their effort to abduct Ben's little sister.

"But you found Rachel, and Ben will be forever indebted to you."

Paul chuckled. "I'll remind him of that the next time we're arguing about peacemaking methods for Sudan or how to negotiate the situation in Darfur."

Before she could reply, his phone rang. He smiled at her and answered on the second ring.

"How are you doing, Ben? We were ready to take the next luxury liner to Nairobi. Are the nurses keeping you so occupied that you've forgotten your friends?" Paul laughed. "Why am I not surprised? A few days? Are you sure? What did the doctor say?" He held the phone away from his ear, and Larson could hear Ben's choice words for Nairobi's hospital and medical personnel. "I agree with them. Why don't you stay there and allow that arm to heal?" Paul shook his head at Larson. "Do you want to talk to Larson for her medical expertise?"

"I'll give him a piece of my mind." She offered her best scowl.

"He heard you," Paul said. "He says a good woman listens to a man's misery."

"Tell him to stay in the hospital and put on a few pounds." He'd looked extremely thin the last time she saw him.

Paul said nothing while he listened. "I understand you're anxious to check in with your men, but can't you do that by phone? I see . . . Well, I'm heading into Darfur in the morning, so I'll see you when I get back." He collapsed the antenna and dropped the phone into his pocket.

Larson laughed. "Nothing's changed?"

"Apparently not. He plans to leave Nairobi in a few days and head here."

"Wonderful. I'll get to enjoy his bad mood."

"He wants a good meal. Obviously hospital life is not to his liking."

She could imagine Ben's roaring about how he'd been mistreated. "As if sleeping on the hard ground for days in the jungle, without decent food, were any better. How long does he plan to stay here?"

"Not more than a day. He wants to join up with his battalion as soon as possible."

"That's not wise." Irritation nipped at her mind. Ben had been wounded badly, and he needed rest, not another firefight.

"I'll let you tell him that."

"I will." She lifted her chin. "But I want to go with you into Darfur. Sarah can handle Ben."

"It's too dangerous, especially for a doctor who is needed here."

"I'm a good shot, and those people need medical attention too. What's the problem, when I've been there with you before? Other medical teams are getting into Darfur."

"True. But I want you to think about the increased danger."

"It's not that bad."

"Then explain why Kofi Annan's interpreter was harassed by authorities after he translated an interview with women who had been raped. The conditions there are so bad that Annan asked if the international community was going to let Darfur become another Rwanda." Paul leaned over and kissed the tip of her nose. "No. You cannot go with me in the morning. A team of doctors is already on the ground in Kibum. Conversation ended."

Larson churned with frustration. She'd risked her life plenty of times before becoming Larson Farid, and she didn't appreciate anyone making decisions for her. "So you can risk your life, but I can't?" As if to punctuate her words, a sudden burst of rain splattered outside the hut. "My skills are needed. You might as well admit it, and besides, we've gone together before." She crossed her arms. "Are you flying a drop or landing?"

"Landing, with plenty of supplies. You saw the latest UN reports. More than half of the population needs food." Paul hoisted a bag of ammo.

"And needs medical attention in mammoth proportions."

He stiffened. A rarity for Paul to let her see she was getting to him. "When it's safer, we'll go back together."

"Promise?" She laid a hand on her abdomen, remembering too late that she should avoid such telltale gestures.

"Sure. Are you ill? Stomach problems?"

If he knew, their conversation would immediately turn to where she'd spend the next seven months. "No, sir. I'm very fit. But don't forget I want to help those in Darfur." She kissed him, not just to hush his uncomfortable questioning but because she loved him.

❖ ❖ ❖

Paul's concern for Larson mounted throughout the day and into the night. She slept more than he could ever recall, and her pale face alarmed him. Still, she insisted that her health was fine.

The following morning he hesitated to bring up the subject. He knew his strong-willed wife. Instead, he would continue to observe her and give his concerns to God—and Sarah.

"Something's wrong," he told the wrinkled woman while they swept out the clinic. "I've never seen her so tired, and

70

she's not eating. Another thing that bothers me is that she's sleeping in the middle of the day. And even though she denies it, yesterday she vomited."

"Give it time." Sarah patted his arm. "She'll be all right, and I'll make sure she rests while you're gone."

"Thanks. My sweet wife will listen to you before she does me."

"Ah, stubborn should be her name." Sarah laughed. "And yours. When are you planning to leave for Darfur?"

"In about an hour. Urgent needs require my attention."

"For Feed the World?"

Feed the World only wanted him to fly food and medical supplies into the Kibum refugee camp and leave the ravaged area, but he felt the familiar tug to be on the ground and help-ing—and seeing his brother. The news reports of the contin-ued atrocities in Darfur only grew worse, and Khartoum was blatantly glossing over the ugly truth. The situation nudged him night and day to do more . . . always do more to help.

"Why don't you drop the food and come back to us?" Sarah asked.

He eyed her curiously. "Why?"

"I fear for you, just as your wife does. Your spirit wants you to stay in Darfur, and that means taking dangerous chances. I know your heart for those persecuted people . . . my people."

"Odd that you call them your people, considering—"

"That they were a part of the jihad that attempted to de-stroy all of us in southern Sudan?" Not a hint of malice crossed her face. "I forgive like Jesus says. Some cannot. But I remember how we suffered and are still suffering. I wish that for no one. Women are treated bad . . . Makes me cry." She shook her head. "My memories are nightmares. I want to for-get and believe each day will be better."

"We all want the same things, Sarah. That's why we must keep praying."

"But you fly over areas where the GOS threaten to shoot you down, and it frightens Larson."

He chuckled. "That's who I am."

"You already know what I think about that."

A martyr syndrome. He'd heard it from more than one person. "You'd miss my teasing."

A wide, toothless grin spread across her face. "I suppose so. But be careful. Larson will grieve for a long time if you are killed."

"She understood my commitment to Sudan when we married, just like I understand hers. That's why we're a good team."

Sarah pressed her lips together and turned her attention to a black snake that slithered across the concrete floor. She swept the venomous creature outside.

"Don't come back," she said.

Paul caught sight of the snake and made his way toward the door to kill it. Sarah tugged on her right ear as he passed—a sure sign that she had something on her mind.

"Are you holding back information from me?" He stopped in the doorway. "Has my wife asked you not to tell me something?"

Sarah carefully rolled up Larson's instruments inside a clean cloth. "Men are always demanding answers and think they know things they don't."

He started to ask what she meant, but she whirled around and left the clinic without another word. Making Sarah angry solved nothing, and he loved her too much to press the matter. Larson did work hard. Maybe she simply needed a little extra rest while he was there to help out. As soon as the workload for FTW calmed down a bit, he'd take her back to the States to visit her folks. That should bring back the color to her cheeks.

SEVEN

───────────── ✦ ─────────────

*B*en stared out the window of the Mitsubishi MU2, the same model of twin-engine turboprop that Paul flew for FTW. Paul had lost two of his planes when the GOS had gotten lucky, but he'd replaced them with the same model.

Sometimes Ben wondered how much money Paul had pulled out of Khartoum when he'd escaped the clutches of his Muslim family. He had to have millions stashed away in the States, most of which he used to purchase food and medical supplies for stricken people in southern Sudan and Darfur. Thoughts that should never enter a man's mind hadn't left him since he'd been diagnosed with cancer. Was there a possible cure? How much would it cost? What about a test drug?

He shrugged. Desperation did strange things to a man. But he'd never ask Paul for money—certainly not to find a cure for a tough warlord like himself. Life had a beginning and an end, and his was trickling away like the sands washing into the sea, whether he liked it or not.

The dirt landing strip beside Warkou came into view. The rains had saturated the earth, turning the area into thick mud. Last year the Bahr al-Ghazal province had gotten little rain, and the resulting drought had brought starvation to many of the villagers. Now, if the government left them alone, they could plant crops and survive another season. Some of the villages had received seeds from humanitarian organizations and missionaries to begin growing their own food again. Ben hoped the new government officials actually kept their word on some things. The idea of villagers growing tomatoes, beans, cabbage, and maize without fear of getting shot sounded good to him. Of course, many of the fertile areas held land mines.

A few villagers watched the plane circle and then come in for a landing. They were curious, but not afraid. This cream-of-the-crop missionary plane always brought aid. Ben chuckled. Ironically, this flight brought a dying man.

After talking to Paul yesterday, Ben had convinced a missionary pilot in Nairobi to fly him to Warkou. Commander Okuk was supposed to meet him there and escort him back to his men. Ben searched the ground, but he didn't see the bullet-ridden truck or Okuk. A half-dozen curses etched into his mind. He hated wasting time and putting up with irresponsible people. He hated more the limited days and hours left in his cancer-infested body. The pain he used to ignore now attacked him harder with its reminder of his finite future.

He could handle the torment, but not the idea of death. His father had once told him that every man needed to have his house in order from the moment he realized the difference between heaven and hell. Ben had put off making any changes, and now he didn't have a spare moment to contemplate rectifying his life. He'd stopped believing in God after seeing more than his share of blood and tortured bodies. Not like his parents, who thought Christianity was the cure for the world's problems. Why waste time and effort to parley with death over the things he couldn't change? He'd always considered himself invincible—a superhero, as they said in the States. *What a joke.*

Every breath found him on a downward spiral, anxious about everything and overwhelmed with what needed to be accomplished. Maybe he'd get lucky, and an enemy bullet would end it all. The glory in that death was a better legacy to leave David—but first his son needed to find out about his father.

The truth ate at him. Ben craved a relationship with his son, and his son needed a father. But would the boy even want to be a part of Ben's remaining days? David had been raised by a fine woman, and Ben wanted to thank her. He could provide only a meager living for them after he was gone. Most of his money went to his younger sister Rachel in California for her education. Perhaps once she finished nursing school and secured a good job, she could help David and his mother.

David's mother does have a name. Daruka. You took her when she was barely fifteen years old, lured her into your arms, and then abandoned her when she got pregnant. How could he tolerate himself? He'd been a part of so much ugliness.

Once he briefed Commander Okuk about the responsibilities of an SPLA leader and began molding him for service to southern Sudan, he'd make his way to Daruka and David. Okuk didn't need to know how critical his leadership capabilities would be until the end.

Too much to do. Too little time.

One thing Ben had come to terms with while waiting for the doctor to remove his stitches was that he had to choose what he could feasibly do in the months remaining.

The thought of turning back to God and promising Him everything if He'd simply give him more time had tempted Ben more than once—just as he'd been tempted to ask Paul for help. But the blood on his hands and the nightmares that kept him awake were enough evidence that God, if He did exist, had no reason to show mercy—or compassion. Death had won, as every man must one day be forced to admit. He'd face whoever or whatever held the afterlife of man with the optimism that hell might not really be a forever pit of torment. After all, it couldn't be much worse than life in Sudan.

I had so many dreams that I kept putting off. He stiffened. Too late now. How gallant, dauntless, magnificent to die a hero's death, rather than to shrivel up in pain until his body fought for his last breath. Ben had always thought he'd been on the side of good, but would his sacrifices benefit the people he left behind?

A few ideals hammered into what little conscience he had left. Larson and Paul deserved more than he could give them. At least Larson had a healthy husband to keep her safe—as long as Paul watched his backside. Feeding the hungry and making sure they had medicine was one thing, but the starving masses didn't care about God, only the ache in their bellies. And the government wanted Paul dead: not just killed, but tortured and mutilated as an example to those who thought Christianity was better than Islam. Ben hoped Paul steered clear of his family. Courageous efforts could get him killed.

Ben owed his military comrades another argument against a unified Sudan instead of the value of this worthless piece of paper called a peace treaty. The North would never honor the peace agreement, and it was time that the leaders of the South accepted that fact. He shook his head. Maybe he was being too stubborn. If any man could bring about reconciliation, it would be John Garang. John was more than a respected leader for the South; he was its lifeblood. He'd single-handedly drawn up battle plans during the war, and he'd have a method of uniting all the tribes. John had carried the banner for southern Sudan for twenty-five years. Ben had served under him all that time, never doubting John's decisions until now, with this foolish idea that the North would actually cease its persecution of the South.

"What is the new government going to do about Darfur?" the pilot asked. "The number of dead is already larger than the number killed by the tsunami in the Indian Ocean. Sometimes I wonder if the peace treaty with the South was just a ploy to distract the international community from the destruction in Darfur."

Ben huffed. He could have easily spouted the relevant facts, but he saw no point in wasting words on a man with a missionary agenda. "Khartoum simply agreed to the terms so they could get back to the business of outfitting the Janjaweed."

The pilot nodded. "I think I understand the situation there, but it seems so complicated."

It is, and I'm not in the mood to explain it. "Depends on the day of the week or which way the wind is blowing or what tribe is ready to kill for pasture."

"My sister lives in the States. Louisiana. When I tell her what's going on over here, she says the GOS are like cockroaches. You run them out of one spot, and they take up residence in another."

"And each time they get stronger and bolder."

"Some days I pray for Jesus to come now and put us all out of our misery, and other days I want the opportunity to spread the gospel to a few more desperate people."

The pilot sounded like Paul and Larson. How would they all feel if they were the ones looking down the throat of cancer?

I'm bitter, and I don't care. Maybe he did a little.

The plane touched down hard into the slippery mud. The impact jarred Ben's spine, and he gritted his teeth and gripped his knees. His dose of painkiller was long overdue.

"Bad landing," the pilot said. "Sorry about that."

"I'm used to rough rides."

Once the pilot had finished the landing procedure, the two men stepped out into the sultry air.

Ben shook his hand. "I appreciate this." He couldn't even remember the pilot's name. "Good luck to you."

"The same to you. I hope this new government changes things for Sudan. I'm sure John Garang as first vice president will do his best."

Ben chose not to comment. John's announcement and swearing-in had happened while he was in the hospital. Kofi Annan could make all the pretty speeches that he wanted about unity for the entire country and about allowing nongovernmental and humanitarian organizations into Darfur—and the United States could keep on making claims about its resolve to see the killing stopped. But when the dust settled, it didn't change a thing. Khartoum had its own agenda.

The pilot climbed back into the cockpit. "Say, you forgot your backpack."

Great. Now he was losing his mind. Ben stepped forward and grabbed the straps of his bag. A streak of lightning pain raced up his spine. Must he be constantly reminded?

The plane took off down the strip, its rumblings drowning out the villagers' jubilant shouts. Ben recognized the faces and waved. When Rachel had lived with Larson, he'd spent a lot of time here. *Rachel.* Should he tell his sister about the cancer or let her find out for herself? He was getting meaner all the time. And he couldn't make decisions either.

Sarah walked toward him. To think that obnoxious old woman would outlive him. She smiled and nodded. "How are you doing, Colonel?"

"Close to normal."

"I guess that's good."

"What do you mean?"

"Your normal can be hard to take at times."

"Sarah, can't you treat me with some respect? Look what I've done for you."

"I appreciate your work, Colonel Alier, but I can still pray for your soul and a change in your attitude."

That again. "Don't waste your breath. Is Commander Okuk here?"

"He was yesterday, but now he's gone." She walked toward the clinic, and he joined her.

"Where did he go? Never mind. Is Larson busy at the clinic?"

"She's not here either."

He should have called and made sure people understood what they were supposed to do. "Where is she?"

"On her way to northern Darfur."

"Paul took her to Darfur? Why, when the work here needs their attention?"

Sarah stopped and eyed him. Not a crease of emotion crossed her face.

"What is it?"

"Paul flew there this morning for FTW and landed. I have no idea how long he'll be gone. Larson followed him in her Hummer. I don't know if he's found out she's behind him yet."

Ben's head now pounded, along with his arm and back. Glancing toward the medical clinic, he wished Larson would step outside and wave to him. "Neither of them has any sense. I suppose Paul refused to take her, and she decided to make the trip anyway. Whereabouts?"

"Refugee camp. Kibum."

"They've gone there together before. What was different about this trip?"

"I don't know, but I'm worried about Larson."

"So am I. What a fool notion to drive there. She'd be a fine prize for the Janjaweed." He didn't want to think about that. "Well, she knows how to take care of herself. Who went with her?"

"Your Commander Okuk."

"So my men are without a commanding officer?"

"I'm sure it's just until she meets up with Paul. I heard him phone your men."

"All right, Sarah. I'll phone Okuk and make sure they're

okay. Maybe he can keep Paul and Larson from getting killed. But he's in trouble for leaving me stranded here. What was he thinking, leaving my men without a commander?"

"What would you have had him do, when Larson asked for his assistance? You'd have done the same thing."

"I have more experience than Okuk. Since when do I have to answer to you?"

Irritation competed with the anguish in his body. He hadn't expected news like this. His priorities didn't involve playing bodyguard. His mission to watch over Larson had stopped when she'd married Paul and Ben had lost his chance. Paul had had "Kill Me" written all over him ever since he'd converted to Christianity. He should have stayed in California and enjoyed his money instead of flying dangerous missions for Feed the World and attempting to evangelize every non-Christian in Sudan. The man had more contracts out on his life than anyone else in the country. And now Larson was hot on his heels in a hellhole called Darfur.

Ben stepped into the clinic. All the bottles, supplies, and instruments were neat and clean. Only Larson was missing—Larson, with her wide smile and crazy stories about her life in the States. Larson, with her large blue eyes and light hair swept back into a ponytail. Larson, who had chosen an Arab over him. Ben whirled around and reached for his backpack to find his pain medication.

Sarah stood in the doorway with her arms crossed over her chest.

"I thought you'd left," he said.

"Did you call to make sure Larson and Okuk haven't run into trouble?"

"Why? They have weapons." The pain increased. He jerked out the bottle and flipped the lid, sending it flying across the concrete floor.

She picked up the lid and handed it to him. "There are things you don't know."

Had Larson and Paul quarreled? Had Paul's family caught up with him? "What happened?"

"I can't tell you."

Now he really wanted to shoot her. "How do you expect me to help when you don't tell me the whole story?"

Sarah glanced out the open doorway. "I gave my word."

"To Paul or Larson?"

"Larson."

Ben popped the pills into his mouth and swallowed them. Slumping into a chair, he closed his eyes. "I'll phone Okuk now and then head back to my men."

EIGHT

---

*P*aul had flown many missions over Darfur. He'd dropped food and supplies to areas where he could not land, and he'd been on the ground assisting humanitarian organizations and medical teams who labored to bring aid to those caught in the web of genocide. Many of those times, Larson had come with him, bringing immunizations for cholera, malaria, measles, and yellow fever, as well as health treatments for the children. The women and children suffered the most. Paul recalled the alarming figures: according to some, ten thousand displaced persons died every thirty minutes. At the sight of the Kibum refugee camp, he wished he'd brought Larson to help. But not today. It was impossible.

Some of the people held cards issued by the United Nations High Commissioner for Refugees. The UNHCR workers punched the refugees' cards as a record of what was distributed, in an effort to ensure the supplies were evenly dispersed. Two lines of people stood in the infernal heat. One line was to register for food, and the other one was for water. Unfortunately, the people could not stand in both lines. So how did they choose? Some of them had donkeys on which to load what they received, but most struggled with water and food containers, glad for what they now had.

The fetid odors of unwashed and diseased bodies,

exacerbated by the lack of sanitation facilities, clung in Paul's nostrils. Larson could have given health and hygiene classes to the women as she'd done before, showing them how to utilize what little they had to keep their families healthy.

The condition of the children in Kibum knotted his stomach, just as it did each time he brought provisions to the camps. They died from disease and starvation that could have been prevented with proper diet and medical treatment. Ignorance played a major role, and more than once he considered heading up a way to educate the women, the grass roots of this forgotten people. His insides churned with the reminder that his family supported the Janjaweed's persecution of the Darfur tribes, just as he once had. One of his brothers was a GOS officer; he'd claim these sordid conditions were the will of Allah.

More like the will of Satan.

Paul swallowed his emotion. He didn't think he'd ever come to terms with the knowledge that God had forgiven him and given him new life. Until the day he died, Paul would do all within his means for these people. Larson had accused him of legalism, until he'd explained that he was driven by love for the God who now called Paul His child. Even if he didn't understand the full concept of mercy and grace, he understood freedom in Christ.

A young girl, not much more than twelve years old, walked by him carrying a crying, naked little boy. The child's ribs protruded from the sides of his frail body, and his swollen stomach indicated infected internal organs, probably from parasites.

"The doctor's tent is there." Paul pointed toward the clinic.

Tears welled in her eyes.

Paul lifted the child from her arms and walked her to the medical line. The little one felt much too light. A small team from Doctors Without Borders, one of whom Paul recognized, were tending to several patients at a time, but the line still stretched around the hut and down the dirt pathway. *Larson should be here too.* Shaking away the guilt, he continued on through the camp, which housed mostly women wrapped in colorful rags and children wrapped only in hope. So many women had buried children; how could they go on?

He and Larson had made the right decision to not have children of their own. They needed to be free from ties that would hinder them from helping these people.

An aid worker, a young man with an American East Coast accent, divided up bags of grain. Paul stepped in to help. He still had plenty of time to make it to his destination.

"Do you have a Qur'an?" a man asked when Paul handed him a small bag of grain.

"No. I'm a Christian."

The man looked at the grain, then stared into Paul's face. "Whatever you have, I want it."

Paul pulled his backpack around to his chest and handed him an Arabic New Testament. The man thanked him and walked away, and Paul headed for the edge of camp. As soon as he finished his business, he'd return to help.

Walking alone over the barren land, Paul scrutinized the flat terrain. He sickened at the sight. FTW wanted a full report for its monthly publication, so he snapped pictures and made mental notes. The land where people had once lived and thrived now held countless graves. The land where people had once grown food, the Janjaweed had set on fire. His path took him to a pile of charred bones, where likely the few surviving animals in the area had perished and the villagers had burned their remains to avoid disease. He breathed in the despair of squalor.

He despised the government's miserable excuses for eliminating these people: from the open resentment of some Darfurans toward government policies, to their black African ethnicity, to the problem of ongoing conflicts among some of the tribes. The victims of the genocide were mostly Muslim farmers who raised cattle and goats in the way of their ancestors. Sometimes Paul wondered if the government had a hidden agenda. Did the ground beneath his feet hold vast pools of oil? More likely, the whole mess was a political necessity to secure those in power.

❈ ❈ ❈

Perhaps he shouldn't have left the refugee camp to meet Nizam. An eerie sensation settled on him. He could be killed for the clothes on his back or for the food some poor soul might think he carried. He'd give everything he had if it would keep a suffering person alive another day. But he had another reason for this jaunt.

Paul studied the horizon. Not a soul in sight. No breeze. No birds. Nothing. Only dirt and flying insects in forty-eight degrees Celcius. Not enough life here to sustain a vulture— unless you counted the human ones. On his left, a solitary acacia tree reached up to the cloudless sky as though praying for relief. To his right lay the ashes of a burned-out village. Forcing himself to take pictures helped occupy his mind.

He reached into his backpack and pulled out a folded piece of paper with Nizam's instructions. His brother had said he'd meet him at noon, five kilometers northwest of Kibum in an abandoned village. Nizam claimed he simply wanted to see Paul and to hear more about the Christian religion, but only on the condition of strict secrecy. Both of their lives would be in danger if the family or government authorities discovered them together.

I hope I'm not playing the fool.

The closer he got to the meeting place, the more he feared walking into a trap. His death would bring a celebration in Khartoum, and honor to whoever had pulled the trigger. He headed toward the ash-ridden village. A donkey carcass rotted beside a destroyed irrigation system. Homes had been burned to the ground, along with whatever meager posses sions the villagers might have had. And the people . . . This had been a farming community, the home of villagers who meant no harm to anyone, despite the government's claims. The hollow eyes of the hungry children in Kibum haunted him. They'd smelled the stench of death and heard the screams and anguish of friends and loved ones. It wasn't fair—not to the innocent children or to the mothers who'd borne them.

His own family had ordered the deaths. *And you are no better than the ones who did this. You once condoned the genocide of all those who opposed the government or its belief in Islam.* How many times had his mind echoed these words?

The accusation that often seized his heart in condemnation was not the voice of God. A verse from the Psalms came to him: *You are not a God who takes pleasure in evil.* As quickly as that verse sped by, another took its place, a verse he'd memorized for these times, when the weight of his past sins threatened to push him into insanity: *Cleanse me with hyssop, and I will be clean; wash me, and I will be whiter than snow.*

God now saw Paul through the eyes of Jesus. The comforting thought relieved his burden of guilt, and he wanted every inhabitant of Sudan to know that peace.

"Abdullah Farid."

Paul stiffened. It was not the voice of Nizam, nor any of his brothers.

"Turn around slowly."

❖ ❖ ❖

Larson bounced along in the Hummer while Commander Okuk drove. Normally she didn't allow anyone but Paul to drive her armored portable hospital, but this was Darfur. She wasn't sure of the way to Kibum, and every moment was precious. And the GPS on her satellite phone wasn't enough to protect her if she ran into trouble. But doubts about the commander's ability to drive crept in as she watched him steer with his knee while he shifted gears with his one arm. Paul had purchased the Hummer about two years ago, and she intended to keep it in one piece.

Deep inside, she sensed Paul was in trouble. This trip was not just a simple delivery of provisions. She had nothing on which to base her fears, only a quivering in her spirit. As much as she prayed about what she liked to call his martyr syndrome—his need to atone for past sins by heedlessly throwing himself into dangerous situations—the symptoms were still there. If only Paul would rest in God's love instead of letting his guilt drive him so. Had Nizam convinced him to do something reckless?

Paul. He'd chosen the name when he became a Christian because of the similarities between his life and the apostle Paul's. But that didn't mean he had to die a martyr's death.

The desolate land rolled past the Hummer, sending up a choking dust to parch their throats. They'd driven out of sheets of rain into this land that cried out for a single drop of water. As during the other times she'd been to Darfur, an unexplainable wariness had swept over her—a suffocating oppression. At first she'd ignored the sensation. Her job was to use her medical knowledge to treat as many people as possible, not to contemplate peculiar feelings. Later she'd labeled the haunting shroud as hopelessness and desperation, but then her thoughts had wrapped around the truth. It was fear. She was feeling the terror of a persecuted people, the constant wondering about when the enemy would reach them. Whether the enemy was an opposing tribe or the government-backed Janjaweed, for those who had given up, the terror was a part of living.

She studied Okuk's face. No scarring from tribal manhood rites, so she guessed his age to be under thirty. But his neck held a wide scar, deep and ugly. Had the wound occurred when he'd lost his arm? It was a wonder the man had survived.

"Do you have a wife and children?" she asked.

"Not anymore."

"I'm sorry." She choked back unexpected tears. Hormonal overload.

"I tried to protect them. The GOS thought I was dead too."

Silence. Should she urge him to talk more, or wait for his leading?

"I've been with Colonel Alier since then. He gave me a reason to live."

"I appreciate what you are doing today. The GOS would like nothing better than to blow us up."

He chuckled. "Some things never change."

They rode in silence for the next half hour. Obviously he didn't want to talk further about his tragedy. She stared out the window. She didn't want to talk about it either. The drought had decimated the terrain. She tried to imagine the land in a time when the people were happy and the rains came in season. Silently she prayed for God's blessings on all those who bore the agony of tragic memories.

"Have you ever been in the States?" she asked.

"No. I'm Dinka. Lived here all my life."

"Darfur reminds me of a place there."

He tossed a curious look her way but said nothing.

"There's an old battleground in Pennsylvania called Gettysburg. Back in the 1860s, a civil war raged through our country."

Okuk nodded. Civil war he understood.

"Over a half-million soldiers were killed. A lot of them boys," Larson said. "One of the bloodiest of battles was fought at Gettysburg. My parents took me there when I was fifteen years old. I imagine it was for me to see what happens when brothers fight against brothers."

"What caused the war?"

"The northern states didn't want slavery, and the southern states claimed they needed slaves to run their plantations. When the South wanted to be separate from the North, war began."

"Like Sudan?"

"There were tragic incidents committed by those who were driven by hate, but not to this extent. At least I hope not. War is horrible for any reason, but some actions are inexcusable. Anyway, I remember getting out of our car at Gettysburg and walking past the spots where soldiers had camped and fought and died. A strange chill came over me. It was as though the dead were crying out for help." She tilted her head, remembering. "I thought I heard the screams of thousands of soldiers. So many that I thought they would pull themselves up from the ground and begin to fight again. I covered my ears—I couldn't stop the sounds of the dying all around me. My parents put me back into the car, and we left. I had nightmares for weeks."

"Sudan is the same nightmare," he said. "I hear my wife and sons."

"Are you Christian?"

"Why should I be?"

"Because God loves you and will give your spirit peace."

"I see just as many Christians die as those who are not."

"But the Christians live forever in heaven with God."

His face hardened, and he did not respond.

"I imagine Ben will be arriving in Warkou soon," she finally said. "He said a couple of days, but that means today. He'll most likely call."

"And I imagine he'll be angry with me. Very angry."

"It's my fault. I asked you to come with me in case of trouble."

He chuckled. "We'll see."

Okuk's satellite phone on the console rang. He snatched it up. "Hello, Colonel Alier. How are you, sir?"

Larson could hear Ben's voice crackling in the receiver. Okuk winced and pulled the phone away from his ear slightly. "I'd like to talk to him," she said.

Okuk nodded, his attention straight ahead as if Ben were right there in front of him. "Yes, sir. I understand, sir. Yes, Santino is with the men."

Ben must be on the mend to have the energy to fire questions. Either that, or he was in pain and too stubborn to take his medication. She wondered why he'd denied her access to his medical records. Face-to-face, she'd ask.

"I'm driving Dr. Farid to Kibum, where she plans to meet up with her husband. Yes, sir. I will return as soon as she's in his company."

This time, Larson touched Okuk's shoulder. "I really want to talk to Colonel Alier."

"Sir, Dr. Farid would like to speak to you. Yes, sir. I understand, sir." He handed her the phone.

She smiled at Okuk. He'd gotten an earful because of her request. "Hi, Ben. Where are you?"

"Warkou. I'm trying to make sense of the mess that's happened here since I left."

"We did our best to manage without you."

"Don't humor me. I'm mad, and you're in the middle of it."

She inwardly cringed. Ben had nearly died, and here she was teasing him. "I'm sorry. I did ask Commander Okuk to accompany me to northern Darfur. Paul landed there earlier today, and that's where I'm going. Once we find him, I'm fine."

"Why didn't Paul take you with him?"

"I don't know."

"Then why are you going? Obviously, he's knee-deep in something dangerous."

Her pulse sped. Her instinct had told her the same thing.

"The refugee camp can use my skills."

"So can the soldiers in Khartoum, but I don't see you driving there."

"I won't lie to you, Ben. I'm afraid for him."

Ben swore. "What can you do? Do you need reminding what happens to women captured by the government or the Janjaweed?"

No, she didn't need reminding. Ben's sister had been through a nightmare during her captivity. Maybe what Larson was doing was stupid, but she couldn't give up her longing to find her husband.

"Say something," he said. "I can't read your mind."

"I think it has something to do with his brother Nizam. They've been writing letters, and Nizam is very persuasive."

"Paul has about as much sense as the dirt under my feet when it comes to his family. He ignores the culture—their mind-set. So are you going to try to stop him?"

"Yes. It will take awhile for him to unload the food and supplies. I'm hoping the aid workers will detain him long enough for me to get there."

"Sarah's worried about you."

"She's simply being overprotective. And you should still be in the hospital. Why not stay in Warkou for a few days and let Sarah tend to you?"

"She'd summon the GOS. That woman hates me."

She laughed. "She doesn't hate you at all. You could try giving her some respect."

He growled like an angry dog. "She doesn't respect me. Anyway, Sarah told me there's a serious problem between you and Paul, but she wouldn't tell me what."

And she won't. "Oh, you know Sarah. She probably got wind of Paul looking for his family."

"You're a poor liar, Larson. But if you don't want to tell me what's really the matter, that's your business."

"Thank you. Why didn't you return my calls?"

"You have your secrets, and I have mine." He paused. "It's twelve hundred. I need to check on my men and see if I can get my hands on a truck to get back to them. Tell Okuk to be careful and to call me when you reach the refugee camp."

The phone clicked in her ear. Ben had no business doing anything but resting and letting his arm heal—not heading back to his men. She should have thought of the situation she was creating when she asked Commander Okuk to come with her. Now she had two problems. Actually, three.

NINE

Paul slowly turned, wondering how many men he was up against. No one stood within sight but the black Arab pointing a Kalashnikov rifle at his chest from about eleven meters away. Not far from the gunman was a large, toppled clay vessel that the villagers had once used to store extra food and water in the event of an emergency. That's where the man must have hidden. Paul had passed right by him.

"Drop your pack and raise your hands!" the man shouted in Arabic.

Paul slid his backpack from his shoulders and allowed it to drop to the dry ground with a thud. He raised his hands and studied the man while he calculated how quickly he could pull his 9 mm from inside his shirt.

"Where's Nizam? He was supposed to meet me here."

"He asked me to make sure you'd come alone. Now use your left hand to pull out the pistol and toss it to me."

Paul hated to concede, but he was fresh out of ideas. "You can see I'm alone. So where is he?"

"Waiting where it's safe."

"Safe from me? You can do better than that. Call him and tell him I'm here."

"Those aren't my orders."

Paul started to lower his arms.

"Keep them up."

"When do I see my brother?"

"In three days."

"Why not now? I've come a long way."

"We saw how you flew your plane to Kibum with food for all those people."

The sarcasm in the man's voice grated at Paul's nerves. "I do all I can for our people. More than what the government does." He considered blasting him about the government's support of the Janjaweed, but the man still held the rifle.

"You talk brave for a man who could die before his next breath."

"I know where I'm going when I die."

"Allah sends the infidel to hell."

"God sends His people to heaven."

The man lifted the rifle. "I know where to send you."

"Did my brother order this?" Paul hoped his voice sounded stronger than he felt. He'd been stupid to fall for Nizam's request.

The man hesitated.

"Did my brother order you to kill me?"

"That is none of your concern."

Paul eyed him squarely. "Then put down that rifle, and tell me what this is all about."

"I already have told you all you need to know. You'll see your brother in three days. Stay at Kibum until you are called."

"And how will you do that?" A half-dozen people knew his satellite phone number, but Nizam wasn't one of them.

"Nizam has his means. Now turn around."

"Why?" Who had betrayed him?

"Do as I say."

"What's your name?" Paul stalled while he considered how to retrieve his pistol lying on the ground.

"Muti."

"All right, Muti. Maybe I'll answer your call, and maybe I won't."

"You must not want to see your brother."

"Maybe my brother doesn't want to see me."

"He's being careful. Enough talk."

"I need my pistol."

Muti sneered. "Go ahead. Even aim it at me. It would give me great pleasure to kill you."

Paul doubted if Muti was working alone, but any others were carefully hidden. He picked up his weapon and gave the man a curt nod before setting off toward Kibum. *Lord, forgive me for being so headstrong. Guide me in what to do. Larson doesn't need to be a widow because I'm not taking the necessary precautions.*

❖ ❖ ❖

Ben lay in a hammock outside the medical clinic in Warkou with his phone on his chest and mosquito netting covering him. If it weren't for all the thoughts hammering against his brain, he'd give in to sleep. The pain pills were the reason he had to fight to stay awake, but he had no choice but to take them. With his eyes closed, he once again mentally listed what had to be done in the next few months and how long each thing would take, leaving plenty of days to spend with David. He should ask Daruka to marry him. That would give his son a name. He allowed his body to drift off to sleep, a welcome reprieve from his pain-filled world.

The shrill ring of his phone roused him from his drug-laden stupor. It rang twice more before he knocked it from his chest and onto the ground. Reaching to wrap his fingers around the phone, he nearly spilled from the hammock.

"Colonel Alier, we have a jeep on the way to Warkou," a man said.

"Thank you, sir. When can I expect it?"

"Early morning. You need a ride back to your men, correct?"

"Yes, sir."

"What has happened to the Rhino's battalion trucks?"

If the jeep hadn't belonged to a key political leader, Ben would have told him to keep his vehicle.

"I have reason to believe Dr. Larson Kerr Farid and her husband are in danger. Because of that, Commander Okuk has taken one of the trucks to a refugee camp in northern Darfur. The other truck is with my men."

"Very good. I trust you are healing well. I wish I had a copter to fly you in."

"I appreciate the jeep, sir. Thanks again."

The phone disconnected, and Ben chose to sleep a while longer. He had plenty of time until the vehicle arrived, and he needed rest to clear his head. He woke at daybreak to the sound of Sarah's voice.

"Colonel Alier, two men are here for you."

"With a jeep?" he asked, now thoroughly awake.

"Yes, and it's not full of holes."

Ben chose not to respond. He never knew what Sarah would say next. He swung out of the hammock, his back screaming in protest. "If you can cook me some breakfast, I'll be on my way."

"You slept a long time." The lines deepened in her face.

"Why, Sarah, were you worried about me?"

She crossed her arms over her chest in a familiar stance. "Yes, I was. If you died on me, I'd have to dig your grave."

"Such a sweet, caring heart you have. At least if I ask you to fix me some breakfast, I don't have to worry about you poisoning me."

"Not this time."

He laughed, less from amusement than to shake off the pain in his back, and turned to greet the men. The driver of the jeep was an SPLA man, Sergeant Thomas Jok, a good man who had once served under Ben. Jok's military status was recognizable only by the ammo belt swung over his shoulder. The other man was an SPLA soldier. Such a ragged bunch, but they had stout hearts. Thomas and Ben shook hands vigorously, and the other man saluted.

"You are healing well?" Thomas asked.

"Takes more than a bullet in the arm to stop me."

"Nothing keeps Colonel Alier from the battle." He smiled broadly, revealing the gap where a tribal ritual had left several lower teeth missing.

"You need to eat before you return."

Thomas nodded. "Thank you; we are hungry. It is an honor to serve you. Everyone respects Colonel Alier. I understand your commander is assisting the Farids in Darfur?"

"Yes. I fear there may be trouble awaiting them."

"I pray God will keep your friends safe. Vice President Garang will ease our suffering soon. Southern Sudan is blessed to have him speaking for us. Our soldiers are now resting, and hopefully they will be able to return to their homes soon."

What homes? The GOS had been burning villages and killing the southern Sudanese since the early eighties. He suspected Garang would have great difficulty convincing the Muslim government to allow the South to build their country and control their own resources. Ben didn't voice his thoughts on the matter. The future would show whether he was right or wrong. Of course, he didn't have a future beyond six months.

Sarah approached them. For an old woman, she walked unusually erect. "I have food for all of you." Smiling at the other men, but not at Ben, she ushered them toward her *tukul.*

Was she upset that Ben wasn't traipsing after Larson? He had a job to do and a responsibility to his men. Before he died, he would make sure that wrinkled woman acknowledged all he'd done for people just like her, who were helpless against the government.

❖ ❖ ❖

Larson wanted to sleep, but each time her body veered in that direction, the truck would hit a rut and jar her from any thought of rest. Commander Okuk said the journey would take almost two days—providing they were lucky and no one stopped them. She needed to sleep. Once they arrived in Kibum, she'd hit the ground running. Saving lives and giving hope to those desperate for medical care offered little time for eating and sleeping. There, she'd exist on adrenaline and the grace of God.

In the past, Paul had organized a church service for refugees waiting for food, water, and medical care. Most of them were skeptical of an Arab who spoke of a God who was not Allah. Paul took the time to assist them through the endless lines and earn their confidence. Then he explained what the Lord had done for them. She appreciated the way he didn't condemn their Muslim traditions but showed his love of Jesus in other ways.

She turned her attention to Commander Okuk. "I'm proud of Paul, and I want to tell him so once we're finished yelling at each other."

"He should be proud of you."

Odd statement, but she was fairly certain that the commander did not trust her husband. Probably because he was an Arab. She closed her eyes. Commander Okuk should rest too, but she knew he'd refuse. They'd drive until dark and get a fresh start at first light. She'd wanted to leave as soon as Paul's plane had cleared the landing strip, but a relentless attack of morning sickness had delayed them for over an hour. Calling Paul made no sense until they were nearly at the camp. He'd be furious with her, but she didn't care. Her biggest fear was that he'd air-dropped the food and flown on into northern Sudan to meet Nizam.

To the left of the Hummer, a few women and children drove some goats toward their path. Larson righted herself and stared at the pitiful parade. What motivated these people to keep planting one foot in front of the other?

"We can't stop," Okuk said.

"I know. We're running behind. But I want every government and every nongovernmental organization in the world to see what is happening here. These people are so needy, and my heart aches for the women and children."

"So does mine." He continued on past the group without a glance in their direction.

A tear slipped over her cheek. She touched her stomach and again wrestled with her decision to find Paul. What could she do to help if his family had already seized him? She refused to think about such horror. Their baby would have an opportunity to know his father—if God was willing to keep Paul safe.

"I grew up on a farm in Ohio," she said, more to occupy her mind than to tell stories from another world.

"Ohio is in the States?"

She nodded. "Where I grew up is really pretty, rolling hills and green fields. Behind our house were seven springs that flowed into a winding creek. As soon as the snow—"

"What's snow?"

She smiled. "It's like rain, but it's white and cold. When I say cold, I mean like the frost on the inside of my little refrigerator at the clinic."

"Okay, but what does snow do?"

"In our winter it piles up on the ground. Big trucks have to clear the roads to drive, while the rest of us play in it."

"Like children?"

"Yeah. You wear coats, hats, and gloves to stay warm. You can pack the snow to build snowmen, or you can make snowballs and throw them at each other."

"Can you play soccer with snowballs?"

She laughed. "Not exactly. I'll have to find some pictures for you."

"Did the snow fall on the creek too?"

"The creek froze all the way through, and you could walk on it."

Okuk threw back his head and laughed. "Now, Dr. Farid, don't make fun of me for not knowing about snow. Is this a Christian story like your Jesus walking on water?"

"Not at all. Both stories are the truth." Now she was laughing. It did sound ridiculous. "Just you wait until I show you the pictures."

He threw her a wide smile and shook his head. "You get some sleep while I drive. I want to think about snow, and water that gets hard enough to walk on."

She closed her eyes and drifted off to sleep, dreaming of sled rides, building snowmen, roasting marshmallows, ice-skating . . . and a precious baby boy who looked like Paul. Three times she woke and asked Okuk to stop the Hummer so she could relieve herself. She hoped he didn't figure out her problem. They made good time, driving late into the darkness. After several hours, Okuk switched off the engine for the night. He took the front seat, and she curled up in the back.

"I need only a couple of hours' sleep," he said. "I'll begin driving before the sun rises."

Larson woke to the sound of Okuk's voice. Sunlight had ushered in a new day. They shared a bottle of water and drove on, each mile looking like the previous one. Again her head began to nod.

"Dr. Farid, we have trouble." Okuk picked up the binoculars and focused on something ahead. His left knee steered.

Instantly her senses cleared. "What's wrong?"

"Those men up there aren't SPLA." He handed her the binoculars.

She recognized the Arab militia instantly by their head-dresses and their wicked assortment of weapons. *Janjaweed.* Some said the word meant "devil riding a horse and armed with an automatic rifle." Along with a few horses, she also saw camels. "Can we radio anyone for help?"

"I already have. The nearest battalion is close to an hour away."

"What do we do?" She took a deep breath to still the rising panic.

He slowed the Hummer. "They're blocking our way across the road."

"You want to outrun them?"

Okuk moistened his lips. "I don't think we have a choice. It's the getting past them that bothers me. This truck is armored, right?"

She nodded. "It would take a bomb to destroy it."

An image of the truck blowing up with them in it sent a chill up and down her arms. This would surely be a test of how well the Hummer maneuvered and its ability to keep Okuk and her alive. She recalled the grotesque stories of what the Janjaweed did to their captives. To women. What if they knew she was Paul Farid's wife? And Okuk? They'd take great delight in torturing him.

She mentally pushed away her fright. "What can I do?"

"Are you a good shot with that AUG 3?"

The heavily armed Arabs spread across the road ahead and lifted their MK 47s.

"I am. Ben and Paul trained me well. You want me to pick them off?" Odd how confident she sounded when fear clutched at her throat.

"All of them. Reach behind the seat for ammo and grenades. Do you know how to use them?"

"Yes. And I can use the grenade launcher." She twisted in her seat and zipped open the bags, then grabbed the duct tape on the floorboard with the grenades.

He cursed. "If only I had two arms. I'm supposed to protect you."

"We'll protect each other." She laughed and duct-taped the magazine together to allow for sixty rounds of continuous firing.

"What's so funny?" he asked.

"You and me taking on the Janjaweed."

"And living to tell about it?"

"You mean bragging to Ben and Paul about it."

They both laughed, and it kept her from crying. She'd heard of men using humor in the face of danger and hadn't understood it at the time. Now she did, though she knew this situation was no laughing matter. She took a deep breath and stared ahead, praying for deliverance. Killing was wrong. The Bible said so, but she didn't have time to deliberate morality in a war zone. It wouldn't be the first time she'd taken a man's life who threatened to kill her or someone she loved.

"We'll call Ben once we're through this." Okuk pushed the automatic button to roll down their windows. "Hand me one of those 'nades," he said. "This one-armed soldier can do a lot of damage."

She laid them in the seat between them. "Which do I use first?"

"The rifle. Farther distance. Then use the grenade launcher. That'll clear the path for a few more rounds of ammo."

Snatching up her weapon, she stuck the assault rifle out the window. "Drive this tank straight through them, Okuk. I'm ready."

TEN

Ben drove the jeep and steered with his good arm while his back and injured arm throbbed. His entire body revolted against the impact of the deeply rutted road, as though he'd been beaten on every inch of his body. He'd be useless in a firefight. Before his trek to the hospital, he'd been able to ignore the aggravating pain, but it had not been this intense. Maybe knowing the stakes behind the pain caused him to hurt more.

"Stay in Nairobi and take treatments," the doctor had said. "This is a rapidly growing type of cancer."

"How much more time would that buy me?"

"A few months, maybe longer."

"That's all? So I'd last the length of the treatments? I'd rather spend my remaining days taking care of business instead of staying here and throwing up with chemo or having my insides burned up with radiation. That's not even an existence."

The doctor closed Ben's file. "Many strides have been made in your particular type of cancer. I've consulted with experts who say the situation is not hopeless. Any day we expect a breakthrough."

"Right. Now you want me to be a laboratory rat?"

"I don't want you to give up. You deserve a chance to live.

What if the cancer went into remission, and you suddenly had years left instead of months?"

My son. Southern Sudan. Ben brushed away the thoughts. "Looks to me like the test results show I'm as good as dead. No, thanks. I'll live what's left of my days my way."

Thinking back over that conversation, Ben questioned whether he should have taken a few treatments to see if the cancer might have lessened in its severity. The possible side effects of the treatment didn't bother him as much as the thought of wasting time—or of someone's finding out about his medical condition.

He gritted his teeth and tried to dodge a rut big enough to bury him in. What good would he be to anyone in his current condition? His vision blurred. Pain pills. Whether he took them or not, he had no quality of life.

Ben stiffened. The reality of what lay ahead of him rattled his mind and spirit. Did he really believe God no longer existed? Many years ago, he'd tried following His ways, but that was in his idealistic youth. He'd actually thought the war with the North could be won easily—because the South had suffered. Then he'd started watching his comrades fall, leaving behind families and friends to mourn their loss. Widows and fatherless children found no glory in those deaths. Pessimism had festered in Ben like an infection in an open wound, and he'd never recovered.

Ben glanced over at Sergeant Jok, riding in the jeep's passenger seat. "I'm turning over the driving to one of you. This arm of mine is bothering me, and driving seems to make it worse. I need to get Okuk on the phone too. My guess is, he and Larson Farid spent the night on the road, and I want to see how they fared." Almost a lie, but it bought him a little time to relax. Sweat burned his eyes and trickled down his face.

Once Ben had changed places with the soldier in the rear seat of the jeep, he pulled out the antenna of his satellite phone and punched in Okuk's number. It rang seven times with no response. Finally he was able to leave a message. He tried Larson's phone, but she didn't answer either.

"Larson. Call me. I want an idea of how you two are doing." The combination of pain and fury over her stupid trek into Darfur with his commander had left him with a pounding headache. "You'd better be calling me back real quick. I don't have time to be worried about you."

For the next hour, he watched the dismal countryside pass him by, each mile the same as the last. The people they occasionally passed were so poor that they looked like the walking dead. He tried Larson's phone again, but nothing. Anger slid down as worry took precedence. He stared at the phone, then decided to try another number.

"Paul, this is Ben."

"Where are you?"

"I'm in a jeep with two soldiers en route to my men."

"I thought you'd spend a few days in Warkou and let Larson take care of you."

"I'm fine. Got to get back to my responsibilities. You have her plenty scared." Was it Paul or Larson who deserved more to stand in front of a firing squad once he faced them for this?

"I'd better give her a call."

"Good luck. She's not answering her phone."

"She and Sarah are probably visiting with the villagers."

"She's not in Warkou."

"Where is she?" Paul's voice took on a slight edge.

"Somewhere between Warkou and Kibum."

Paul blew out an exasperated breath. "Are you telling me that she's driving here? Is she alone?"

"Commander Okuk is with her. What's going on between you two?"

"Nothing. I had something to do here besides delivering food and supplies, and I believed it was too dangerous for her to join me."

"*Dangerous* is Larson and Okuk driving to the camp. Besides, she's been there before. Doesn't make sense why you didn't take her."

"It's not important. When did she leave?"

"Late yesterday morning. I imagine they stopped for the night."

"They should have been here by now."

"My thoughts exactly. I'll radio around and see what I can find out."

"Thanks. And get back to me as soon as you hear something. My wife is going to get an earful for this one."

Paul sounded more than a little exasperated. *Good.* His frustration matched Ben's.

"And you two didn't have a fight?"

"I don't know where you got that. She hasn't been feeling well, which was another reason why I didn't want her here."

Great. Larson's sick and driving to a disease-infested refugee camp. "She'll turn up soon."

"I hope so. I'm worried, Ben. This isn't like her. And with cholera threatening to break out in full force here. I just don't want her in this mess until she's recovered from whatever has her feeling bad."

"You don't have much choice since she's nearly to Kibum."

"I'll try to contact her. It's too late for her to turn around. I hate to think of them out in the middle of nowhere, stranded or worse."

"Let me know if you hear from her." Ben ended the call.

He dropped the phone onto his lap and rubbed his face. Larson might be married to another man, but he still cared for her. He'd never understand what she saw in Paul. Ben shook his head. Paul was a good man; he just took too many risks for a man who had a contract out on his life.

Comdr. Jeremiah Kedini had a battalion in northern Darfur. Ben leaned over the front seat and grabbed the radio.

After several tries, the commander responded.

"Colonel Alier here. I have a commander of mine and Dr. Larson Kerr Farid on their way to Kibum. They are not answering their phones. What can you tell me?"

"Received a call from Commander Okuk." Kedini sounded breathless, like he was running. "He spotted about a dozen Janjaweed on camels and horses and needs help. We're heading there now, but we're about fifteen minutes away. I hear the guns."

"Get back to me."

"Yes, sir."

Ben stared at his phone, deliberating about what to tell Paul. He lifted the canteen to his lips and swallowed a mouthful of tepid water. If Larson were his wife, he'd want to know the whole story. But she wasn't. He got Paul back on the line.

"I've contacted a unit a few hours from you. They're scouting the area and getting back to me."

"Did he report any trouble?"

"No more than usual."

"What does that mean?"

"We're in a war zone."

"I'm sorry, Ben. I keep trying her phone and watching for the Hummer."

"I'm sure she's fine. They might have gotten tired or stopped to help some people. I'll keep you posted." If something happened to Larson, he'd never forgive himself.

❖ ❖ ❖

Paul slammed his fist into his palm. Ben had lied to him. The tension in his voice gave him away. Larson was in danger, and neither Paul nor Ben had the means of helping her. But she was in the Hummer, and it was fully armored, and she had the AUG 3. Paul and Ben had spent hours drilling her on the rifle's features. *Just keep your finger on the trigger so it keeps firing.* She had the laser aiming system too. Every reassuring detail about the Hummer and the assault rifle repeated in his mind over and over. All the while, he trembled.

Okuk was a good soldier, but with one arm what could he do? Paul paced the length of the camp, his heart too heavy to pray more than a plea to spare her and Okuk's lives. He should have told her the truth.

His original reason for landing in Kibum suddenly roared as selfish. Nizam hadn't shown up, and the meeting in three days had "death trap" written all over it. *Stupid.* He could have been killed yesterday. Paul expected a full set of marching orders from God before he'd agree to meet Nizam again. Yesterday Muti's fingers had itched to pull that trigger—not the type of messenger a man sends to welcome his brother.

But he shouldn't be thinking of anyone but Larson. Pulling his phone from his pants pocket, he tried again to reach her. No answer.

"How about some company?"

Paul offered a thin-lipped smile to Chuck Butler, a once-retired pediatrician from London who now volunteered with Doctors Without Borders. His trademark hat covered in fishing lures, together with his thick, dark-framed glasses and his compassion for children, made for an eclectic mix of a man.

"You look as if you need a friend," Chuck said. "You're about to wear out our dirt road."

"What I need is a miracle." Paul dropped the phone back inside his pocket.

"You mean the suspected cholera?"

"That wasn't what I was referring to, but I did wonder about some of the diarrhea cases today."

"I think we can get it under control. Hard to keep sanitization as a priority for these people, but we're giving daily classes on how to avoid the disease. People are dying of thirst, and they drink whatever they can find."

"Desperate people resort to desperate means." His mind focused on Larson.

"We could share a couple of bottles of water and talk about it." Chuck pushed his glasses up a sweaty nose.

"I'm not good company."

"Try me."

Paul smiled. "All right. I've paced this camp long enough. Why don't we find a place to sit for a few minutes?"

Inside a tarp-covered area with boxes of everything from rice to powdered milk, the two men took refuge from the merciless sun and drank their water.

"What's troubling you?"

"My wife is on her way here with only a one-armed soldier to protect her." He glanced quickly at Chuck. "Commander Okuk is a fine man. I didn't mean for that to sound condescending."

"I hear the concern in your voice. When do you expect her?"

Paul capped the bottle of water and rested it on the ground beside his feet. "By my calculations, she should have been here."

"Why didn't she fly in with you?"

Paul frowned. "I wanted her to stay in Warkou this trip. I had business to tend to, and she's not been feeling well." He shook his head. "My business here had some possible danger too—more than usual. And I knew she'd work much too hard and not rest."

"She followed you, huh? I can check her out when she gets here. But she should have an idea what's wrong and treat the problem herself."

"She insists that everything's fine."

"Why don't you tell me the symptoms? That way, when she gets here, I can discuss it with her and get her on the mend."

Paul nodded. "She wants to sleep all the time."

111

"Any fever? Headaches? Diarrhea?"

"None of those. Just tired. She's not eating much either, and something is making her vomit."

Chuck wet his lips and gazed out through the tent's opening. "Anything else?"

"She's been very emotional, and my Larson is—or was—the most logical, clearheaded woman on the planet."

"When was her last period?"

Paul was startled. He clenched his fists a few times to get the blood flowing again. "I . . . I don't know for sure." His mind raced. When *was* it?

Chuck wagged a finger at him. "Sounds to me like Larson might be pregnant. You should consider having a talk with your wife when she gets here."

"Before or after I wring her pretty little neck?"

"Preferably before." Chuck grinned. "Aren't you Christian?"

"Yes. I've been praying all day, and I'm fresh out of words."

"I thought you people had a direct line to God."

"We do, but there are times He doesn't respond as quickly as I'd like." *I sure hope He's listening.*

Chuck had to be wrong—a wild guess. A pregnancy wasn't supposed to happen; they'd taken precautions. He and Larson had discussed at length that children would disrupt their ministry.

❖ ❖ ❖

Larson's heart slammed against her chest. Her fingers shook so badly that she couldn't pull back on the trigger, but once the Janjaweed lifted their weapons, she simply reacted as Paul and Ben had taught her.

"Launch a couple of 'nades, then switch back to rifle mode." Okuk must have had more faith in her than she did.

Through his open window, Okuk hurled a grenade into the lineup of men like a major league pitcher. She did the same. The grenades whistled and exploded. Men and body parts blew out of the thick gray smoke. Larson leaned out her window, aimed, and squeezed the trigger again.

Okuk stomped on the gas and drove straight toward the tattered soldiers as automatic rifles pumped bullets into the Hummer's sides. Camels screamed, and one fell in the vehicle's way.

"Get out of our way," he shouted, and veered around the animal.

Larson realized she'd gone through thirty rounds already. She flipped the assembly upside down and loaded the other end. Sweat streamed down her face. Several Janjaweed stood in front of the Hummer. Hate radiated from every muscle of their faces. The Hummer picked up speed. How much could the vehicle take? Certainly not a direct hit from a grenade.

Her finger held tight to the trigger, mowing down one man after another. A sharp sting pierced her shoulder. She screamed.

ELEVEN

———— ✦ ————

*P*aul peered under a stick-covered shelter at three small children. One of them, a little girl, giggled and covered her mouth. Paul crawled under the makeshift haven and watched the children in fascination. His worries about Larson temporarily receded.

"Am I funny?" he asked in Arabic.

The little girl giggled again, and another child joined in. Paul held out a small yellow rubber ball, one that a humanitarian worker had given him. The girl stared curiously at the ball with large, dark eyes. Their sparkle had not yet been quenched by the perils of her ethnicity.

"Go ahead. You can have it." Paul slid his palm closer.

She wrapped her fingers around the ball and slowly drew it to her. She tilted her head and brought it to her lips.

"It's not food. The ball is a toy." He took it from her hands and juggled it a few times. *What next?*

"Need some help?"

Paul glanced up. "Hi, Chuck. I'm trying to figure out how to explain to these kids what to do with a ball."

"We can demonstrate it."

Paul lifted a brow.

"Pretending to be a kid is the best way I know to relax in

this godforsaken hole." Chuck sat down in the dirt outside the shelter and spread his legs. "Here, roll the ball to me."

A few seconds later, the two men were rolling the ball back and forth between extended legs. A couple of Darfuran woman passed by and eyed them strangely. Paul wondered if they'd like to join in, but they kept on walking.

"Do you want to try?" Chuck asked the children.

When the little girl appeared eager, Paul picked her up and positioned her in the same spot where he'd just been. Chuck rolled the ball to her, and Paul helped her send it back. Then Paul led another little girl to Chuck's side and showed her how to place her legs in a *V* and play the game. Shortly thereafter, the little boy joined them.

"Child experts would commend us." Chuck peered over the top of his glasses, sweat slid to the end of his nose. "I'm sure they'd assign fancy terms to the process of children putting aside their autonomy and learning to share. I use to do that sort of thing in London, but now I simply try to save their lives." He bent to snatch up the ball, which had escaped one of the children. "Some humanitarian specialists could spend hours discussing the merits of Sudanese peoples observing children at play as part of peacemaking efforts."

"If only it were that simple."

When Chuck left to return to the medical tent, Paul played with the children until they all tired. Afternoon shadows crept in like a cunning thief bent on robbing his hope of Larson's arrival. Where was she?

She still wasn't answering her phone.

As he stood in the middle of the camp on this twenty-first day of July and stared down the endless road, he recalled the nights he had recited to her from *The Rubaiyat*. One of Omar Khayyam's verses rolled through his head.

Oh, threats of Hell and Hopes of Paradise!
One thing at least is certain—This Life flies;

One thing is certain and the rest is Lies;
The Flower that once has blown for ever dies.

Paul refused to think of her being hurt, or worse. Soon, she and Commander Okuk would roll into camp in the black Hummer. Paul had spared no cost to make sure she'd always be safe. But he wasn't God, and harsh reality was the only guarantee in his life. He caught his breath. Ah, how quickly cynicism choked the life out of his faith. It happened far too much of late, and he couldn't bring himself to do anything about it.

Larson. The woman he loved more than life itself. How many times had he taken her for granted when he should have showered her with gifts for putting up with his miserable self? They were an odd pair—products of wildly different cultures, brought together by their shared commitment to the oppressed Sudanese and by a love only God could give.

He recalled the first time he'd met the renowned Dr. Larson Kerr. He'd flown in a shipment of food and medical supplies to Warkou, a village that had been bombed repeatedly by the GOS. He'd asked the fearful villagers for Dr. Kerr, expecting a man to emerge from one of the many *tukuls*. Instead he'd found a feisty woman—a feisty, beautiful woman whose blue eyes shone with vitality and passion.

Shortly thereafter, a battalion of SPLA soldiers had entered Warkou, and he'd met Col. Ben Alier, the warlord who'd despised Paul and his Arab background. Ben had looked for a reason to blow his head off. And he'd nearly done it when government soldiers flew in, attacked the village, and kidnapped Larson's young assistant, who was also Ben's sister. Ben, Paul, and Larson had put aside their distrust for each other and teamed up to find Rachel Alier. By the time the young woman had been located, Paul and Larson had fallen in love, and Ben had gained a fragile respect for the Arab Christian.

Paul treasured his wife a little more each day. Tonight his heart ached for her.

Oh, my habibi.

Chuck had planted a seed that concerned him. If Larson were pregnant, she needed to leave the country. Neither she nor the baby would be safe as long as war and disease raged— and his family sought to kill him.

A child . . . *his* child. Even though he'd believed fatherhood wasn't a part of God's plan for their lives, the idea of a boy or girl sharing his and Larson's looks fascinated him. A warm sensation moved through his body at the thought of watching his daughter or son grow. A child was a gift from God, not a mistake or a nuisance, and he intended to take care of his gift.

If not for the SPLA's presence near Warkou, he was certain his family would have marched into the village and filled him full of holes by now. Too many times, Paul had taken comfort in the fact that rebel troops were protecting Larson and the village. But his confidence defied logic. His family knew he was in Warkou. Why hadn't they bombed the village and wiped it out? What stopped them? The peace treaty? Earlier this evening, while pondering who could have given away his phone number, he—

Paul's phone rang and interrupted his ponderings. The screen lit up with Ben's name.

"Paul, I've heard from Okuk."

"Are they all right?" Paul's voice threatened to shatter.

"Okuk is fine. Larson will be all right. A bullet took a hunk of her shoulder and sailed out the other side. According to Okuk, the bleeding's under control, and she said the bullet missed the bone. She instructed him on what to do with her medical supplies."

"I have to talk to her."

"I understand. Let me know how she's doing. I assume a doctor is there to bandage her up."

"Ah, yes. I'll call you later." He remembered his comment to Chuck about "wringing her pretty little neck," an American phrase that he'd picked up from a movie. Maybe five years from now he'd consider that—but not tonight.

Paul punched in Larson's number, all the while praising God she was alive and praying for her to get to the refugee camp soon.

"Hi, Paul."

"*Habibi,* are you in much pain?"

"Not too bad. You know me. I'm tough. I'm sorry about all this, really I am. I was afraid you were walking into a viper's pit with your brother, and I thought I could stop you."

He cringed. "Almost right. But you are the one who's suffered because of my foolishness. What's important is that you get here and let Dr. Chuck tend to your shoulder."

"Okuk says we'll be there in about two hours." She paused. "I have to tell you something when we get there."

"The Hummer's destroyed?" He attempted to sound humorous to keep from breaking into tears.

"Not at all. That jewel saved our lives."

Paul heard a laugh in the background. "What's so funny?"

"Oh, Okuk is expounding on my expertise with the AUG 3. Your lessons and Ben's may have saved our lives too." Her voice faded.

"*Habibi,* we'll talk later. Right now you need to save your strength. I love you. If I'd have been honest with you, none of this would have happened."

"I love you too. So very much. We will work this out." She gasped. No doubt the pain was intense. "Do you want to talk to Okuk?"

"Yes, please." Paul had to know what had happened.

A few seconds of silence gave Paul time to gain control of his shaken emotions.

"I'm here," Okuk said.

"How much blood has my wife lost?"

"Not too bad. She was very brave."

"Can you tell me how you were attacked? Are you driving, by the way?"

"I can drive and talk with one arm." Okuk chuckled. "A band of Janjaweed lined up in front of us on the road and opened fire. We returned it, along with a few grenades, and raced through them. Dr. Farid used that rifle like a trained soldier, but sticking her arm out the window to fire caused her to get shot. We got away, then Comdr. Jeremiah Kedini arrived about twenty minutes later and cleaned up the rest of the Janjaweed. Your wife talked me through what to do with her arm."

Paul took a ragged breath. "Thanks. I will never forget this. I owe you plenty. Just be careful, and I'll be here waiting." He disconnected the phone and dropped it into his pocket.

They couldn't arrive soon enough. Later he and Larson would sort through their differences that had nearly gotten both of them killed. Later he'd talk to Ben about which of his trusted friends might have betrayed his phone number to Nizam. And later he'd listen to what Larson wanted to tell him, but he probably already knew. For now, he'd find Chuck to alert him to her injury.

He took a deep breath and wished he could confess his miserable soul to the One who granted forgiveness. Maybe later. If he'd done what he should, none of this would have happened. Tomorrow he'd fly his wife home to Warkou or on to the hospital in Nairobi if need be. From now on he intended to be a husband, not some idiot chasing men who wanted him dead. His work involved piloting for FTW, evangelizing and discipling nearby villages, and helping his wife with her medical practice. If they decided to work more with the Darfurans, then they'd do it together safely. Surely God didn't want him risking his wife's life for the sake of sharing the gospel with those who didn't care.

Ben phoned Okuk for an update. He couldn't rest until he knew Larson was in Kibum and under the care of a doctor.

"She's sleeping, and her color is good," Okuk said. "I insisted she take something for the pain."

"Good." Ben wiped the sweat streaming down his face—not so much from the heat as from his own pain. The reminder of his cancer assaulted him constantly.

"One of the last things she said was about her worry for you—that you might have a relapse from your wound. I also think she's concerned about how she upset her husband with her insistence upon this trip into Darfur."

Sounds like her. Larson's concern for others was one of the things he loved about her. But she was another man's wife, and he was nothing more than a dying man with illusions. He shook his head. "Maybe it knocked some sense into her. She can't help people if she's dead."

"Colonel, I'd have killed her myself rather than have her face the Janjaweed."

"Whether they knew who she was or not, they'd have made sure she suffered plenty before she died."

"I'd have killed her for you, not for her husband," Okuk whispered. "I don't trust any Arab, even one who drops food and supplies for our people."

Ben started to defend Paul, but Okuk would not have understood. As far as the commander was concerned, all Arabs were a murderous lot. Until meeting Paul Farid, Ben would have agreed, but he doubted if Paul could ever do anything to prove his loyalty to Okuk—other than give his life for the South. Possibly not then.

Ben remembered his fate in the months ahead. Okuk and Paul would need each other. "Paul has saved my life more than once, and he risked his neck to find my sister. I trust him, and I hope someday you'll see that he's not like the others. They're out to kill him too. In fact, they'd rather find him than attack us."

"Sir, have you ever wondered why Warkou is no longer attacked like it used to be?"

"We have troops in the area to deter them. Besides, you and I both know that the North signed the peace treaty so they could concentrate their efforts in Darfur. I am convinced of Paul's loyalty, and I advise you to trust him. If you feel this way, why did you consent to drive his wife to Kibum?"

"To find out what he was really doing."

"I've taught you to trust no one but yourself and to obey your officers. But in this matter with Paul Farid, you're wrong."

"Yes, sir." He paused. "Larson's waking up."

"Keep me posted."

"I will."

Ben closed his eyes. Larson would be all right; he had to believe that. So much for him to do in so short a time. If only the pain pills worked better.

TWELVE

The Hummer's headlights shined a pinpoint of light from far off and inched closer through the slow shadows of night. At first Paul thought he was seeing a mirage, but the sound of the approaching vehicle was no delusion. He raced to Chuck's tent and summoned him before hurrying to meet his wife.

As the vehicle grew closer, he stood in its path and pointed to the clinic, where Chuck awaited them.

He'd seen plenty of blood in his day, but not his wife's. When Okuk opened the Hummer's rear door, Paul sickened. All of this could have been prevented if he'd told Larson the reasons why he'd wanted her to stay behind in Warkou.

"I'm all right." Larson's words slurred. "I'm fine. Oh, I'm so sorry, Paul, to cause this much trouble."

He scooped her up into his arms and cautiously lifted her from the seat into the evening air, thankful that the sweltering heat had cooled. His lips brushed across hers. "Hush. I won't hear any of that nonsense. This whole thing is my fault. Chuck is right here, and he'll fix you up just fine."

She laid her head against his chest, and he swallowed a lump the size of Sudan. He felt certain that her emotions, along with her body, had taken a beating in the last twenty-four hours.

Inside the tent, a diesel-fueled generator powered light for Chuck to treat her bloody shoulder.

"Paul says you haven't been feeling well." Chuck unwound the bloody gauze wrapped around the top of her arm.

"Nothing important."

"Why don't you let me be the judge of that? He says you've been tired and vomiting."

Paul studied her pale face. She glanced up at him. *She's afraid.* Had he done something to lose her trust? Or had she contracted a disease? "Talk to him, *habibi.*" He held her other hand and kissed it.

"I . . . I know what's wrong with me."

"Tell me so I have an idea what I'm dealing with here." Chuck pulled out a sterile needle for an IV.

"I'm pregnant." She turned her attention to her upper arm, then back to Paul.

"Congratulations," Chuck said. "Any spotting or complications?"

"No." She continued to stare into Paul's face. "Only the typical morning sickness."

Paul gave her a smile, one he truly felt. Contrary to what he'd always expected, the prospect of being a father brought a surge of pride and excitement. In the next breath, fear for Larson and his child alerted him to what must be done. But he refused to show his trepidation. "Why didn't you tell me? We could have celebrated."

"I was afraid you'd send me to Nairobi or the States. I couldn't bear leaving you or Sudan."

"I love you, and I'm happy about our baby. We'll talk through all of this when you're feeling better."

"Are you, Paul? You're not angry with me?" She attempted a light laugh. "How many women do you think get pregnant on the pill in the heart of Sudan?"

"Just my wife." He bent and kissed her. "Now let Chuck patch up that arm."

An hour later, while Larson slept, Paul stepped out into the night with Okuk. "I can't thank you enough for what you've done for Larson and me. I don't want to think of what might have happened."

"Neither do I," Okuk said. "If it hadn't been for her good aim and that truck of yours, we wouldn't have made it. The soldiers who came were a help too."

Paul nodded. "I agree." The weight of fatherhood hit him again. "I'm going to be a father."

Okuk laughed. "Are you trying to convince yourself or me?"

"I'm not sure." He laughed. "I never thought I wanted children with my family after my hide, but I feel good. It's going to take some time to get used to the idea. I feel so stupid that I didn't put it all together."

"Enjoy the moment. I remember . . ." Okuk took a breath. "I remember my children."

"Are they gone?"

"Yes. About five years ago."

Paul stared into the man's face. Although darkness separated them, he prayed Okuk heard compassion in his voice. "I'm sorry. I despise the loss of innocent lives in all of this turmoil."

"Thank you."

"I'm worried about the danger for Larson. But Warkou has been fairly safe recently with soldiers nearby. I must believe God will guard and protect her."

Commander Okuk coughed.

"I'll be forever indebted to you, Commander," Paul said. "If not for your bravery and quick thinking, well, I don't want to discuss that possibility. Do not ever hesitate to ask anything of me." He reached out to shake the man's only hand.

Okuk grasped Paul's hand. "Your wife has kept many of us alive. And you have brought food and supplies to our people. It was an honor."

"Thank you. Guess we could use some sleep." Paul yawned. "I'm staying right by Larson's side in case she needs something."

"One of us should call Colonel Alier."

"I will." *He needs to hear about the pregnancy from me.* "In fact, I'll call now. Good night, Commander."

Paul headed back to the clinic. He thought he heard Okuk mumble something, but he was too tired to inquire what.

❖ ❖ ❖

Ben had dozed only sporadically since returning to his battalion. Between the pain and his concern for Larson, every nerve seemed fixed on hearing his phone. If she needed additional care, Paul wouldn't hesitate to fly her to Nairobi. Maybe he should do that anyway.

Why didn't Paul or Okuk call? Ben drifted off into a light sleep . . . dreaming of Larson . . . despising himself for still loving her . . . and dreading what lay ahead.

He was startled at the sound of his phone and reached for it.

"She's going to be all right," Paul said. "The doctor here said the wound would heal just fine."

"That's good to hear." Ben dare not give away his heart. "Don't you think you should take her to the hospital in Nairobi?"

"I'm waiting to make that call in the morning. The doctor here didn't think it was necessary, but things could change."

"A little communication between you two might help."

"I agree. It started tonight when she told me something. I'm going to be a father."

The news scraped across Ben's heart. "How do you feel about that?"

"Very good. Not sure how we'll make the transition and what we need to do in preparation for a baby, but I'm very happy."

"Congratulations." Ben needed to say more, but what?

"Thanks. I'm sure you want some sleep, so I'll call you in the morning and let you know how Larson's doing."

After the call disconnected, Ben couldn't sleep. Larson pregnant with Paul's baby. The news disturbed him. He should be happy for them; instead, he felt miserable. Without delay, he had to find David and establish the relationship that should have begun twelve years ago. If he couldn't be part of Larson's life, at least he could be part of his son's.

※ ※ ※

Paul took Larson's hand and brought it to his lips. The sun had risen hours ago, but Chuck had made sure she slept on. Larson opened her eyes, those fathomless, sky-blue eyes.

"I'll make this up to you once we're home." He brushed a wayward strand of hair from her face. "No more secrets between us. From now on, we're open and honest about everything."

"I hope so. I've had a few scares in my day, but this one was a nightmare. Thank God for His deliverance."

"If you're feeling better this afternoon, we'll go home. Do you think we should fly on to Nairobi?"

She shook her head. "Chuck said I didn't need additional care, and I'll watch for any signs of infection."

"All right. Just close your eyes and rest. Oh, Ben said congratulations."

She smiled. "I wondered how he'd take the news."

"Like the strong man he is." Paul kissed her forehead. "Back to sleep."

"But I'd like to go home now."

"I want to make sure you're okay before we do that." He squeezed her hand lightly and laid it across her stomach. "When will she move?"

"She?" Larson smiled. "I'm thinking *he*."

"No, my sweet princess. It will be a girl with blue eyes and lips the shape of an angel's kiss."

"Oh, I could listen to you for hours." Her gaze met his, and he caught his own reflection. "I didn't answer your question. Your son will need to be four or five months into development before we can feel him moving."

He smiled. Yes, they were a stubborn pair. "A Book of Verses underneath the Bough, A Jug of Wine, a Loaf of Bread—and Thou Beside me singing in the Wilderness—Oh, Wilderness were Paradise enow!"

"Do you have all of *The Rubaiyat* memorized?"

"Only the portions that remind me of my beautiful wife."

She closed her eyes. "I'm so very lucky and so very tired."

"Chuck said the injection would make you sleep. When you wake, I'll be right here, and we'll talk about our flight home."

"I love you."

He watched her body relax and the lines around her eyes disappear as the medication eased the pain. If his life ended today, he hoped his last image on earth would be of his beloved wife. Not a lovelier, more courageous, more fiercely devoted woman in all the earth. And she was his.

His satellite phone rang, breaking into his thoughts.

"Nizam is ready to meet with you."

Paul stood and stepped outside the tent. He recognized Muti's voice. "How did you get this number? And I've changed my mind."

"You no longer want to talk to your brother? He is eager to speak of old times and to learn about Christianity."

How had he fallen for these lies before? "Why didn't Nizam call me himself?"

"He is a busy man."

"And so am I."

"Oh yes. Sorry to hear about your wife. I've been told she will survive."

A tremor passed through Paul as fury assaulted him like a sandstorm. He prayed for God to take away his murderous thoughts. Did his brother have something to do with the Janjaweed's interception of Larson and Okuk? "If Nizam were really interested in seeing me as a brother, he would not have sent you with a rifle. Tell him to contact me." He disconnected the call and slipped the phone back into his pants pocket. A few deep breaths helped calm the torrent of anger racing through his veins.

His family had no intentions of giving up on finding him. He'd disgraced them, and they'd offered $500,000 to whoever killed him. That was not a small sum, and with the poverty in Sudan, the reward would catch the eye of any man. He gasped. If his family was watching them closely enough to know about Larson's injury, they might be planning an attack on Kibum. He needed to get her out of there within the hour.

Paul dare not trust anyone but his wife and Ben—and most of all, God.

❖ ❖ ❖

Ben drove his truck toward the village of Yar, where Daruka and David lived. He'd avoided it in the past, sending Okuk and Santino there when he'd suspected information about his whereabouts was being leaked to Khartoum. So far nothing had been confirmed, but his men were watching the villagers from a distance. Ben believed the mole would become bolder if left to carry on without the obvious threat of the SPLA.

His usual confidence eluded him. *Must be the medication.* He remembered in years gone by how he'd looked for reasons to stop here, much as he once did at Warkou. Now he avoided both villages. *Women.* He should have stuck to fighting and left them alone. How ironic to love one woman but have a child with another. But what mattered at this stage of his fading life was his son. Children were the seeds of hope for Sudan. From them would grow a generation of strong, courageous leaders—people who refused to bow down to the tyranny of militant Islam and all that religion represented.

Ben inwardly chuckled at himself. His impending death had brought a sense of purpose and even nobility to him. All the ideals he had once discarded for the life of a soldier now sped to the top of a self-imposed priority list. Today he began with the most urgent one.

He swung his attention to Okuk. One of the critical issues facing Ben was how Okuk felt about Paul. He'd handle that later. "I'm not sure how long I will be here. Can you wait by the truck while I handle a matter?"

"Yes, sir." Villagers gathered close to the two men.

"Keep alert, Commander. See to it that no one diverts your attention. When I return, I'll ask what you've seen." Ben whirled around, despite the torment in his back.

Since the cancer news, Ben had carved out time to mold the commander into a champion, instead of a soldier who let others do his thinking for him. Okuk had to present himself as quick and alert. Perhaps the commander realized the assigned vigil was a part of his training. If not, he soon would. The mole was no doubt watching Ben's and Okuk's every move.

Making his way past curious adults and gawking children, Ben walked toward the *tukul* where Daruka had once lived with her parents. She'd been a beautiful girl—high cheekbones, smooth ebony skin, and a wide smile. He assumed she'd married and had borne more children. But dealing with a jealous husband would not deter him when it came to his son.

As though tribal drums had announced Ben's arrival, Daruka's father stepped from the *tukul*. Deep lines aged the face of the once spry man. Ben hid his surprise; the man wasn't much older than Ben.

"Colonel Alier, it has been a long time."

Ben nodded. *He knows of my promotions.* "Yes, it has. How have the years been to you?" Birds called to each other, as though mocking Ben's attempt at polite conversation.

"Always full of hope for tomorrow."

Still a Christian. "Yes, sir. And your wife?"

"She died during the year of the heavy rains that chased us from our homes."

"I'm sorry. She was a fine woman."

"I miss her, but she is in a better place. What can I do for you?"

"I'd like to speak with Daruka or speak to her husband to ask his permission."

The man studied Ben for several moments before responding. "She lives with me as before."

"Is she married?"

"No."

Strange, when Daruka possessed such rare loveliness. Perhaps she was a widow. "And her son?"

Again the man studied Ben. "Why?"

"It's time."

"She's inside." He turned to the hut's opening. "Daruka, Colonel Alier would like to talk to you."

Ben's heart knocked against his chest like a new recruit facing a firefight. He must do this.

Daruka stepped into the sunlight, her head held high. He remembered the girl who had cowered in his sight, only wanting to please him. Today her large, dark eyes defied him with a hint of anger . . . and something else. Did he see pity? Her beauty nearly took his breath away. He almost felt like he was being unfaithful to Larson.

"Hello, Daruka."

She crossed her arms over her chest, but her lips quivered. Good. His presence had affected her.

131

"Colonel Alier. What do you wish to discuss with me?"

"I'd rather talk in private."

She moistened her lips. The years had been excellent to her. Why wasn't she married?

"We could walk to the river."

The two wound their way through the village. A plethora of memories rushed through his mind, so many that he struggled to push them aside. Had he truly loved her at one time, or had he simply used her?

"How is David?" he asked.

"Why should you ask after all these years?"

A child ran up beside him, obviously intrigued with Ben's camouflage clothing. "Go to your mother," Ben said, and the child hurried away.

"You frightened him," she said.

"I intended to."

"What kind of father would you have been?"

"Does it matter?"

"It should. David is twelve years old and taller than I am. He's a fine boy, strong and smart—all without you." She glanced away. "His grandfather and his uncle took your place." Her response did not resemble the compliant girl he'd once known.

"I was told that you had done a fine job."

"Why didn't you see for yourself instead of asking others?"

His stomach burned. "I was fighting a war to keep you and my son safe."

"And I wonder why you are here after all this time. You must believe in the peace treaty and have nothing to occupy your days."

"I'm here to see my son."

"He believes his father's dead—a soldier for the SPLA who died a hero's death."

"I plan to change that image."

Daruka stopped in the path and faced him. "If you do this, he will know I lied to him. He will want to know why, and I will tell him the truth."

"What is your version of the truth?"

"You deserted us. I accepted the fact that the only feeling you ever had for me was lust, but to abandon your child was cruel. I'm asking you to leave the village and never return. David doesn't need you."

"I want to see my son."

"The answer is no. He's better off without you."

Ben glared at Daruka. He hadn't expected her to stand up to him. Perhaps display a little resentment, but not open hostility. "Please."

She was startled. "The Colonel Alier actually says please. I find this hard to believe."

"I have my reasons." He thought of touching her, but hesitated.

"Don't try to soften me with your manipulation. My son comes before life. So if I did allow you to see him, would it be twelve years before you showed your face again?"

"I plan to become active in his life. Please think about it." He found no reason to threaten her. But he'd rather she supported him instead of his searching out the boy among the villagers on his own.

"I will not." She whirled around, and he grabbed her arm.

"I have a right to know my son."

"You had a right twelve years ago but not today." She peeled his fingers off her arm. "Take your charms and your claims to my son somewhere else."

"Mother."

Ben swung his attention from Daruka to a tall young man behind him. He stared into the eyes of the Ben Alier he used to be. Realization held him captive.

"Mother?"

"I'm fine, David."

Ben smiled at Daruka. "So this is your son? Would you introduce me to this fine-looking young man?"

She hesitated and moistened her lips. "Ben, this is my son, David."

"How old are you, son?" Ben asked.

"Twelve." David's voice had started to deepen, but not yet to a man's level.

"David, this is Col. Ben Alier." She whispered Ben's name as though the sound of it might bring the truth to light. He felt her hate as though it were a fiery inferno.

Ben and David shook hands—a firm handshake. Ben understood why Daruka had asked him to leave. He and David shared the same body build and stance, not an easy fact to ignore.

"I'm a friend of your mother's," Ben said.

"I've heard my uncle speak of you and all you've done to fight the government soldiers. Now that peace has come, I'm sure you will be an asset to our new government."

Ben smiled. Intelligence glistened in his son's eyes. "It's good to be appreciated." He turned to Daruka. "Thank you for offering to cook for me and my commander. I'd like to talk to your son while you prepare the meal."

Daruka glared at him. "Colonel Alier, you are such a busy man. I'm sure spending time with a boy would be bothersome."

"Not at all. I welcome the change. After all, the youth are our future."

"Enjoy your time with David for now. It will not last."

THIRTEEN

---

*L*arson noted the heat of the day more now than she could ever recall. Twice a day she stepped into the makeshift shower outside her and Paul's private hut to rinse off the heat and grime. There, her slightly rounded abdomen brought the reality of her pregnancy to the surface. Paul said she didn't have a stomach yet, but Larson saw the difference. They needed to make definite plans about their future, but she dreaded the conversation. He'd given no indication of allowing her to stay in Warkou.

Indignation rose one more time. She was a grown woman with more responsibilities than most. He had no right to tell her where she and the baby would live.

Yes, he does. He loves this unborn child as much as I do, and he wants us both safe. How could one little baby cause such a quandary, such a perplexing mixture of fear and joy at the same time?

If not for the elderly man awaiting her attention, the young mother after him, and whoever else might stand in the doorway of the clinic, she'd give in to a nap.

Since they'd returned from Kibum, Paul had doted on her as though she might shatter. She didn't like the sacrifice of her independence or the mere suggestion that she might resort to the behavior of a helpless female. So frustration had set in, and she hated her disposition. And Paul had yet to explain what had happened with his brother.

"Mama needs a little rest?" Paul studied her from his corner where he used his laptop to catch up on the rest of the world.

She forced a laugh. "Shall I find a nest to spend the next six and a half months?"

"Somehow I can't picture you sitting for any length of time."

"Neither can I. Mother hens have a tendency to get fat."

He stood and walked across the room and wrapped his arms around her waist. "I cannot imagine how you'll look with a big belly."

"Like I said, fat. This reminds me of a story."

Paul moaned. "Is it a good one?"

"Absolutely. This happened on my granddaddy's farm."

"They all do."

"But this one is different." She leaned into his arms and snuggled tightly, allowing her irritation with him to dissipate. "We had this white hen that had sat for days on her eggs. Every time I got close to her, I tried to stick my hand under her so I could count them, but she always pecked me. I couldn't understand her sour disposition. One day I traipsed by the henhouse to see what she was doing and found the nest was empty. I looked everywhere, thinking the dog might have gotten her and the eggs. Anyway, I looked out onto the front yard of our house and saw a bunch of dandelions. Well, if I couldn't find my hen, then I'd pick my grandma some flowers."

"And you did?"

"No. Those dandelions were baby chicks, and that hen just strutted all around, letting them play and me make a fuss. My point is, my hormones are causing me to be nasty, but once our baby is here I'll be back to normal."

He lifted her chin, and she smiled into his incredible dark eyes. "Are we having more than one little Farid?"

She shuddered. "I hope not. I haven't decided what we're going to do with this one yet."

"Do you want to talk about it later?"

"Maybe." She sensed the flood of emotion threatening near the surface. *Rats.* What she wouldn't give for her overwhelmed body and mind to level off. "Paul, I don't want to leave Sudan."

He held her a little tighter. "I know, *habibi.* But what is best for our baby?"

"Being raised by both parents."

"Are you wanting us to move to the States?"

"I couldn't do that. Besides, I don't think I'd fit there anymore. Remember when we visited my parents on our honeymoon? I felt like a square peg in a round hole. It was a wonderful visit, but everyone there is so . . ."

"Safe?"

"Yes. Safe and comfortable." She laughed. "No adventures there."

He kissed her forehead. "Isn't security what we want for our baby? Surely not this constant threat of danger. Even with the peace treaty, the country rumbles in violence. We can't forget my family's threats either."

She nodded and squeezed her eyes shut to keep the tears at bay. "I despise myself."

"Makes me feel protective."

"I think I'm going to get really mean with this pregnancy."

He laughed. "Then I'll send you back on the road to Kibum. The conflict in Darfur would be settled by a woman single-handedly. Wouldn't the Muslims love that?"

"I'd make history."

"I'd rather you give birth to a baby somewhere far away from here."

"Oh, Paul. I can't leave Warkou, and I don't want to argue."

"Me either." He kissed the top of her head.

"I'd love to spend the entire afternoon in your arms, but I have a patient."

"I know, except I'm going to hold you thirty more seconds, Dr. Farid."

"We didn't settle a thing about the baby, unless you've agreed to let us continue to live here in Warkou and raise our child with the people we love. I mean, with the peace treaty and John Garang as vice president, things here are bound to settle down. Education will come to the children, and the international community will help all of us."

He pulled her tightly into his arms. "I love you. We'll continue to pray and see where God leads us."

"And I love you." But she feared he hadn't changed his mind about her leaving Sudan. She laid her hand across her abdomen. Would she show a lack of faith by leaving the village and not trusting God to provide a safe place for their baby? She wished she knew the answer.

❖ ❖ ❖

"If you don't tell David that I am his father, then I will." Ben stood with Daruka at the edge of the village beneath a starlit sky. In the distance a hyena called, as though laughing at Ben's ultimatum.

"You've never answered me why this is important to you."

"I regret not being a part of his life."

"Have you realized you are growing old, and you may die a lonely old man?"

Her question was dangerously close to the truth.

"I have many, many friends. This is a personal matter that bears no more explanation than I've given you. Why haven't you married?"

"I never met anyone who suited me." She stayed three feet away from him.

He laughed. "I'm flattered. I remember marriage was important to you." Even with the cloak of darkness wrapped around them, he sensed her bitterness.

"I was a girl thrown into a woman's role. Motherhood has molded me into a much stronger person."

Ben stared down at the small-framed woman. "You have changed, and I admit for the better. I have a possible solution."

"Nothing short of your leaving in the morning would satisfy me."

"Marry me."

She drew back. "Are you crazy?" Her words pierced the night air and seemed to hush nature's sounds. "Why would I exchange my life for that of the wife of Col. Ben Alier, who beds every woman who catches his eye? How many other children do you have? Let me remind you that nearly thirteen years ago, you left my bed while I slept. You abandoned me after I told you I was carrying your child. Why should I consent to telling David about his father? Why would I even consider marriage to you?"

"To establish David's future. By carrying my name, he will be honored and given many opportunities."

"Unless the northern government decides to make an example out of him."

"Daruka, I can provide for both of you, and in the event of my death you'd be no worse off than you are now."

"No, Ben. I can't do that. You're a warlord, not a husband and father. Besides, I'd be afraid of AIDS."

He'd just had that test. "I don't have it. In fact, I was tested before coming here."

She gasped.

She believes me. "I'll be faithful. You have my word."

"Your word?" Bitterness swept through her laugh. "You expect me to believe your word means anything to a woman?"

"Would you consider being married in name only?"

"You'd consent to such a relationship?" Her tone softened. At last he'd touched her heart.

"I want to be a father to my son. We can tell him together about us, and I promise I'll never touch you if that is what you want."

She stood motionless, as though paralyzed. Slowly she walked back toward her *tukul*.

"Daruka, what is your answer?"

She slowly turned and faced him. "I . . . I have to think and pray about it."

"Fine, but I need to hear from you soon. I'm staying in the village until this is resolved."

"We'll talk when I'm ready."

※　※　※

Larson studied the young man assisting Sarah to disinfect the clinic and spray for mosquitoes. Santino Deng, Sarah's nephew, had served two years with Ben. Santino wasn't a blood relative, but Sarah considered him as her own, and it was obvious that he loved her. The young man wanted to learn more about government policies—go to school and help his country. His dream was to study at the University of Nairobi, and perhaps one day return to his country as a political leader. Sarah had talked about Santino for a long time. Since most of her own family had been killed, he was like a true son to her.

"How long do you intend to stay with us?" Larson asked Santino.

"A few months. Your husband indicated that you needed a bodyguard in his absence." Santino towered over his aunt and Larson. Although Dinka culture did not hold women's work in esteem, he had washed clothes and children in the few days he'd been in Warkou.

"Ah, I see." Larson understood her protective husband.

Maybe he had decided that she could stay in the village. "We've had a few close calls lately."

"My job is to make sure there are no incidents." He laughed, a deep-throated sound that reminded her of a lion. If indeed the animal ever laughed.

"I remember when Santino stayed close to my side for me to protect him," Sarah said.

Santino scooped up a handful of soap bubbles and planted them on his aunt's nose. "Now it's my turn to keep you safe."

❖ ❖ ❖

Paul hung up the phone. This was the second call he'd received from Nizam's people since he and Larson had returned from Darfur. Today, as in the other calls, Paul had refused to meet Nizam. As in the other times, the caller's number had been foreign to him. The man had identified himself as a friend of his brother's, but not Muti. According to the caller, Nizam was most eager to see his brother and wanted to arrange another meeting place.

"There's no point in continuing this ruse," Paul had responded. "I'm not a fool. Don't waste my time by calling me again."

Paul thought of all the things he wished he'd said. None of it worthy of his faith. He snatched up his Bible and headed for the riverbank. The paperwork for FTW could wait. The vicious thoughts clinging to his brain needed to be cleansed. Ever since Larson had been shot, hatred for those he had once called family and friends swelled like an incurable disease. If he didn't surrender his loathing to God, his relationship with Him would suffer.

It already has.

Help me, Father. I want to give it all to You, but it is so hard. Let me bring it to You in small pieces.

How much Paul missed Abraham, the old man who had

led him to Christ. He'd died shortly after Paul and Larson were married. When Paul had still lived in Khartoum, Abraham's right hand had been severed by the GOS for lifting it in praise to God. When that didn't stop the old man from worshiping, the government had imprisoned him in a ghost house. Paul recalled his first meeting with Abraham—when he'd been given orders to kill the infidel. Abraham's eyes had radiated a peace and love that shook Paul to his core. The old man wasn't afraid to die and said so, not with defiance but with tenderness. Fear of Abraham's strength and courage had stopped Paul from harming him. Instead he'd found the courage to ask why the old man wasn't afraid to die. Whatever Abraham had, Paul had desperately craved it.

Abraham's son, Bishop Malou, had become a close friend to Paul and Larson, but he was near Juba training Episcopalian pastors and would be gone a few more weeks. Seeking the counsel of Abraham or Bishop Malou would have been a tremendous blessing. Where would Paul be if he had followed his father's orders and killed Abraham?

The decision made in the ghost house had changed Paul forever. His purpose in life now exceeded the realm of his family's opulent wealth. Without a Bible or anyone else to answer his ever-increasing questions, he had grown closer to God through Abraham's friendship. Paul understood that his family and the government would not rest until he was dead, but his new faith meant so much more. He'd transferred his massive wealth to a bank in New York, helped Abraham find safety, and then fled Sudan for the States. Once there, he'd slowly made friends and become active in a church. After changing his name from Abdullah to Paul, he'd gone to work for FTW. His drive to help Sudan hadn't ceased.

Someday he wanted to tell this story to his son or daughter, if he lived that long. Paul shook his head. This bitterness had to stop. Abraham had never displayed the anger that Paul sensed was about to overtake him.

Take away this decay of my soul.

The words had no sooner left his mind than his phone rang again. Considering that only six people on the face of the planet had the number—now seven, since one of those six had given the number to his family—he expected to see a familiar number. Not so.

"Abdullah?"

"Nizam."

His brother chuckled, the familiar light laugh that made Paul smile, but caution immediately reined in his memories of a loving brother. "I hear you want to talk directly to me?"

"I hear you want me dead."

"No, brother. The others do. Not me. We were close, and I miss the good times we once had."

"Where is your loyalty to Allah?"

"That's what I want to discuss with you."

"Nizam, you could be killed for this conversation."

"Which is why I had a trusted friend make the calls to you."

Paul thought back to the meeting with Muti outside of Kibum. What had stopped his brother from meeting him then? "Your trusted friend nearly killed me. I think you're drawing me into a trap."

"No, I swear."

"Then what are you suggesting?"

"For us to find a place to meet where no one will suspect us."

"I cannot trust you."

"What must I do to convince you, brother? I think God might be with the Christians, but according to the Qur'an, that is blasphemy. Where do I get my answers? I need proof. If I am to face death for this belief, I must understand why."

Paul longed to believe him. His heart raced with the possibility that Nizam might come to know Jesus. How could he refuse him?

"I suggested that you read a Bible."

"I haven't found one yet."

"Then how can I believe you are serious?"

"I feel something inside me that is moving me to find answers. Please, brother."

Paul swallowed his excitement while his mind shouted that he was a fool. "Where could we meet?"

"Anywhere. I will come."

"The States?"

"Yes, of course. I can come to Los Angeles or to your home in Malibu."

How did Nizam know about his beach home?

"I prefer Feed the World's new headquarters in Los Angeles." He would have security there.

"Good. Very good. I will find the office. When?"

"This has to be discussed with my wife."

Silence greeted him.

"I believe women are equal with men," Paul said.

Silence still.

"She will come, of course," Nizam finally said.

Paul held his breath. This was happening far too quickly. "We'll discuss it. I need a number to reach you."

"I'll call you in five days. It is not safe here."

"Who gave you my number?"

"A trustworthy friend. You have nothing to fear. I must go now."

Paul had nothing to fear? Was this a hopeless illusion? Or was it an open door for him to tell Nizam about the true God? He stared down at the Bible clutched in his hands. His thumb pressed into the leather cover.

Surely God had ordained this call.

FOURTEEN

---

*A*morning Ben mulled over his plans to deceive
Daruka. The agony in her face the previous
evening had chipped at his conscience but not changed his
mind. Today she looked close to tears and avoided him and
Okuk. Frustrated with the whole situation, he sent Okuk to
question the villagers, looking for GOS sympathizers. With
the way Ben felt at this very minute, he'd set the mole on fire
in front of them all.

Last night Daruka had spoken the truth about Ben's ne-
glect of David, his abandonment of her, and his selfish pride.
But David had Ben's blood flowing through his veins, and
time was running out. If Daruka agreed to marry him, would
he be obligated to tell her about the cancer? He'd rather not.
Let the disease take its course as though he were oblivious to
his miserable health.

He'd lain awake and asked himself repeatedly if he'd ever
loved her. He wanted to ease the guilt by finding a spark of
something akin to affection. Except he hadn't loved her, only
made sure she was happy and willing to give herself to him.
Dare he be honest with her about that? No. He could lie; that
was easy enough. He could lie for a few months to have his son.

Now, as Ben watched Daruka walk to the river, he realized he had to have an answer. He pulled himself up from the

weather-worn chair. Like a lightning bolt, the pain in his back reminded him of his future—or rather, his lack of one. He had to convince Daruka to marry him. Give her anything she wanted. Promise her the moon, if that's what it took to know David. The boy deserved to have a relationship with his father. But was all this effort for David or for himself? He pushed back the unwelcome thought.

Daruka stood among a half-dozen women, laughing and talking until she saw Ben. She stiffened as though reminded of all the heartbreak he'd caused. They were probably discussing him.

"Daruka, can we talk?"

She walked toward him, her face devoid of emotion. Beauty graced her features, but she had hardened with what life had dealt her. Most of which was his fault. He glanced behind her to the other women, who stared at him with disdain. Rage curdled in his stomach. Perhaps they needed a reminder of what he'd done for southern Sudan. Or maybe they'd learned the truth about him and Daruka. She balanced a basket of bananas and pawpaws on her head, giving her a regal look. He and Daruka fell into step with each other toward the coolness of a huge tree. He waited.

"Ben, I have an answer for you."

"And it is?"

"I want David to decide if we should marry. After all, he's the reason why you suggested it. You will have to prove to me that you are trustworthy."

"That is a reasonable request."

"You will not touch me. If you desire a husband-and-wife relationship, then you have some changes to make."

"I agree to all you've said. Shall we ask David together?" Confidence swelled in him. Every boy wanted a father.

"He's with his teacher."

"Good. Education is the key to Sudan's future. How long will he be with her?"

146

"Until the sun is directly overhead. I want you to understand that whatever David wants is what I'll do. I ask you to abide by his decision."

Ben nodded. He'd won; he'd really won. "Can I keep you company until he returns?"

"If that suits you. I must care for my father now. He's old and sick, and it is my duty to make sure he eats and rests."

"I remember you used to take care of your grandmother."

"I did until she died."

"Tell me more about David's teacher. What does she teach?"

"Her name is Rosemary, and she is teaching David Arabic, English, Swahili, math, geography, and the Bible. She teaches the women too. I'm learning to read and speak English. She also shows us how not to get sick from the water."

"What is your name?" he asked in English.

"Daruka."

"How old are you?"

"Younger than you."

They laughed together.

"Will you marry me?" Ben asked in English.

"Not fair question. No trick Daruka."

"You are too smart for me." This time he spoke in Dinka.

Her shoulders lifted and fell. "I'm not very smart, especially when it comes to you."

Her feelings had drifted through her words, and he doubted if she'd intended it. For a moment he regretted what he was doing.

Once David returned from his schooling, the three sat together on the hard dirt in the *tukul* and ate the bananas and pawpaws. Her father had left the hut the moment David returned. Daruka had alerted him to the discussion with her son.

She took a fleeting glance at Ben, then turned her attention to the boy. "David, I have something to tell you." She handed him some freshly baked bread made from ground maize. "This is not easy for me because I know it will not be easy for you."

The boy tilted his head slightly to the right, just as Ben had always done. He could never deny David was his son.

"When I am finished, you will have a decision to make."

David narrowed his eyes, like Daruka. "Please, tell me. I see you're upset." He nodded at Ben. "Should this be said in front of Colonel Alier?"

"Yes. It must." She took a deep breath, and Ben placed his hand on her shoulder. She drew back as though she'd been burned. "David, I told you that your father had been killed while fighting with the SPLA. I . . . I lied to you."

He sat erect. "Why? Why would you do that?"

"You see, your father was unable to take care of us. Not because he didn't want to, but because he was committed to keeping us safe from government soldiers."

"Then my father is alive?"

"Yes." She hesitated. "He is Colonel Alier."

Ben met a silence so powerful that it seemed to clang in his ears. He searched David's face for signs of a response. The boy studied him with unreadable emotion.

Suddenly the boy stood. "All my life I dreamed about my father. I thought maybe he hadn't been killed. Maybe he'd been imprisoned, and one day he'd return to us. I was such a fool. My mother worked hard to care for me. She told me stories about my father—my brave father, who loved me enough to die rather than see me forced into Islam or become a slave. But you chose not to see me or my mother. For that I hate you."

David disappeared through the hut's opening and into the brilliant sunshine.

❖ ❖ ❖

Paul craved the counsel of his friend Tom, who directed FTW in Los Angeles. Tom was the one man who understood how he viewed life and his relationship with God. When Paul had first arrived in LA and attended a Bible church, Tom treated him shamefully and asked him to leave the fellowship. Tom worked as an attorney at a large firm and believed he practiced Christianity as Jesus desired. But he despised Arabs and Muslims. One Sunday morning, the pastor asked Paul to give his testimony and share with the congregation why he'd changed his name from Abdullah to Paul. Once Paul finished, Tom made his way down the aisle, apologized, and hugged him like a brother. Soon afterward, Tom took a directorship at FTW. The two men had been close ever since.

With the weight of what to do about his wife and baby, and now Nizam's request, Paul's mind was about to explode.

He walked through the clinic as Larson was taking temperatures and blood pressures for two ill patients who had journeyed from an isolated village south of Warkou. Their blood tests indicated yellow fever. She'd kept the patients isolated from others entering the clinic, fearing further outbreaks of the dreaded disease. Paul's presence seemed to irritate her.

"I'm going to call Tom."

"I'm surprised you haven't already." She frowned but did not glance his way.

"Oh, I told him about the baby, remember? He's betting on a girl too. I'm just confused, not sure what to do about a lot of things."

She recorded a blood pressure reading. "I can take care of the baby just fine. I proved that on the road to Kibum."

"You got shot, Larson. You were nearly killed." He glanced at the sling on her arm.

"I'm still quite capable."

"I've seen you handle yourself in all kinds of situations—"

"Then what's the problem?"

149

He saw the battle in her eyes. "Your safety is more important than what you do here."

She slammed the notebook containing the patients' records onto the table. "My work is vital to the survival of a lot of people. I know you don't value what a woman does—" She glanced at her two patients in the other room.

Thank goodness they didn't understand English.

"What are you talking about?" Paul moved closer. Perhaps if he could touch her, she'd calm down.

"Should I spell it out for you?"

"Go right ahead."

"You were brought up with the understanding that women are second-class citizens. The culture reeks with it. Now I'm pregnant, and my worth has been demoted to that of chattel. You might think I'm your property and can decide my future, but it won't happen, Mr. Farid."

"That doesn't even deserve a response."

Her eyes blazed. "I don't think you value my work here—"

"What are you talking about? Now you've really made me mad. I don't know what else to do. I tell you I love you. I do everything I can to show you how I feel. I tell you I'm looking forward to the baby. I tell you how much I respect and honor your abilities as a doctor, and you accuse me of treating you like chattel?" He snatched up his phone. "Enjoy your solitude."

He must have walked two miles before his temper started to subside from a boil to a simmer. Were all pregnant women just short of insane? If this was the case, they'd never have another child. What made her fabricate all of those accusations? He'd been Christianized, Americanized, Westernized, and surely civilized.

A half mile later, he punched in Tom's number.

"How is the little mama?"

"Don't ask."

Tom chuckled. "Ah, the hormones have hit, and Larson

150

has turned into the Wicked Witch of the West."

"Who?"

"Never mind. It would take too long to explain."

Paul described the situation with Larson and the baby, then the dilemma with Nizam.

"And you want me to tell you how to proceed? I can pray, but I'm fresh out of good advice." Tom paused. "Seriously, I understand your concern for Larson. If she were my wife, I'd have escorted her out of Sudan a long time ago. Then again, she views her work as a ministry, just as you and I do our work with FTW. It's a tough call."

"I can't talk to her about it sensibly. She simply turns into this woman I don't know."

"My guess is, she's as concerned as you are about the danger."

"And too stubborn to discuss it."

"Both of you are champions at stubbornness. Paul, love her. That's all you can do right now."

"I can, and while I'm at it, I'll mark off the days on the calendar until the baby arrives."

"I shouldn't laugh, but this is funny."

"Thanks for the sympathy. Then there's my other problem, with Nizam."

"Do you think he's serious? I mean, arranging a meeting with a man who's sworn to kill you is a dangerous undertaking."

Paul shook his head and squinted into the setting sun. "When he said he'd meet me anywhere, I suggested the States for his reaction. I figure he's either serious about changing faiths, or he's willing to go to any length to kill me."

"What does your heart say?"

"To trust him. We were always close."

"What does your head say?"

"That it's a trap, and Larson may end up a widow with a child to raise."

"Paul, what is God telling you?"

"I honestly have no idea, but I can't walk away from my brother."

"I'd be glad to talk to him. In fact, there are countless Christians around the world who'd counsel him."

"I don't think he'd talk to anyone but me. But I can give you all the numbers he's used to contact me."

The rain had soaked Paul by the time he returned to his and Larson's hut. He changed into dry clothes—frustrated with the rain, Larson, Nizam, and life. He wasn't ready to talk to Larson yet, and showing up at the clinic invited another confrontation. She'd pushed him a little too far.

One nasty retort after another flashed across his mind as he considered what he could have said to her. That was always the case with him. He glanced at her Bible and realized he should open it, but fury stood in the way. He could finish up his paperwork and e-mail it to FTW, except he'd have to retrieve his laptop from the clinic.

He stood in the doorway, listening to the rain beating against the thatched roof and pouring onto the ground. Anguish invaded every corner of his heart. He needed to construct better living quarters, but Larson felt they should live as much like the villagers as possible. He hated the tightly woven mosquito netting that seemed to suffocate him, and the snakes that wiggled into the hut. He wanted indoor plumbing, air-conditioning, and electricity. He wanted glass windows so he wouldn't have to listen to the *eek eek* of the tiny bats that settled around the hut's opening at night, or the barking of hyenas, or the roar of lions. He was tired of battling mosquitoes and the million other disease-carrying insects. In short, he craved the advantages of civilization. None of which were possible in the heart of southern Sudan.

How could he love a woman and be so angry with her at the same time? She'd taken all his feelings for her and tossed them into his face with claims that held no shred of truth.

He'd taken the time to listen to her side of why she should stay in Warkou. Why couldn't she try to understand how he felt?

The culture thing dug into his skin the most. She knew how he detested Islamic practices regarding women, how he struggled to bring Christianity to those enslaved by those beliefs.

He had to stop thinking about their argument. It solved no purpose but to divide them further. Waiting in the hut until she finished for the day made sense. He'd cook something she enjoyed. Lately she craved the boxed macaroni and cheese. Nasty stuff, but she inhaled it. Maybe a full stomach would soften her temper.

❧ ❧ ❧

Larson adjusted the sling on her right shoulder and counted the patients waiting to see her. Men, women, and children needed her care, and a young woman she'd never seen before sat on the floor at the end of the line. She looked no older that thirteen or fourteen and appeared to be pregnant.

Somewhere outside the clinic was Paul. She'd been furious with him, and for the life of her she couldn't figure out why. If not for these people needing medical attention, she'd find him and beg his forgiveness for all the horrible things she'd said. What had she been thinking? Her hormones were chipping holes in their marriage.

Her ears tuned for the sound of the Hummer over the rain, as if Paul would leave her. Of course, he wouldn't. But she wouldn't blame him if he did.

Perspiration dripped from her forehead. *Drat pregnancy.* Her body was not her own; neither was her mind. She wanted this baby, didn't she? What kind of a monster resented the privilege of bringing life into the world? But this baby interrupted her life's work among the Sudanese. God had given

153

her the gift of healing, and a few years ago, He'd called her into His family. Why this change? Her and Paul's life had purpose; they sacrificed and lived in constant danger. Had they disappointed God? If only she understood why He was doing this.

A man needed stitches removed from his leg, and she instructed him to stay out of the river until the wound healed. A woman had burned her hand while cooking. In a decent medical facility, Larson would have ordered skin grafting. A little boy who had been born blind cried incessantly with a stomachache. His swollen liver alerted Larson to a more serious condition. If only she could run more tests here at the clinic. One patient after another received the best care Larson could provide. Finally she was alone with the teenage girl.

"How can I help you?" she asked, first in Dinka and then in Arabic.

The girl's face tightened.

"Are you in pain?" Larson bent to where the girl sat on the hard floor.

"Baby is coming," the girl responded in Arabic.

The one day that Santino had escorted Sarah to another village to visit a friend, Larson needed them. And Paul—well, she'd run him off.

Oh, God, is this my punishment for lashing out at my husband?

"I need to examine you, to find out how the baby is doing." Larson helped her onto the examination table. Agony ripped through Larson's arm.

"*Shukran.* Thank you."

"What is your name?"

The girl stiffened. "I can't tell you."

"How far apart are the pains?"

"They don't stop."

Larson held her hand. "May I pray for you?"

"Allah is angry with me."

154

"I don't pray to Allah. I pray to the living God." Larson gently coaxed her to lie down. "We'll talk later about my God."

After explaining the examination procedure, Larson discovered the baby was breech. *I really wish Sarah were here. My arm hurts so.*

"I have to turn the baby around." Larson caressed the girl's face. "This might hurt, but then the birth will come."

Tears rolled down the girl's face. "I want to die."

"Why? Soon you will have a beautiful child to love."

"I'm not married."

Larson realized the futility of the girl's life. Her Muslim family would make certain both she and the baby were eliminated. Once the child was born, Larson would convince her to stay at the clinic until she could arrange for safety elsewhere.

"I'm going to turn the baby." Larson hoped the umbilical cord was not wrapped around the infant's neck. "I'll be as gentle as possible."

The girl cried out. Larson's wounded arm felt like someone had lit a torch to it.

"There, it's done. Now it shouldn't be long before your baby arrives. Where is your village?"

"Far from here."

"There's no need to be afraid of me. I won't tell anyone about this. You're safe."

"My family may be looking for me."

"Who told you about the clinic?"

"My uncle broke his leg a few years ago, and he was brought to you." She gasped as the baby struggled against her body to be born.

"Squeeze my hand until the pain is finished."

In less than an hour, the girl gave birth to a tiny boy. Larson wrapped him in a clean cloth and laid him in the girl's arms. Children giving birth to children. How horribly cruel.

"He's beautiful and healthy," Larson said. Suddenly she wanted her baby now. She wanted to hold him and make sure nothing would ever happen to him.

For the first time, the girl smiled. "Each time I felt the baby move, I wondered if it was a boy or a girl and what it would look like."

"What are you going to name him?"

She shook her head. "No name. Neither of us will live."

Larson's emotions plummeted, and she touched her own stomach. "Please let me help you. You can live here until my husband and I find you a new home."

"Where would I go?"

"We'd help you get farther south or out of Sudan."

A shadow in the doorway grasped Larson's attention. She whirled around to face two men with assault rifles.

FIFTEEN

———— ❦ ————

*B*en listened to his men boast about what they intended to do now that peace had come to Sudan.
He'd heard it since January, when the peace treaty had been
signed. Fools. The conflict would never end. Just wait until
one of them stepped on a land mine and see what kind of
sympathy the government gave them. They'd encountered a
firefight last week; they'd be fighting tomorrow. The government lied to the international community while open warfare continued. And he didn't want to get started on the
situation in Darfur.

His mind rested on the many women and children taken
as slaves. Where were they held, and how were they going to
find their way home? Both sides had used child soldiers, and
many children still carried guns—especially in Darfur. Ben
had used them in the past, but Paul and Larson had convinced him to let the boys go. For years, he had believed that
using the boys was a necessary part of the war. He needed soldiers, and most of the boys were willing. But in his effort to
build the South's army, he hadn't realized he was killing the
future of his country. He knew now that without counseling,
those abused by the atrocities of the war might never recover
from their ordeals.

The lack of education in Sudan was another source of contention. A people who lacked sufficient schooling lacked sufficient leaders. A twenty-year vacuum existed in which the children had not been schooled. So what happened when the current leaders, like himself, could no longer fulfill their duties? He didn't trust any of the government officials but John. If any one man could bring about changes, it would be Vice President John Garang.

Slowly his thoughts drifted to Daruka and David. After the boy's rejection, Ben and Okuk had made their way back to the Rhino Battalion. At least with his men he fit. While the two had been gone, his men had exchanged fire with a few government soldiers, which led Ben to believe that someone from Yar had informed the GOS of his location. Every time he thought about the hatred he'd seen in David's eyes, a knife twisted in his heart. More so because David had been right.

Ben attempted to shove aside the memory and convince himself he didn't care. He sunk onto a chair outside his tent and winced. His life had lost what little meaning it once possessed. Now that he knew his son had no use for him, Ben's grandiose ideals about a father-son relationship had died before they had a chance to flourish. All that remained to him was a ragtag army and a civil war that many wanted to believe had ended. He'd get drunk if the doctor hadn't told him not to mix the pain medication with alcohol. But why should that matter anymore? He deserved a stiff drink for all he'd been through, and it wouldn't change cancer's death sentence.

"Okuk, bring me a bottle of whiskey."

"Yes, sir."

"Day after tomorrow we'll leave at first light. We're going back to Yar. All of us. We're going to find that mole and make an example of whoever has betrayed us."

❖ ❖ ❖

Paul heard a scream and several rounds of rifle fire. *Larson.* He snatched up his pistol and darted out into the pouring rain toward the clinic. With Santino gone for the day, Paul had failed to keep his wife safe. Not twenty meters away a black man guarded the clinic's opening with a Kalashnikov rifle. He wore a *ghutra* headdress.

"Drop your weapon." Paul aimed his pistol.

The moment the shooter raised his rifle, Paul fired into the man's head, sending him sprawling into the mud, with blood filling its own puddle.

"Stop, or I'll kill the woman," a man from inside the clinic called out in Arabic.

"What do you want?"

"To leave here with the white woman."

"Go, but leave her." He moved closer. The many accountings of what happened to captured women hammered in his head. "You're surrounded out here. Leave now and you'll live."

The man laughed. "There's no one with you. And if you want the woman to live, you'll not try to stop me or follow."

"Can I talk to her?"

"Paul, I'm all right," Larson called in Arabic. "He's shot a young girl and the patients. I think they're all dead. He's asked me to bring medicine for a man who's been shot." Her voice trembled. "I'm sor—"

Her words broke and she cried out.

"Leave her alone." Paul fought to keep his composure. "What can I give you for the woman? I'll pay any price."

"No money. I need her with me."

"Let me go with you, and when she's treated your friend, I can bring her back."

"I'm finished talking. Toss your pistol in front of the hut."

Paul did as he was told. "I'm backing away."

"If I find that you've followed us, I'll put a bullet in her head."

"I understand." Fear paralyzed every inch of him.

Larson stepped from the hut with a rifle stuck in her back and her bag of medical supplies in her left hand. Where was her sling? Who would help her change the bandage on her wounded arm?

The man sneered at Paul. "She's mine now."

"I'll get her back." *And make you pay for what you've done to my wife.*

"I don't think so."

She turned in the pouring rain and looked at Paul. He saw the longing in her pale face. "I love you," she said in English. "See if the baby inside lives."

The man grabbed her wounded arm and pushed her ahead of him. Paul watched until she was out of sight. Snatching up the pistol, he shoved the dead man away from his path and hurried inside the hut. A young girl lay on the floor. A pool of blood trailed from the examination table to her still body. She'd been shot in the back. He bent and turned her over to discover an infant wrapped in her arms. A very much alive baby boy.

He needed to go after Larson. The baby needed tending. Sarah wasn't in Warkou. He glanced into the other room at the patients and saw they were dead. Anger flooded his senses and threatened to overtake any logic. He gathered up the baby and sheltered him from the rain before hurrying outside. He'd take him to a nearby hut and go after Larson.

God, keep her safe. Don't let anything happen to her.

❖ ❖ ❖

Ben loaded a box of ammo into the back of the mud-caked truck. When he'd first come back from the States and joined the SPLA in the eighties, he used to worry about a grenade or a strategically aimed shot blowing him and his men to who-knows-where, but not anymore. He and his men did their jobs and buried the casualties.

Kicking one of the bald tires, he calculated how long until one of them blew. The engine sputtered like an old man, and the oil was never changed. He and that old truck had a lot in common. Chances were the truck would last longer.

He itched for a good firefight, and he hadn't killed an Arab since one of them had put a hole in his arm. Ending Paul's problems by putting a bullet through Nizam's heart had crossed his mind. A quick glance at his men breaking camp showed that the rest had done them good. Paul had sent food and cases of good water, and they'd eaten well. Hard to fight with a hungry belly.

"Colonel Alier, we'll be ready to leave at dawn," Okuk said. "They're in good spirits."

Ben laughed. "The spirits I had last night gave me a horrible headache this morning."

"I hope this goes well for you."

How much about Daruka and David had Okuk figured out? "What do you mean? We all want to put our hands on that mole."

Okuk swallowed. The scar across his throat widened. "I overheard your talk with Daruka, and I've kept the information to myself."

"And?"

"That's all, sir. Sometimes I still hear the cries of my family."

Ben studied him for a moment: his one arm, raspy voice from a slit throat, and courage. "You have much to learn, Okuk, but you are a fine soldier. A commander who understands the men around him earns respect from his soldiers and his superiors."

"Thank you, sir."

"Make sure your insight never clouds your judgment."

The day wore on along with the perpetual blinding rain. Ben briefed Okuk on his strategy for finding the man or men who'd joined forces with the government soldiers. As the pain in his back intensified, Ben found it more difficult to concentrate.

"Okuk, I will be assigning you more and more responsibilities in the coming weeks."

"Are you leaving us?"

"Possibly."

Okuk grinned. "For Juba? Colonel, you deserve leadership in rebuilding the South."

Ben sat back in his chair while the rain splattered against the tent. "I'm not giving any details. Just want you to know that I'll be working you hard and expecting more."

His phone rang. A quick glance showed it was Paul.

"I need help," Paul said. "Larson's been taken by a man who shot and killed three of her patients."

Ben stood. Hadn't she been through enough? "How many men?"

"Only two. I killed one. The other one headed northeast with her on foot. I'm trailing them now. Santino is in another village with Sarah. Should be back today."

"We're on our way. Give me your location."

Within the half hour, Rhino Battalion moved out over water-filled roads to find Larson. Would he always be choosing between Larson, Daruka, and David? Ben drew in a deep breath and reached into his pocket for the pills that kept him moving one more hour.

※　※　※

Larson struggled to keep up with the fast pace of her abductor. She fought hard to see through the screen of rain while she attempted to figure out how to escape. How badly hurt was this man's comrade? What would happen to her after she treated him—or watched him die?

Paul. How insensitive she'd been to him. If only she could take back the cruel things she'd said earlier. But he knew of her love; she'd seen it in his face. He'd be close behind them, doggedly pursuing them more viciously than a lioness tracking her kill.

Larson's arguments and reasons for staying in Sudan didn't seem as important after seeing the man ahead of her shoot the young girl and her other patients—and possibly the baby. Given the time, Larson would have shared the Good News of Jesus with the girl. Senseless murders. Every day the tally rose, taking so many innocent. The predators never satisfied their lust for blood. If only the international community could see what was really happening, maybe things would change.

I will survive this, and my baby—our baby—will not live in this terror. Oh, dear God, help me so my baby will live.

The medical bag filled with instruments of healing also held a 9 mm pistol. And she wouldn't hesitate to use it.

"How far are we going?" she asked.

"Doesn't matter."

"What happens to me once I've treated your friend?"

"I haven't decided. You'd bring a good price."

"I'm a doctor. Surely that means something to you. Others will die if I can't help them."

"Shut up." He struck her wounded shoulder with the rifle barrel.

Stumbling into the mud, she bit her tongue to keep from crying out. The handle of the pistol in her bag lay against her baby. She drew in a deep breath in an effort to manage the piercing pain and thanked God for the heavy rain. The man would not try to rape her in this miserable weather, and Paul would have a clear set of tracks to follow if he stayed close behind them.

Where did these vicious men come from? With a signed peace treaty, why didn't they attempt to settle down? Didn't they have families and a home? A suspicion crept into her mind and she shivered. Could this man be sent from Paul's family to force him into their clutches? She caught her breath. *I can do everything through Him who gives me strength. I can do everything through Him who gives me strength.* She shoved away the despairing thoughts. God was in control, not the man holding a rifle to her back.

They continued on in the rain for what she believed was around two hours. She thought they were headed northeast, and she knew a battalion of SPLA soldiers used to be camped in that region. Water dripped from her and weighed down her clothes. Twice she asked for privacy, but the man denied her and laughed. At least the rain cleansed her the moment her body finally sought release.

Soon it would be nightfall. Had it been stubbornness on her part to stay in Sudan? On the other hand, if she escaped this abduction and left the country, did that action show a lack of trust in God? She'd had her share of scares before, but the tiny life growing inside her compounded her fears.

Paul, find me, please. I can't bear spending a night with this man.

SIXTEEN

———— ✦ ————

*W*ith the fast-approaching darkness, Paul hurried his pace and followed Larson and her abductor's trail. The rain had stopped for now, which made the going easier, and he could see until night overcame him. Voices alerted him. He stopped and crouched low, then listened to men speaking in Arabic. Slowly, he moved forward until he was able to peer through the bushes into a small clearing. A fire touched on the features of three men outside a makeshift shelter consisting of a tattered UN blanket strung over brush. Paul stared into the shelter. In the shadows, he saw the outline of Larson's body.

Paul pulled out his phone. "I have them in sight," he whispered.

"According to my GPS, we're directly west of you," Ben said. "Once we've surrounded them, you make your move."

"Got it." Paul disconnected the call. His gaze focused on the movement in front of him. None of these men had respect for his wife. Yet they needed her to save a man's life.

"This man is nearly dead," Larson said from inside the shelter. "He needs more than what I can give him."

"Do not let him die," one of them said. "If he lives, then we might let you live too."

Bring her out of the shelter.

"I've removed the bullet and stitched the hole, but he's lost too much blood."

"You heard the deal."

Paul listened to what the men intended to do to his wife, and none of their claims had anything to do with letting her go. From Ben's position, he had to hear too. Two men who loved the same woman would not allow these animals to lay a hand on her.

One of the abductors peered inside at Larson and the injured man. Paul aimed his pistol. Just let that snake take one more step toward her.

Lord, protect her.

"Muti, is the woman yours first?" The question came from a man near the fire.

Muti. Is my brother behind this? Acid burned Paul's throat. Of course he was. Larson's abduction was his own fault.

The man stepped back from the shelter and rejoined the group. "I have my orders. We'll not go unrewarded."

"Does our brother still live?" another man asked.

"For now," Muti said. "I don't think he'll last much longer. Abdullah did not marry a skilled doctor. Look, I found a gun in the medicine bag." He held up Larson's pistol and laughed.

Paul kept his gaze fixed on Muti, waiting for the moment to send a bullet into his murderous heart.

Suddenly Larson stood at the tent's entrance. "The man has died. I told you he'd lost too much blood to survive."

Muti grabbed her by the shoulder and pulled her into the light of the fire.

"You will pay for this, and so will your infidel husband."

Paul signaled to Ben's soldiers with the soft cry of a jungle bird, and they stepped into view. Muti's men lifted their weapons.

"Put your rifles down now!" Ben shouted.

Muti pulled out a knife from his waist and held it at Larson's throat. "Do you want me to slit her throat while you watch?"

"Touch her, and all of your men will die," Ben said.

"And we'll take her with us." Muti sneered. "Move back, and I might let her live."

Paul crept behind the shelter. He'd stop the man or give his life trying. Lightning flashed across the sky, and in the next instant thunder roared. Rain pelted all of them. Paul inched closer, his pistol aimed at Muti's back. As long as he went undetected and the sound of rain masked his movements, he might be able to snatch the knife from Muti's hand. Within seconds, Paul stood behind him. He reached around the man and jerked back the hand holding a knife to Larson's throat. The knife flung to the right, and Larson stumbled to the ground. Rifle fire cracked, and the other two abductors fell. Paul lifted his pistol to Muti's head.

"Don't kill him." Ben grabbed Paul's hand. "We need to know who's behind this."

Paul heard Ben and understood, but the thirst for revenge threatened to take over. "Did you hear what this animal was going to do to her?"

"Paul, I want to deal with him." Ben pressed Paul's arm firmly. "Put down the pistol."

Paul lowered his weapon. "Take him before I kill him."

He reached for Larson and helped her to her feet. She eased into his embrace, her sobs matching the heavy rain.

"Twice now I've almost lost you," Paul said. "And it's my fault. Nizam is behind this."

"Our baby has to be safe," she said. "I don't know what we are supposed to do, but we have to do something to protect our child."

"Take her to the truck," Ben said. "I'll be there after I deal with this man."

"His name is Muti," Paul said. "He held me at gunpoint outside of Kibum. Claims to speak for my brother."

"Do you really think Nizam ordered my abduction?" Larson asked.

"I imagine so." Paul whipped his attention from her to Muti. "Ben has ways to make you talk. You're a fool not to co-operate."

"Nizam did not order this." Muti's voice was layered with scorn.

Paul glared at him. "Then you'd better tell all you know."

Leaving Muti with Ben, Paul took Larson's hand and followed Okuk to the truck. Again lightning flashed, and the downpour flooded over them.

"I'm ready to go home." She shivered. "I want this nightmare over. Every time I think of the patients they killed inside the clinic, I'm ready to join up with Ben and carry a rifle instead of a doctor's bag. All of this talk about peace from the government, and your brother's claims to want to know more about Christianity, are nothing but lies."

"The infant is alive." Paul held her close. "I left him with a villager."

She was silent for a moment. "I want to keep the baby." Her words were edged with emotion. "I'm not sure why, but I have to care for that motherless child."

"With one of our own on the way?"

"Yes. It may not make sense to you, but I feel God is asking us to raise him as our son. He is the heritage of Sudan, the hope for reconciliation." She touched his face in the darkness. "Try to understand me, Paul."

"My *habibi*. If this is what God wants, then this is what I want too."

But what of Muti and Nizam? Would Paul bring death and destruction to everyone he touched?

❖ ❖ ❖

Ben made his way to Daruka's *tukul*. He'd hoped to have secured information from Muti by now. Last evening Ben had tried convincing the man that things would go easier on him if he cooperated. But Muti had only laughed.

"Tell me who ordered Dr. Farid's abduction," Ben said.

"You already have my answer. But I might give you information in exchange for my release."

Ben had burned with rage. John Garang once said that he didn't want negotiations; he wanted dialogue. And Ben wasn't getting anywhere with Muti.

This morning he'd left six of his men with the prisoner, and he'd brought four with him and Okuk to talk with the Yar villagers. He'd ordered his men to make friends with them, not frighten them. Once his men gained their confidence, Ben hoped to learn who had linked hands with Khartoum. Maybe his poor health had softened him a little, but he no longer felt the need to terrorize a village in order to find moles. There were other means to draw out information. However, Muti was of the breed that deserved a slow death.

Standing outside Daruka's *tukul*, he realized the foolishness of his previous plan to establish a relationship with David at any cost. His desires hadn't changed, but his methods needed a fresh approach. Daruka had expressed her dislike of him on his last visit, and she'd not be happy about this one either. And David . . . the more he thought about his son, the more he saw they shared the same quick temper. The key was to convince Daruka to marry him, with or without David's permission. That way he could slowly prove himself to the boy, much as he wanted his men to persuade the villagers. With renewed confidence, Ben stepped into the *tukul*.

"Why are you here again?" Daruka asked. "And why are your men in the village?"

"I'm here to convince you to marry me."

She pressed her trembling lips together. "Ben, leave us alone. I told you before. I will not marry you unless David agrees."

"Can't you convince him to give me a chance?"

"So you can run off and leave us again?"

"I'm finished with running from my responsibility to you and my son. I have my duties with the SPLA, but my home would be with you and David. You may have no feelings but anger toward me now, and rightly so. But isn't there something inside you that would consider giving me another chance?"

He saw the turmoil in her face. Had she loved him all these years?

"Daruka, I want to spend the rest of my life as your husband and David's father. Unless there is another man, why not give me an opportunity to prove my faithfulness?" He touched her shoulder. "I have business in Juba mid-August. You and David can come with me. When we're finished, I'll take you to Nairobi. You've never been to a big city, and I'd like for you and David to see it."

A tear slipped from her eye, and she whisked it away. "I don't know, Ben. It's been so long. I wonder why you never married. Am I being a foolish woman to want to believe your heart has always held something for me?"

Could he go through with this? Deceit marched across his mind. "We had good times back then. We can again."

She focused her attention on something to her right. "David has not spoken of you since you left."

"Where is he now? I want to talk to him."

She pointed in the direction where she'd been staring. "He's watching the goats. We are fortunate to have been given them, and he takes great pride in making sure they are safe and in good pasture."

"All right." He took a deep breath to steady his nerves and manage the pain in his back.

"I'll pray for you . . . for God's will."

Her words warmed his heart. He wasn't worthy of this woman, but he would take care of her properly. "Thank you."

Ben walked under the shade of ancient trees and on through tall grass. He caught sight of David with the goats.

No wonder Daruka was proud of him. With no one around, he stood erect and guarded those goats as though they were gold. Ben stopped and watched his son. He held a club firmly, and his gaze darted about for signs of trouble.

Suddenly confusion anchored in him. What should he say to this boy who was a stranger to him? Their last meeting had ended in disaster. This time he'd be as honest as possible.

"David, can we talk?"

The boy stiffened. "What about?"

"Your mother and me." *You are so much like me at your age.*

"I will listen, but that doesn't mean I want you as my father."

Ben started to say he didn't have a choice, but swallowed his response. "I want to right the past and marry your mother. She's done a fine job raising you, and I'm grateful for her love and sacrifice. I can't undo what happened before you were born and the years I've missed, but I can begin right now to take care of both of you."

"Are you leaving the SPLA?"

"No, but my role has changed with the signing of the peace treaty. The fighting has diminished as both sides seek to work out their differences." Ben no more believed his words than he trusted the new government.

David studied him, his face as troubled as Daruka's. "I like it that you speak to me as though I were a man instead of a boy."

"I believe you deserve it."

"Does my mother want to marry you?"

"Only if you give your permission."

"Will it be a Christian marriage?"

"If that is your mother's choice."

"Do you love her?"

"Yes. It took me a long time to realize that." Ben had lied all of his life, but this falsehood was one of the hardest. Yet to

171

have David, he'd sell his soul to the devil. He already had.

David nodded. "I want my mother to be happy."

"So do I."

"And you promise not to leave her again?"

"I will honor my vows to your mother. I do need to lead my men and continue my duties with them, but my home will be in Yar."

David crossed his arms and glanced away. "All right."

"Shall we tell her together?"

"I think so."

❖ ❖ ❖

Larson enjoyed having Santino and Sarah with her at the clinic. Talking with them helped her cast aside her fears for those she loved.

"I thought things were supposed to change with Vice President Garang working with the government." Sarah straightened the chairs and benches.

"So did I. But life continues on as usual. Strange, when the peace treaty is supposed to allow us to breathe easier." Larson unlocked the cabinet containing her precious medicines and slipped her hands into sterile gloves.

"Nothing is more beautiful than the paradise we have here," Santino said. "Unlike Colonel Alier, I have faith in the new government."

"I want to," Larson said. "But it's difficult to trust anyone since Paul's family have sworn to kill him. I'd like nothing better than to raise our children here, but a few problems need to be resolved first."

"Has your husband heard if Muti has given Colonel Alier any information?" Santino folded a few ragged towels.

"Not to my knowledge." Larson took a deep breath in hopes her queasy stomach soon settled. She was more than ready to stop throwing up and simply gain her baby weight.

Sarah planted her hands on her hips. "If he hasn't, then I imagine he's not alive."

Santino laughed. "Aunt Sarah, you have never liked Colonel Alier or his tactics, but in this instance, you might be right."

"Muti still lives. Paul is talking to him now in hopes of finding out who ordered my abduction, since Muti claims that Nizam knew nothing about it." She studied Santino for his reaction.

"I've never seen your husband interrogate a prisoner, but I don't think he can do so effectively. It's not a job for anyone with compassion."

Larson wondered about that very thing. She hadn't questioned Paul about it. His former life in Khartoum stayed right there, and she had no intentions of digging up past sins when she had plenty of her own. "I'm not sure what he has in mind."

Santino's gaze unnerved her. Maybe he actually thought Paul was capable of torture, despite his words to the contrary. "Muti has to be broken in order to end the attacks upon you, Paul, and all of your friends."

"My husband is not a violent man. There are other ways."

Santino's eyes narrowed, and he returned to stacking the mound of rags.

Larson glanced at Sarah, who offered a sad smile. Normally the older woman voiced her opinions whether anyone wanted to hear them or not.

God, I know You are in control and that Paul listens to You.

Determined to end the topic of conversation, Larson walked across the room to the small reed-woven cradle containing her tiny son. Placing a kiss on the sleeping baby's forehead, she felt tears near the surface. Where had all of this love come from for one so small and helpless? She smiled, remembering her and Paul's bantering discussion about a name choice.

"We can call him Latte for the color of his skin." She'd swallowed a giggle. The baby's father must have been Arabic.

"Not my son." Paul picked up the baby, who was squirming with hunger. "However, we could call him George Bush Farid."

Larson wrinkled her nose. "As much as I support our president, I don't think that's a good choice. Do I need to remind you that we're living under a Muslim government?" She tapped her finger to her chin. "My father's name is Tom, and so is your best friend's."

"Smart woman." He offered formula to the baby, who greedily drank from the bottle. "I'm partial to Abraham too."

"Then we have it. Thomas Abraham Farid."

He smiled into the baby's face. "Do you realize we will have two children six months apart?"

"More like five months."

They laughed.

Larson enjoyed the memory. Yet still no decision had been made about moving from Warkou. Temporarily, Santino served as her bodyguard, which eased Paul's fears and made her feel better too.

Larson stood up from the cradle. "Isn't he the most beautiful baby in the whole world?"

Sarah joined her and hugged her waist. "All little gifts from God are beautiful, especially our own."

Since her abduction and Thomas's mother's death, Larson often considered living somewhere other than Sudan. Strange how instant motherhood had changed her perspective. She didn't understand her new feelings, the unconditional love that held little room for selfishness. Torn between her passion for Sudan and the safety of her family, she asked God for direction. But would she trust Him enough to obey His guidance?

SEVENTEEN

*W*ho ordered my wife's abduction?" Paul grasped Muti's jaw and stared into the man's dark, beady eyes.

Muti shook his head. "I'm not talking. Go ahead and kill me."

"Maybe I'll attach a bomb to you and let you die a hero's death."

The man challenged him with a defiant glare.

Paul forced a laugh. "Ah, yes, you'd much prefer a delusion of paradise."

"I should have killed you when I had the chance."

"And now it's my turn." Paul wished he had the guts to use torture techniques. He'd been schooled well by his older brother in what gave the best results. But he hadn't been able to inflict any of those methods then, and neither could he do so now.

When he died with Christ, the old passed away. Odd, that in this tent with Muti—a man whose hands were stained with the blood of the innocent, a man who sat in his own filth and shouted murder to the infidel—that Paul recalled a phrase of Scripture.

I was no better than Muti, and God called me to be His own.

Father, must this all be so hard? Do I kill him so he will not kill my family?

"You are weak." Muti chuckled. "You refused to kill me before, and you can't now."

Paul shook his head and turned toward the opening of the tent, not wanting Muti to see how he trembled—not in cowardice but in fear of not obeying God. He whirled back around. "You have no idea what real strength is."

"I see what it isn't."

"Your life is not in my hands, but those of the soldiers who hold you here. I will leave this camp today, whether you tell me what I want to know or not. Once I'm gone, how long will these men keep you alive?" He leaned in to the foul-smelling man. "You want to make a deal? Tell me who ordered the abduction of my wife. Nizam? One of my other brothers? My father?"

Muti's stoic face and cold eyes were his only reply.

"You're making a serious mistake," Paul said. "I will leave within the hour. If you value your life and change your mind, let me know." He stepped out into the drizzly afternoon and drank in the fresh air, glad to be unencumbered by a man who'd rather die than give up his beliefs in a false god.

Commander Okuk approached him, and Paul pushed aside Muti's repulsiveness from his mind.

"There's been a terrible accident." Commander Okuk's expression hardened. "Colonel Alier just informed me that John Garang has been killed in a helicopter explosion."

Paul's pulse raced. "Are you sure?" Could Ben have obtained false information? *Not John Garang, Lord. He wanted to make so many changes. He welcomed Christians.*

"The colonel said the information came from a reliable source. Six other Sudanese and seven Ugandans were also killed in the crash."

Paul's stomach churned. How would the Sudanese community respond to this tragedy? "I don't want to believe it."

"Neither do I."

From inside the tent, Muti laughed. "Allah be praised," he called.

Okuk pulled out his 9 mm.

"No, Okuk. I'm not done with him yet." Paul started to touch his one arm, but he thought better of it. The commander did not like him, and both men were upset with the dire news. "Why not gather your men and tell them about the explosion?"

A murderous scowl cemented in Okuk's face. "If you don't kill that jackal, then I will. Nothing would give me greater pleasure than to skin him alive."

❖ ❖ ❖

Ben attempted to draw Daruka into his arms, but she refused him. Years ago she'd met John Garang, and her heartache was doubled. The hope of southern Sudan, and a leader she'd personally revered, was gone.

"Let me comfort you," he said. "I know how much John meant to you—to all of us."

Her face softened, and she stepped into his arms. "I'm being selfish. Your sorrow must be more than mine."

Grief and anger pierced his heart and mind. *John Garang is dead.* Rebecca, the vice president's wife, had to be devastated with the loss of her husband. For years she'd lived with the knowledge that his life could easily be destroyed. But this? After the signing of a peace treaty? Now that her husband's hopes for Sudan were finally taking form, he'd been snatched away.

For Ben, life was spiraling down to an unfathomable depth. His gun would not bring back his lifelong friend or cure the cancer raging through his body. In the past, he'd shoved away hopelessness, believing it was the fodder of weak men. Now he sensed the snake of despair uncoiling in his body.

"What will happen to our people now?" Tears streamed down Daruka's face. "John Garang fought for years for our people, just like you have. I'm frightened that heavy fighting will begin again."

"There are good men who are deciding important matters right now. We have to hold on to our faith in the South's leaders."

"And in God. He will not forsake us."

Ben tightened his hold on her frail body. He remembered when he'd left her years ago after learning she carried his child. She hadn't believed in God then. Perhaps his abandonment and the task of raising David had caused her to turn to God.

"I'm shocked about the news too. And as much as I hate to leave you and David, I need to be with my battalion. I must be there to stop my men from panicking."

Daruka lifted her tearstained face and offered a shaky smile. "I would not try to keep you. Our people have always looked to you for leadership, and now more than ever before."

"I'll be back." He meant it.

"Please be careful."

They were her first gentle words to him since he'd tried to convince her to marry him. Ben felt closer to love for Daruka than he ever had before. But he chased away those feelings as soon as they entered his mind. His heart still belonged to Larson. Her image stayed with him . . . always would. *And I must focus on the trials of southern Sudan, not my needs.*

Ben's gaze settled on David, who had heard and watched what had transpired between his parents. The solemn look on the boy's face reminded Ben of the overwhelming responsibility of Sudan's youth to their tumultuous country.

"David, take care of your mother. I'll be back as soon as I can."

Ben saw the suspicious look in the boy's eyes.

"I give you my word," Ben said. "Bishop Malou will marry your mother and me. I'll make the arrangements while I'm gone." He released Daruka and grasped David's arm, then pulled him into a hug. It was the first time he'd ever held his son.

❖ ❖ ❖

Larson fed Thomas his formula and noted how her infant son had begun to fill out. Little rolls of fat around his neck and legs indicated a strong, healthy baby. Still, she fretted over the unknown: her complete lack of knowledge of his mother's prenatal care and the circumstances surrounding the girl's pregnancy. Larson and Paul planned a trip to Nairobi soon to have Thomas tested for disease and other health issues. HIV rested foremost in her mind.

She giggled at Thomas's vigorous sucking noises. His little world centered on a bottle and nipple. Larson's mother would claim he'd soon be ready for meat and potatoes.

Realization struck her. She hadn't contacted her parents to tell them about the baby growing inside her or the one in her arms. As soon as she finished feeding her famished son, she'd make that call. With so much happening lately, she hadn't phoned Mom and Dad for fear they might detect the danger stalking Larson and her precious family. But for now, she felt safe with Santino close by.

Profound love for little Thomas seized her. How could her heart have this much room for another baby, or still another? She kissed his cheek and blinked back the wetness. Who would have ever thought that the tough and independent Dr. Larson Kerr might find real love and marry? More surprising was the fierce love she held for her children. All those years on the farm experiencing the innate passion of mamas had not prepared her for the feelings enveloping her now.

Her granddaddy had owned a sow that no one could go near whenever she had a litter of piglets. That old sow would have eaten anyone or anything that might be a threat to her babies. Larson didn't particularly want to compare her feelings to those of that old, surly pig . . . but she surely understood a mother's protective nature.

The phone rang, interrupting her pleasant thoughts, the ones that took her away from Sudan's problems. A quick look at the caller ID showed her it was Paul.

"Good morning, honey." She laughed. "Your son cannot get enough to eat."

"My *habibi*, I miss you."

She detected sadness in his voice. "Is something wrong?"

"I'm afraid so. John Garang was killed in a helicopter crash yesterday."

Larson sucked in a breath. "He was in office for only three weeks. Was it an accident?"

"I don't know. I doubt it. Anything I could say would be speculation."

"Do you want me to check your laptop and see what I can find?" All the lightheartedness of motherhood vanished with this grim reminder of reality.

"I'd appreciate that. You're feeding Thomas?"

"Yes, but he's had plenty." She lifted him to her shoulder with the phone tucked between her ear and other shoulder and rubbed the baby's back.

"I'm heading back to Warkou, so call me after you've had a chance to see what the international community and Khartoum are reporting. Better call your parents too. They'll be worried once they hear the news."

"I agree. Did Muti tell you who ordered my abduction?"

"No, and Commander Okuk has probably killed him by now."

"I'm sorry." She sighed. "I'll search out the information and get back with you as quickly as I can."

Larson sat with Thomas until he burped like an adolescent boy. As she went through the motions of finishing her son's feeding, tears slipped from her eyes and down her cheeks. Not like the emotion she'd experienced moments before over the joys of her role as a wife and mother, but utter sorrow for a man who many had believed was the savior of southern Sudan. She feared John Garang's death was no accident, and without substantial proof to the contrary, the southern community would not accept it as such either.

She carried Thomas to the open doorway and welcomed the sunlight streaming through the treetops like liquid gold. The day's rains would come soon enough, but for now, she accepted the light as a gift from God, a glimpse of Himself before the skies darkened. The days ahead held no promise of peace or freedom from political unrest, but God would still be walking with them under blue skies or gray.

Perhaps her musings came from grief and melancholia. But they seemed more of a confirmation of how God helped her through each day.

After laying Thomas in his cradle, she powered on Paul's laptop for the latest world report on Sudan. Instantly she read how the tragic news had shattered the hopes of many southern Sudanese. With a heavy sigh, she called Paul.

"I have information about John Garang's accident," she said. "At least, what is being reported."

"I'm ready. Tom's already contacted me to get my opinion about it all."

Larson had scanned the reports before calling him. Placing her cursor at the top of one news release, she selected the items Paul would want to hear now. "Vice President Garang was killed in a helicopter crash in southern Sudan after a meeting with Uganda's president. Many southern Sudanese are suspicious of the northern government, since Garang survived a twenty-one-year civil war." She read further. "Ugandan President Yoweri Museveni has called for an official investigation. Then another report says Museveni should not have allowed Garang to leave in a helicopter that late in the evening. Still another states that the Lord's Resistance Army in Uganda might be responsible.

"Who knows, Paul? In my opinion, it looks like the responses are led by anger and sorrow rather than facts, and more than one group had reasons to see Garang dead. Whatever really happened is not clear, but the North and the SPLM are working together in an investigation."

"What a mess. I'm assuming there's rioting as we speak."

"Definitely in Khartoum."

"If the world wants to find out who killed him, they need to pinpoint who had the most to gain from his death."

"What's Ben saying?" Larson stood from the chair and walked to the doorway, where clouds already scurried across the sky.

"He's angry. Doesn't know who to blame, so he's blaming all the factions."

"That's Ben." She paused and stuck her hand out to catch the first few drops of rain. "What do you think?"

"Disappointment. Anger. Fearing all of this means a major setback for southern Sudan and the situation in Darfur."

Larson searched for anything to lessen the burdens on her husband's mind. "Don't you think that if an investigation proves Khartoum planned the crash, the international community will come down hard?"

"For certain the SPLA will retaliate, and the bloodbath will resume again. I think I need to keep in daily contact with Ben in hopes of discouraging anything that resembles full-scale war. Of course, if the government is behind it, they have covered their tracks."

"I agree." She decided to forge ahead on a matter that concerned her. "Have you heard from Nizam?"

"No. Since Muti is in custody, I'm hoping the matter is ended."

"Paul, he will not stop trying to see you until . . ."

"He is successful? Don't you think I see what is happening?"

She took a breath to keep from saying what she really thought. "Let's talk about something else. Do you think Ben looks okay?"

"I suppose. You're the doctor."

"He should have stayed in Nairobi a while longer. He's pale and thin."

"Can you gain access to his medical records?"

Larson bent to adjust the mosquito netting on Thomas's cradle. "Not without his permission, and we both know the likelihood of his consent to that."

"Maybe his upcoming marriage will put him in a better mood."

"What? Ben's getting married?"

"That's what the old warhorse told me. Remember him speaking of David while we waited for the AIM pilot to pick him up? Ben has been talking to the boy's mother, and they've decided to marry."

Relief washed over her. "I hope they're very happy."

"Makes me wonder if the signing of the peace treaty had a lot to do with it. He should be able to relax now and enjoy his wife and son." Paul paused. "Let's just pray Garang's death is not a catalyst for bloodshed and that it doesn't destroy Ben's plans for the future."

EIGHTEEN

***

$\mathcal{B}$en shifted from one foot to another. He'd repeatedly told himself that he shouldn't be nervous about
marrying Daruka, but the burning sensation in his belly was
worse than being outnumbered by enemy soldiers. Did all
men go through these doubts while in the middle of a marriage ceremony?

The smell of a butchered white bull roasting over a fire
met his nostrils. He didn't deserve the village's tradition in
honor of him. Would this day ever end?

Paul and Larson were seated somewhere behind him.
Their presence—or rather, knowing Larson was witnessing
his marriage—affected him. A part of Ben wanted her to
never forget him. At times he wished he could hate her,
wished she'd say or do something that would turn him
against her. But she had yet to fall from her pedestal. Not a
day passed that a memory didn't yank at his heart. There'd
been a time when he'd have gladly killed Paul to have her.
They were territorial lions who both wanted the same mate,
but those days had ended when Paul had proved his mettle
and saved Ben's sister from a life of slavery in northern
Sudan. Now Ben called him friend.

No doubt Larson thought Ben's feelings for her had
wasted away when he'd announced his plans to marry

Daruka, but he doubted if Paul was so easily convinced. What a foolish man he'd become. Must be the painkillers playing havoc with his mind. Too bad a drug hadn't been discovered that could manage heartache . . . or death. Time might have eventually resolved his problems, but when his numbered days came to a halt, the cancer would take care of all that tormented him.

Paul had wanted to fly him and Daruka to Nairobi for a honeymoon, but Ben refused and didn't tell Daruka. He didn't want to leave David. Even now he considered taking the boy with him back to his battalion. If fighting broke out in the aftermath of John Garang's death, he'd have his son escorted safely back to Daruka.

From the corner of his eye, he saw David beside him, his shoulder span wide and his height not far from Ben's. Pride and regret hammered at his heart. Deserting his son had to be one of the worst things he'd ever done. Now, love for his son fueled all of his actions. Daruka could never learn that Ben's feelings about his life were torn in so many directions that he often didn't understand himself.

On the other side of him stood Daruka, a beautiful woman and a prize for any man. If only he cared for her as he should. She deserved more than a loveless marriage and fast-approaching widowhood.

She must have sensed him staring down at her, for she looked up and smiled. He smiled back. After all, he must give the appearance of a lovesick groom instead of a man consumed in misery. Until a few days ago, he hadn't gained her confidence.

"Do you have other children?" she'd asked one night when they were alone.

"No." Not to his knowledge, anyway.

"And you haven't ever married?"

"Never." He turned to her. "We will need to take our time as husband and wife. But I am anxious to be married."

In the shadows she shook her head. "Even though I don't want you to touch me?"

"Yes. I meant what I said. I want to take care of you and David like I should have done a long time ago."

"I appreciate all you've said and the things you've done for David and me."

"I'm surprised you don't have a husband. You're a beautiful woman."

She wrapped her arms around herself. "Some things about me have never changed. The girl grew into a woman, but her heart has always been the same."

Ben knew exactly what she meant. Compassion settled upon him. "I'll earn your trust."

"Good. I want us to be husband and wife . . . as God intended. David needs to see us happy together."

"I feel the same way." Ben took her into his arms and rested his head atop hers. She didn't resist.

Now, as he faced Bishop Malou on his wedding day and prepared himself to make promises he couldn't keep, Ben questioned his own sanity. For a moment, he considered doing the honorable thing and walking away. But what was the honorable road? Daruka loved him, David needed a father, and cancer was eating away at his body. Ben steadied his gaze on Bishop Malou, and the man lifted his chin. Could he see the lies? The truth waged war in Ben's mind. If he endured this ceremony, he could live the next few months in the company of his son. That was all that mattered.

Bishop Malou turned to Ben. "Repeat after me. I, Benjamin Alier, take thee, Daruka Wol, to be my wedded wife, to have and to hold from this day forward, for better or for worse, for richer, for poorer, in sickness and in health, to love and to cherish, from this day forward until death do us part, according to God's ordinance; and thereto I pledge thee my troth."

The bishop's voice roared as though someone might find

187

fault with his words. Ben forced conviction into his vows and hoped no one heard the deceit. Sometimes he feared everyone saw through his lies.

❖ ❖ ❖

"I'd like to take a trip to Nairobi in a few days." Santino fell in step with Larson as she walked from her *tukul* to the clinic—his daily habit, whether Paul accompanied her or not. "I need to register for classes at the university. Take some tests and see where I'm at."

"I agree. You shouldn't wait, and classes fill up quickly." Larson smiled into the face of the tall young man whom she and Paul had grown quite fond of. "Education is your most important asset in helping your country—that, and a sound faith in God."

"Thank you. Can Paul be here while I'm gone?"

"I'll talk to him about it. How good of you to consider our needs when you have your whole future to plan for."

"I take my role as your bodyguard seriously," he said. "I want to make sure Paul is able to handle any problems in my absence."

She laughed at his seriousness. "I wouldn't let him hear you say that. He's very proud of his arsenal."

"And the Hummer."

"Oh yes. Both of us are quite fond of that truck." A chill crept over her arms at the memory of what had happened in Darfur.

"I've never understood why Paul keeps all of these weapons, then speaks about Christianity to the people."

How many times had she and Paul discussed the same issue? Neither of them had an answer. They didn't fill the role of missionaries, but they were Christians living their faith in a third world country. "My husband believes in protecting those he loves and the helpless. We don't want to see anyone killed, but if we're attacked or if someone we love is threatened, we fight back."

"I think I understand. Your beliefs are sometimes strange to me. From some Christians I hear 'Love everyone and live in peace.'" He shrugged. "But the government soldiers are afraid of your husband's power." He smiled. "Aunt Sarah is working very hard to convince me about your Jesus."

Larson swung him a curious look. Did Santino really understand her and Paul's commitment to Christ and what obedience to Him truly meant?

"What is your faith?"

"You would have difficulty understanding my beliefs."

"Try me. I haven't always been a Christian, and I've lived among the Sudanese for ten years. Paul and I have encountered many tribal customs and beliefs. I would not be surprised."

"Someday I'll explain my religion. I promise."

"I'll remind you. So let's get back to your trip to Nairobi. Have you mentioned this to Sarah?"

"This morning. She's happy but has a few tears. I realize she enjoys having me live with her, but she's anxious for me to begin my schooling."

"That's natural. She wants the best, but that means saying good-bye." Larson palmed her hand against her forehead. "Oh, I don't know what I've been thinking. Would you like Paul to fly you to Nairobi?"

"I feel uncomfortable even mentioning such a huge undertaking since you two have been so good to me."

"Nonsense. You've been such a help to us. Why don't you visit with Paul about it now? He's taking care of Thomas."

Santino hesitated. "You and Aunt Sarah would be alone in our absence."

"I'll talk to Ben. He'll have a solution."

"If Colonel Alier can arrange for a soldier to guard you, then I'd welcome a flight to Nairobi."

Santino stopped on the path and glanced back at Paul and Larson's hut.

"Go on and ask him." Larson laughed at his hesitancy. "I have e-mails to answer and a list of medical supplies to make for when Paul takes you to Nairobi." *And I can send a sample of Thomas's blood to make sure he's healthy. Dear God, he has to be okay . . . no strange diseases . . . no HIV.*

❖ ❖ ❖

Paul carried Thomas along the path to the well. The women would be pumping water for the day, and he wanted to show off his son. A whimper alerted him to a possible problem, but a quick look showed him that Thomas merely wanted attention—which he instantly received. Paul studied the face of his son. Perfect in every way. God certainly had a sense of humor to give him and Larson two babies within months of each other. To think the Farids had believed their lives would be childless.

Larson and Paul had yet to reach a decision about where they should live or where the new baby should be born. His thoughts teetered between California and Nairobi. The States held all of the latest conveniences, but Nairobi was closer. He'd move with them. Living separate from his family meant not fulfilling his responsibilities as a husband and father. Everything he read in the Bible demonstrated the importance of those two God-given roles. His senses were tuned to listen for God's voice in hopes of a clear and quick response, but He remained silent.

"Paul, do you have a minute?"

He turned to the sound of Santino's voice. "Good morning. Didn't I just see you with Larson?"

Santino stiffened. "We had a brief discussion, and she suggested I come to you."

Thomas whimpered again, and Paul boosted him to his

190

shoulder. He was getting this fatherhood routine down pat, even learning how to swaddle his infant son. Something about being bundled tightly in a blanket kept Thomas content. Paul believed he'd be an expert by the time the next one came along.

"I need to register at University of Nairobi before the next school session begins in September." Santino hesitated.

Paul laughed. "And flying there is much faster than trying to get a ride."

"Yes, sir."

"When would you like to go?"

"At your convenience. I don't want to take advantage of your kindness."

Santino's training with the SPLA had instilled exceptional manners. "Is Thursday morning all right? I want to make sure I have a couple of soldiers here."

"Thank you, sir. Would you like for me to contact Colonel Alier or Commander Okuk and make arrangements?"

"I'll take care of it. Larson and I appreciate your hard work. If you need a job when school is not in session, let us know."

"I will . . . and thank you for providing for Aunt Sarah. She took me in when my parents died."

Paul nodded. "She's a fine woman and a great help to us."

Santino disappeared down the path to the clinic. *Good man. He'll be a strong leader for this country—once he's converted to Christianity.* Sarah had shared with Paul that her nephew had not acknowledged the work Jesus had done on the cross. In the skies above Africa, Paul would share the gospel with the young man.

The trip to Nairobi would also provide some time to look into housing possibilities for his family. Perhaps Sarah could move with them. Her presence would be a source of comfort to him and Larson.

Thomas broke into a wail, one that the whole village

could hear. Paul continued to pat his son's back in hopes of calming him down without the aid of the village women or Larson. Something warm trickled down the back of his shirt. Then came the smell. Next came the giggles of too many women. Maybe he had much to learn about being a father.

NINETEEN

---

*B*en swallowed a pain pill before Daruka returned from her garden. He found it increasingly difficult to steal away and take the prescribed drug without her knowing. The agony in his back seemed to grow worse. Night was approaching, an hour past the time he normally slipped away for his medication, but she'd been talking and then had gone to pick vegetables.

Sleep often eluded him, and the sexual appetite of his wife demanded strength that he no longer possessed. Something had changed her view of him once the wedding vows were spoken. He couldn't refuse her, but how long would it be before she discovered her husband did not possess the vitality of other men his age? Daruka gave him her undivided attention, and David spent every waking moment with him or with his goats. Ben smiled despite his physical discomfort. Since the wedding, his new family's company was the first peace he'd known since attending college in the States. Strange, he must admit that for the first time in his life he'd found a portion of happiness.

Daruka walked toward him, carrying a basket of maize. As their people had done for centuries, she'd grind the grain to make bread or porridge.

"Where is David?" Ben took the basket from her arms.

"He's sleeping tonight with his cousins."

Her brother's sons. David needed good friends, especially when Ben passed on.

She tilted her head slightly and studied him.

"Are you sick?" She touched his cheek.

He chuckled. "Perhaps. If you consider how you're wearing me out at night."

She glanced away, a slow blush rising up her neck and face. "I waited and prayed for you for many years. And now that you are my husband, I want to make sure I keep you."

Ben's stomach twisted. They'd have a few months—not years—together. "You are more priceless than any man could ever hope to have." That statement was true. He'd even considered the men he knew who would look after Daruka and David once he was gone.

"Daruka, you understand that my position with the SPLA is a dangerous one."

"Yes, you are everyone's hero. I pray for you always that God will protect you."

He smiled and set the basket on the ground. Holding out his arms as a father would do for his child, he silently urged her to step into his embrace. "You think much too highly of me, but I like it."

"Our son is proud too."

David's respect meant more than another promotion or an invitation to help build Sudan. *My son.* "He is such a fine young man."

She pulled away from him. "But you are not well. You eat very little, and you don't sleep at night."

"I've never slept soundly. Army life does that to you. I'm fine. Really."

"What are those pills you take during the day and night?"

How could he lie his way out of this one? He moistened his lips.

"Ben? What are you not telling me?"

194

"Nothing." His voice thundered. "I'm fine."

Her eyes widened.

"I'm sorry, Daruka. I shouldn't have shouted at you." He pulled her back into his arms. All the while, white-hot fire shot up his spine. "The pills are nothing for you to be concerned about. One day I'll tell you why the doctor prescribed them, but not today."

"Dr. Farid? Your friend in Warkou?"

He kissed her forehead. "No. The doctor in Nairobi who took care of my arm."

"Does it still hurt?"

The barrage of questions shortened his temper, and he fought to keep from unleashing it. "Sometimes it bothers me."

She nodded as if she understood. "Why are you losing weight?"

He gripped her arms. "Daruka, please." He cursed. "Stop all of these questions."

She broke from his hold and rushed into the shadows of evening. In her wake, shame wagged an accusing finger at him. He had no right to talk to her as though she were a new recruit. She'd done him a tremendous favor in marrying him, even if she didn't comprehend her sacrifice.

Ben waited nearly an hour before going after her. Suddenly he remembered that a lion had been spotted near the village two nights before. Snatching up his rifle, he hurried to find his wife. A few years ago, he'd upset Larson, and she'd stepped too far from the village and into the path of a lion and a lioness. He wouldn't make the same mistake again.

❖ ❖ ❖

Paul landed with Santino at Wilson Airport, eleven kilometers outside of Nairobi's city center. This small airport was a base for missionary planes and those heading into the

Masai Mara for safaris. After summoning a taxi for the young man, Paul asked him how long he planned to be in the city.

"I'm not sure what is involved with registration at the university, and I'm certain there will be tests to take. I also want to look for a job and a place to live. But I can get a ride back to Warkou." Santino smiled. "Thank you for flying me in."

"Call Ben if you need me to come after you. He'll get the message to me." Paul clasped Santino on the shoulder. "I wanted more time to talk to you about the gospel."

Santino laughed, his wide smile radiating youth and idealism. "You, Dr. Farid, and Aunt Sarah. I'm thinking about the things you tell me. I just need more time."

"I respect that, but the decision to follow Christ is not one made with the head alone." Paul patted his chest. "It comes from here too."

Santino nodded. "Sometimes I feel it."

After the taxi picked up Santino and Paul paid the fare in advance, he made his way to the Nairobi Hospital, a structure of white concrete and gray stone that was always expanding. No wonder Nairobi was proud of this facility.

Larson had drawn blood from Thomas this morning and had made arrangements for the lab to perform various tests. But first, Paul made inquiries about the maternity ward and toured the entire area. A man needed to know where the grand events took place. The green floors glistened like a mirror, and each staff member smiled like he was a dignitary.

Paul hadn't shared his worries with Larson, but Ben looked poorly. The more he thought about it, the more he believed he should try to talk to Ben's doctor. Granted, the hole in his arm had been serious, but the man appeared to be weakening, and his weight loss alarmed his friends.

Once he'd delivered Thomas's blood samples, he learned the doctor's name who had performed the surgery on Ben's arm. Dr. Phillip Khamati greeted Paul warmly, and they spoke freely until Paul asked about the particulars of Ben's health.

"That's patient confidentiality." The doctor leaned back in his chair. "Without written permission from Colonel Alier, I can't tell you anything about his condition."

"Could you give the information to another doctor?"

"The same rules apply."

Paul fumed. "He doesn't look well."

Doctor Khamati didn't move a muscle. "If he has a problem, then he needs to see me or your wife."

"How did you know my wife is a doctor?"

He smiled. "Colonel Alier must have told me. But your wife's reputation is worldwide. I'm sure you are very proud of her, as she must be proud of your determination to feed the starving masses of Sudan."

"Thank you, doctor. But we were talking about Colonel Alier, not me or my wife. We have seen a drastic change in his health, and we want to help. I'm sure you must have run plenty of tests to detect any serious conditions while he was here."

"I did. However, as I said before, this is confidential information."

"My wife and I noted that he takes pills on a regular basis."

"I prescribe medication to my patients as a matter of treating their illnesses."

You're holding back the truth. "You and I both know that Colonel Alier would rather die than admit he needs help."

Did Paul see a twitch in the doctor's face?

"The decision for him to see a doctor is not for you or me to make."

What are you and Ben keeping from us? "Should I tell him I was here?"

Dr. Khamati stood from his desk. "That is up to you, Mr. Farid. If you will excuse me, I have patients to see."

197

Later, as Paul rode about the busy city with its mixture of sights and sounds, contemplating where he and his family might live comfortably, the conversation with Dr. Khamati repeated in his mind. For certain the doctor knew what was wrong with Ben. Paul was tempted to use his connections to obtain Ben's medical records, but that would solve nothing. If Ben kept a secret, then he had a good reason why, and his privacy needed to be respected.

What is wrong with you, Ben? Does Daruka know? Or have you locked a secret inside your head where no one will ever learn the truth?

❖ ❖ ❖

Larson sat at Paul's computer in the clinic and read an e-mail from her parents in Ohio.

Dear Larson and Paul,

We've taken the plunge and bought a computer. Actually, all we wanted was to send e-mail to you. Our friends say that you can send pictures through this cyberspace thing. Can you and Paul do that? We want to see what little Thomas looks like. Can't imagine our Larson with a tummy, but we want those pictures too.

We're enjoying the Internet. Some of the things we read about Sudan are not what we want to know. Do you two have any idea how dangerous it is there? Mercy, Larson. Haven't you learned a thing since you snapped your leg trying to break a horse? You two can't save the world, so why not get out of there? And how are you going to give birth in the jungle? Or is Paul planning to fly you into Nairobi when you go into labor?

My dear daughter, you used to make my hair gray. Now I fear it will all fall out. I'm sure that got a chuckle out of both of you. Please keep us posted on what's happening—well, not all of it. Do you have guns? Never mind. I don't want to know that ei-

ther. But Daddy says to tell you that if you do have a gun, keep it
oiled and cleaned in case you need it.
Love,
Mom and Daddy

Larson laughed. If her parents had any idea what really happened in their daughter's life, they'd send in a Special Forces Team to yank all of them out of there. She'd never tell them about the brushes with death or the hardships, but she would tell them how much she loved Sudan.

Dear Mom and Daddy,
Paul flew into Nairobi today with a young man who's been helping us at the clinic. His name is Santino, and he's decided to attend the university there and needed to register for classes. I thought about going too, but the rainy season has brought me many extra patients.
I'm looking forward to the chocolate and Kenyan coffee my dear husband always brings me back. And I'm curious to see what he brings Thomas. Paul is hilarious with the baby. He talks to him as though he's an adult and reads to him in Arabic and English.
The morning sickness has finally subsided. Now I suppose I'll get fat. I don't think I've gained much weight yet because my clothes still fit. Paul wants to take before and after pictures of my developing shape, so I'll send them on to you, along with pictures of our precious Thomas Abraham.
Please consider making a trip to Nairobi after the baby arrives. Kenya is beautiful, almost as beautiful as our beloved Sudan, and we could take a safari.
Got to run now and get the clinic ready for the day.
Love,
Larson

"What does the computer say today?"

Larson swung around to see Sarah and waved. She clicked "send" and sent her message to her parents into cyberspace. What a great feeling to be only a click away from Mom and Dad.

"A computer doesn't say anything. It provides a way for people around the world to communicate and find information."

Sarah walked to Larson's side. She peered into the screen just as Larson shut it down. "Does it tell you how to make people well?"

"No, I had to go to school for many years to learn how to heal people. But it does help answer medical questions for me when I'm confused about a patient's health. So I guess the answer is yes."

"If I ask it a question, will it answer me?"

Larson nearly laughed, but she could hear the seriousness in Sarah's voice. "What do you want to know?"

The old woman's eyes narrowed, and she pressed her lips together.

"Sarah, is there a problem?"

"I think God doesn't want me to use a computer. He is supposed to answer my prayers."

"You're right. He is. Do you want to talk about something? Is it Santino leaving?"

Sarah shook her head. "This is between God and me."

"I can tell you're upset. If there's anything I can do, please let me help."

"No, Larson. I have to do this my way."

TWENTY

*B*en hurried through the village on the well-worn path his wife had used since her childhood. He envisioned her bare feet curling around the trodden grass and following where it led without a single thought. Attempting to ignore the excruciating torment in his back, he picked up speed and tightened his grip on the rifle barrel. He well remembered the young Daruka, who disappeared into the tall grass and forest when she had difficulty managing unpleasantness. Tonight he had been the cause of her distress.

If anything happened to her, it would be his fault. Ben had heard the roar of a hungry lion during the past two nights. It lurked beyond the village's *tukuls*, close enough to wake the bravest man from his sleep. The villagers had posted extra guards, and so far no one had been killed, but a lion had eaten one of the cows. The predator did its best hunting at night. Wildlife in Sudan had diminished with all the fighting, and the few animals remaining were hungry.

Ben wanted to believe Daruka would have left behind her girlish behavior of handling uncomfortable situations, but in this way she was still the fifteen-year-old girl he'd left behind.

"Daruka." Panic resounded in his voice.

He saw the line of village men who guarded the perimeters

of Yar against predators, whether two-legged or four-legged. Even with their torches, they couldn't see everything. That is what alarmed him the most.

"Daruka, don't be foolish. A lion is out there. We can talk about this."

He peered in every direction. His emotions had leaped beyond anger to worry.

A woman screamed to the right of him.

"Ben, help me!"

He whirled around and lifted his rifle, aiming into the monster of darkness. His heart hammered in his ears. *Not Daruka.* She stood for all the things in his life that were good—not as a sacrifice for his temper. Where did he shoot?

Shouts from the village guards and dancing torches moved in Daruka's direction. They had spears but not guns.

"Is she safe?" Ben thrashed through the grass toward the men several meters away.

"Daruka is with us, but we have not found the lion."

Relief instantly calmed him. "Thank you. I'm heading your way." Ben stopped and took in a few deep breaths to still his heart and manage the pain in his back.

The grass rustled to the left of him. He inhaled the scent of lion—an animal he feared more than an outnumbered standoff with the GOS, though both went for the throat. The lion stalked within a few feet of him.

"Shine your torches over here," he said.

But the lion was closer than any spear or fire torch, and Ben couldn't see it, only smell and feel the animal's presence. The lion roared, settling in for the kill. The village men shouted as they rushed toward Ben. Time, Ben's ageless enemy, offered no mercy. A faint light outlined the lion's body. Ben fired. Then again.

Moments later, the men raised their torches and spears over the lion's lifeless body. Ben recognized the warrior etchings cemented in their faces. He knew the thrill of the kill and the awe of victory. They'd talk about this for days to come. He'd rather forget it. Give him a two-legged enemy any day.

Ben searched in every direction for Daruka. He found her standing apart from the men. Her sobbing rose over the night air, a woman's way of dealing with terror.

He made his way to her side and wrapped his arm around her waist as he'd seen Paul do for Larson. Daruka needed comfort from the man who had promised to love and care for her. "Are you all right?"

"Yes, Ben. I'm so sorry. You could have been killed, and it would have been my fault. I was so scared."

The truth of who was at fault slammed against his conscience. "Promise me you will think hard before leaving the village at night."

She nodded. "I was so foolish. I acted like a child. When I'm upset, I have to face whatever disturbs me. Tonight I nearly got both of us eaten by a lion."

Ah, to be devoured by a lion sounds better than to be devoured by cancer. "But we're fine now, and the animal is dead. I hurt you with my harsh words and stubbornness." He couldn't think of another word to say, and he refused to tell her the truth. "Let's go home, Daruka."

She leaned her head against his chest. "I love you. I'm sorry I pressed you about the pills."

He squeezed her trembling body to his. "I love you too." And for the first time he thought maybe he did.

❖ ❖ ❖

Paul gazed down at the dirt landing strip beside Warkou. *Home.* He'd looked at beautiful houses in Nairobi yesterday afternoon and today. He could well afford any of them for his family, but he couldn't bring himself to indulge in such opulence. Spending a fortune on a home and furnishings and hiring servants to care for it made little sense to him while his people suffered from disease and starvation. When he and Larson had married, they'd agreed to live simply so they could give more to others. If the two of them chose to live in Nairobi, they'd find something that fulfilled their needs without the high-dollar price—and the guilt.

Once Paul was certain of flying into the wind, he flew over the village—a habit he'd acquired when they'd married to let Larson know he was home. Another circle of Warkou, and he pulled the landing checklist from the upper left-hand corner of the cockpit. He might live in a third world country and fly in and out of a cleared splice of dirt, but that didn't mean he ignored any safety guidelines.

When the wheels touched down, mud flew everywhere. If not for the daily rains to shower off the mud, he'd consider building an airplane car wash. He chuckled. In one breath he'd frowned on extravagant homes, and in the next breath he wanted an airplane car wash.

Familiar children ran to greet him, knowing he'd have food for them. The fresh smell of pineapples had teased his taste buds all the way here, but they were for the children— along with a case of granola bars. Larson would have her normal chocolate, rich coffee, and a special treat he'd stored in an ice chest.

Paul climbed down from the cockpit and sliced through a pineapple to hand each child a piece. He'd wait for another day to pass out the granola bars.

"Thank you," echoed around him.

"Don't thank me. Thank Jesus." Paul swung a little girl up into his arms.

"Amen," a boy said.

Paul laughed. His heart warmed with the love of home. How could he and Larson leave? But they must.

"And what did you bring us?" Larson strolled his way, carrying Thomas.

Paul set the little girl on her feet and enveloped his wife

and son in a hug. "Would you be so glad to see me if I didn't bring you anything?"

An irresistible smile met him that said more than welcome—a smile that bannered her love and everything they'd gone through together. They shared a timeless bond that surpassed what many couples even knew existed, and it meant more than the times they had barely escaped death or had traveled to remote villages to help the needy. If he died today, he would rest in the joy of this gift that God had given him.

"Well, Dr. Farid, what if I did fail to bring you something?"

Her shoulders lifted and fell, much like a little girl ready to pout. "I'd be disappointed, but I'd get over it. What did you bring for Thomas?"

He grinned. "Clothes, diapers, baby formula, bottles, a crib for us to put together. The directions are supposed to be easy."

"Us?" She giggled. "I work with surgical tools, not fix-it tools. My granddaddy used to say that I was two screwdrivers short of a toolbox."

"What? I don't understand."

She laughed. "No matter. It's an American thing. I'll explain it later."

"Actually, I bought two cribs."

"Did you buy out the stores in Nairobi?"

He squinted. "How did you know? The plane is packed. I went a little crazy on the clothes, bibs, a funny little thing that looks like a nipple."

"A pacifier."

"Yes, that's it. You'll just have to see for yourself. And I got a car seat for the Hummer."

She planted a kiss on his lips. "Thank you." She stepped around the plane and looked inside. "So much for the simple life, Mr. Farid. We could open a baby store."

"I didn't buy everything. And I brought my wife something special."

"Oh?" Her eyes sparkled mischievously.

"Besides the coffee—and I did enjoy a wonderful latte at Wilson Airport in your honor—I found dark chocolate, white chocolate, and milk chocolate. All to appease your every whim."

She laughed again. "You know how to pamper me—and make me fat."

"There's more. I bought ice cream, your favorite kind with pieces of chocolate-chip cookie dough and peanuts. Had to special order it."

She wiggled her shoulders like one of the kids gawking at them. "Yum, I think I'm in heaven." She patted her tummy. "Did you hear that, sweetheart? We're in for a real treat."

He reached for Thomas. "I missed you. I always miss you when we're not together." Searching her face, he realized a truth. "Wherever we live, it has to be together."

Tears welled in her eyes, a common occurrence lately. "I agree, but where?"

"I looked around Nairobi. We could live there, if you liked the city."

She nodded. "But it would be so hard to leave Warkou. And I'd still worry that you'd be planning a meeting with Nizam. Promise me, Paul. Please, there's no reason for you to ever see him or another member of your family."

"But what if the Holy Spirit is prompting him, like He did me?"

"Have you so quickly forgotten the past few weeks?"

He shook his head. "Not at all. But I've nearly given up on God giving me direction."

"We can talk later, I suppose. Denying it all does not settle a thing."

"I feel the same, but we no longer have just the two of us to think about. God has other plans."

"Indeed He does." She patted her stomach again. "He is growing."

"*She* is growing. I'm sure of it." He was about to say more, but his phone rang.

"Hello, brother. Is this a good time to talk to you?"

Paul raised a brow at Larson, as though his brother had just overheard their conversation. "Nizam." Larson took Thomas from his arms, and he walked away.

"I hear children."

"Yes, I'm walking away for privacy. How are you?"

"I've talked to your friend Tom Messinger in California. You gave him my number?"

"I did. All of the numbers that you and Muti have used to call me. I asked him to contact you when you'd be sleeping."

"I see. He asked if I had questions about your Jesus."

Paul tried to detect anger or frustration in Nizam's voice, but his brother spoke as though others were listening. Suspicion coiled in Paul's heart. "And did you?"

"Yes, but I also told him I'd rather talk to you. He said both you and he would have the same answers. Perhaps different words, but the same meaning."

"He spoke correctly."

"I have an Arabic Bible."

If Nizam spoke the truth, he could be killed for having it in his possession. "Are you reading it?"

"Yes, brother. Today, while turning pages, I found a man in the New Testament section by the name of Paul. I read a great deal about this Paul. I see now why you took this man's name."

Dear God, please touch my brother's heart and claim him as Your own. "I pray God speaks to you through your reading."

"Perhaps I am acquiring an understanding. But these teachings of your God are blasphemy to Allah. I fear I am already destined for hell."

"Then why do you continue to read?"

"I ask myself the same question when I pray to Allah. At times I think my only hope of paradise is to give myself to the cause of Islam."

"I'm sure al-Qaeda would assign you a mission."

Nizam chuckled, a nervous shake that hinted at something else, but Paul was afraid to speculate what.

"My fear is that I'm not ready to die," Nizam said.

"And you are not ready to leave this life until you have the assurance of the real God and acceptance of what His Son did for our sins when He died on the cross."

"Allah has no son. Blasphemy, my brother."

"You will have to determine those things for yourself." Paul swallowed hard. Oh, that Nizam was earnestly seeking answers instead of setting Paul up for death. "As for me, I serve the Lord God who gave His Son Jesus Christ for my sins."

"I hear your conviction, but what if you are wrong?"

"I'm not, which is the source of my real joy. Will you continue to read the Bible?"

"Possibly. I want to see you, Abdullah."

"Paul. Abdullah died when I became a Christian."

Again Nizam chuckled. "I want to speak with you about these things. As I said before, I will meet you anywhere. Will you still see me in California?"

Paul struggled with a response. He glanced at Larson with the children. Dare he risk leaving her a widow for the opportunity to lead Nizam to God? Whom did Paul serve? By refusing his brother, he cast aside his trust in God's protection. Though sometimes he wondered if the Nile would run red with the blood of the innocent before the Creator of the universe stopped the senseless killing.

"Nizam, call me in a few days. I must discuss this with my wife. There is much at stake here, when I consider you may be setting a trap for me."

"This is no trap. I do not comprehend why I am taking this path that may get me killed. But I must find the answers. I will call you in a few days."

Paul disconnected the call. He held the phone in his hand

and stared at it as though God might speak to him. *Nizam. Do you really want to know God? Or do you seek to kill me like the others?*

TWENTY-ONE

❧

Five days had passed since Nizam had called Paul, and every time her husband's phone rang, Larson feared it was her brother-in-law. She wanted to believe that Nizam sought answers about Christianity, that he was sincere. But she didn't trust any member of a family who had made it known publicly that they were out to kill Paul. She'd learned of the reward money and what her husband could expect in the torture chambers. Paul had committed an unforgivable offense by turning his back on Islam, and now he was an infidel who deserved death.

Larson had gathered enough information about his family's religion to understand that the extreme groups condoned lying for the cause of Allah. To her, Nizam represented a form of terrorism worse than the most deceitful of men. But God called His own to love—to give of themselves as He had freely given Himself without regret.

Her spirit burned with the quandary: not simply an unresolved situation but a heartrending dilemma. She could not hold Paul back from obedience to God, even if it cost him his life. And her husband's potential sacrifice was what frightened her the most.

"Spend more time in prayer and in God's Word," she had said to him before Sarah arrived at the clinic this morning.

"He wants you to have the right answers."

"Silence is all I hear." The calls of birds outside the clinic punctuated his words.

"Do we already know the answer and are ignoring it?" Her own question hit her hard, for she already feared what must be done.

"This is by far the most difficult choice of my life." He stood from his chair at the computer. "I've asked for prayers from all over the world."

Larson studied her husband, memorizing every line and curve of his face. "What would Jesus do in this situation? What would the apostle Paul do?"

"He'd pray for guidance."

"Which we have done together. I wonder if, in the silence, God has instructed His angels to clear a protected path to Nizam."

Paul nodded. "I'm not afraid to die, but I am concerned about you and our little family."

"We have to trust, Paul. If God is leading you to witness to your brother, then you have no choice. But my love for you says differently. I want you beside me for many years, not written about in some book of martyrs, like Jim Elliot and Nate Saint."

His curious glance caused her to smile. "They gave their lives for Christ in South America back in the fifties. Later, the ones who killed them became Christians."

"There was a purpose."

She blinked, her throat burning. "Then you have your answer."

He pulled her to him. His eyes told of his love for her. But even more so, his eyes told of his love for God. "I love you, Larson. I'll be careful."

※　※　※

212

Ben glanced at David, seated beside him at the military outpost. The youth listened to the talk of soldiers. Some boasted of past firefights and others talked of the future. David asked few questions and studied each man. He had the marks of leadership and a good mind. Tonight Ben would discuss the activities of the day with him and give him an opportunity to voice his thoughts.

He'd hesitated to bring David after the incident with Daruka and the lion. She'd be lost without their son and concerned about safety for both of them. The natures of men and women washed over him. Often men were the ones who stepped out in courage to protect their homes and provide for those they loved, while women waited at home—and worried. A man's role was easier.

Ben's life had always been filled with confidence and certainty, until cancer attacked. Telling Daruka about his health had crossed his mind. At least she'd understand the necessity of the pills and why pain racked his back. Yet filling her life with misery in the knowledge of his impending death sentence seemed grossly unfair. She'd no doubt realize he'd married her for their son, and Ben refused to hurt her any more than he already had.

"Father, thank you for bringing me with you."

He'd never tire of hearing his son address him. "I wanted you to see what my life is about while it is relatively safe."

"I hope the new government doesn't interfere with the rebuilding of the South."

Ben nodded. "Before Vice President Garang was killed, I'd been invited to work with a team of men who seek to do that very thing."

"Who took the vice president's place?"

"A man called Salva Kiir Mayardit, a military man. We shall wait and see about him. He does support a separate South, and I like that."

"I think you should be the man to lead the rebuilding.

You're a colonel and have been educated in the States."

Ben laughed at his son's declaration. "I think my reputation as a man with a temper might shadow my qualifications."

David shrugged. "Then the government shouldn't make you angry."

Ben clasped him on the shoulder. "Ah, I think you will be a much better leader." He stood and cringed with the pain.

"Father, where do you hurt?"

"Oh, I'm simply getting old. My bones have seen a lot of fighting."

"I'll pray for you."

My wife has raised a Christian son. Ben hoped the boy's faith didn't end up being a sign of weakness. "I have something to do, and I don't think it's the place for you." He smiled. "I'll be back shortly."

Ben strode toward the tent where Muti was kept until Ben or Okuk grew mad enough to kill him. The Arab refused to reveal any information and had resigned himself to death. Torture had little effect on him. The idea of bargaining power had settled in Ben's mind, and today he wanted to work on Muti from a different angle.

Rain began to fall in heavy drops, eating away at the mud on Ben's boots. He shoved aside the image of his shortened life washing away all of his pride and self-respect.

Standing in front of the guard, Ben watched water drip off the bill of the soldier's cap. The guard saluted and didn't flinch.

"Is the prisoner alive?" Ben asked.

"Yes, sir. He's talking."

"Has he been given anything to eat today?"

"No, sir. Only a cup of water."

"We'll see if he lasts the day. Has Commander Okuk been to see him?"

"Yes, sir. Twice."

Ben stepped inside the small tent. Muti was gone.

❖ ❖ ❖

Paul adjusted the strap of his backpack and hastened his pace alongside Bishop Malou. They made their way to the bishop's truck, a war-shot, rusted vehicle that had to have rolled through the factory line during the Vietnam War.

Bishop Malou possessed a powerful countenance. Larson often said she could feel God's presence in the bishop. "Like a Sudanese Billy Graham. His eyes seem to see the things about me known only to God."

Paul recognized the same trait. The difference was, he hadn't put words to the effect of the soft-spoken man's demeanor. Respect for the bishop spread across southern Sudan, but the man's home was here in Bahr al-Ghazal province, and here lay his heart.

Finally Paul caught up with the tall, slender man. "If my legs were longer, I wouldn't have this problem."

Bishop Malou tossed his ragged bag into the back of the truck. "If your legs were longer, we'd get this truck loaded faster."

Paul laughed, hoisted a bag of rice, and slid it alongside other bags and boxes of food. "And if you'd let me buy you another vehicle, we'd both get to where we're going much faster."

They leaned over opposite sides of the truck bed, the sun bearing down on them in the near-liquid heat. Sweat dripped from both of them onto their soaked shirts—Paul in his Ohio State football shirt and the bishop in a red cotton T-shirt.

"How far down the road do we go before you unload what's bothering you?" the bishop asked.

"What makes you think anything is wrong?" Paul pulled two cold bottles of water from his backpack and tossed one at him.

The bishop caught it and screwed off the lid. "I feel it. Man, don't you know by now that I have an extra sense?"

"You don't want to hear what I call your extra sense."

"But I'm right, so let's get this truck moving, and you can talk to me."

Fifteen minutes down the rutted and narrow road, Bishop Malou swung him a grin. "I'm prayed up and ready for you to ask for advice."

Paul chuckled. "I see that humility is not one of your virtues."

"I'm working on it." They hit a hole, and the bishop focused his gaze on the road. "Is this about Larson and the baby, or your brother?"

"Larson and I are fine. Better than fine. We're praying about where God wants us to live and raise our family—be it here or somewhere else. The problem is Nizam. I've decided to meet with him. Larson agrees. My brother should have called over a week ago for my answer, and he hasn't."

"Are you afraid something has happened to him?"

Paul yanked on a loose string on his backpack. "The longer the delay, the more I second-guess my decision. If he's decided to remain Muslim, then I'm back to dodging poisonous darts from him, which I'm used to. Someone gave him my satellite phone number, and I've never discovered who. If my brother presses the point of talking with me in person and learning about Christianity, then I must follow through with our meeting. Either way, I could end up a dead man, leaving Larson to raise our children alone."

"Our families are always a concern. But the whole dilemma goes back to our priorities, and God comes first. The way I look at it is, when God calls us home, it doesn't matter what we're doing. What scares me is not being in His will."

"I have come to the same conclusion, but waiting on Nizam's call is making me a crazy man."

Bishop Malou threw him a deadpan stare.

"All right. I'm crazy anyway." Paul watched a herd of gazelles give the truck a toss of their heads. "I hope my brother has not compromised his safety."

"Whatever the outcome, God has already spoken it."

"Well, I wish Nizam would let me know what he's thinking so I could plan my future." Paul threw in the last phrase to see the bishop's reaction.

Bishop Malou shook his head and chuckled. "The future, he says. We'd all like to see where tomorrow leads."

But Paul felt as though a traitor stood all too near and attempted to change his tomorrows. He desperately wanted to know who'd stolen his phone number and given it to Nizam. And if his brother had secured information, who else might be stalking his and Larson's steps?

"I have a story for you."

"Go ahead. It will take my mind off my problems."

"A young man in Darfur was running from several Janjaweed mounted on horses. The young man raced to a compound, but there wasn't a place to hide. The only person in sight was an old man grinding millet. He had a huge pile of the grain beside him.

"'The Janjaweed are after me,' the young man said, 'but where can I hide?'

"The old man pointed to the pile of grain. 'Underneath here.' The young man had no choice but to crawl under the grain. Moments later the Janjaweed rode up to the compound.

"The leader greeted the old man respectfully. 'Have you seen a young man running?'

"The old man nodded. 'Yes, I have.'

"'Where did he go?'

"The old man pointed to the pile of grain. 'He's in there.'

"The leader of the Janjaweed laughed, and so did those who rode with him. 'Old man, we are not stupid.' Shortly thereafter the Janjaweed rode away, thinking the old man was crazy.

"The young man crawled from under the pile of grain. He trembled so badly that he could barely speak. 'Why did you tell them where I was hiding?'

"The old man smiled. 'Grandson, do you not know that it is the truth that sets you free?'"

❖ ❖ ❖

The patients who lined up to see Larson cut into her naptime, but that was the case most days. She wanted to sleep all the time, and when she wasn't craving a place to lay her head, she pranced around with the need to relieve her bladder.

Oh, hormonal and bodily function overload were real treats.

Larson glanced at the clock. *The hospital will have the results of Thomas's blood work.* The doctor planned to send the information by e-mail, but when would she find the time to check it? Sarah had her hands full with a crying baby whose mother had walked through the brush for two weeks to get to the clinic. As in most situations where a desperate mother brought a sick child to the clinic, there wasn't much Larson could do but make the little one comfortable and pray with the mother. From all indications, this child would not live. Fever and diarrhea raged through its little body, and dehydration had taken its toll.

A man midway through the line seized her attention. He held his left arm against his stomach as though it were broken—or he hid a gun. Larson's thoughts always spun with bizarre what-ifs, and she'd had enough close calls lately.

"Sarah, can you come here a minute, please?"

The old woman brought the whimpering baby with her. Larson turned to speak with her privately. "Step outside with the baby and find one of the guards. Have him join us with some complaint that needs my attention. There's a man waiting who looks a little suspicious, the one holding his arm to his stomach. I want to make sure we aren't in for any surprises today. Stay outside for a little while so nothing looks strange."

"Santino should be here. He'd protect us." Sarah turned and headed for the doorway.

A thickly built soldier stepped into the clinic. "I'm sorry to interrupt, Dr. Farid, but I have a severe pain in my stomach."

"We can't have that." She pointed toward the line. "Anywhere is fine, but preferably not at the end. Our soldiers need to be feeling well as soon as possible."

The soldier eased in beside the man holding his arm. Larson inhaled sharply and focused her attention on her patient. *My job is healing. His job is allowing me to do it in one piece.*

Shortly thereafter, Sarah reentered the clinic. The baby had ceased its weak cries. Larson studied the child long enough to determine she was either unconscious or had died.

"Sarah, I need to see the baby."

The old woman looked at Larson and shook her head. Some days Larson hated her work. She sent Sarah to console the mother and make arrangements for burial. Warkou's burying ground had far too many residents.

Through the mixture of Dinka, other tribal dialects, and Arabic, she heard the soldier and the man beside him talking. All seemed well. A few moments later, she learned the man did have a broken arm, but he carried a knife inside his shirt. The soldier took possession of it until she finished setting the bone.

The day ended late, and she still hadn't been able to access her computer to find out about Thomas's test results. Long after sunset, she cuddled her baby boy and held his bottle while she searched through her e-mail. The message from the doctor in Nairobi sat in her in-box. She kissed Thomas's cheek, desperately wanting her baby to be healthy. A veil of sadness overwhelmed her as she recalled the baby girl's fate earlier in the day.

Finally, Larson clicked on the message. One glance captured what the hospital had determined. All of Thomas's blood levels fell within the normal range. No HIV, no indica-

219

tions of serious disorders. He was a fine, healthy baby boy, and she'd do whatever she could to ensure he stayed that way.

TWENTY-TWO

———————— ✹ ————————

*B*en raged through the camp in search of Muti. He and Commander Okuk tore through tents and studied the trails for footprints. Their prisoner had escaped through a knife slash in the rear of the tent. But who was the accomplice? Ben interrogated each soldier with the threat of death in his every breath. Guards had done their job, and no one had seen anyone suspicious in or near the camp. Ben even went through each soldier's belongings in search of money that might point to treachery.

Another mole existed, and this time it was among his men. His soldiers had served under him for years, and the Rhino Battalion stood as one of the finest. He'd trained them hard, and they'd defended their homeland well. Recalling each man's actions in firefights, Ben could not accuse or find fault with a single one.

When their efforts proved futile, the two men made their way back to Ben's tent.

"Okuk, think hard. Did you see or hear anything that might give us a clue as to what happened?" Ben needed a pain pill, but Okuk and David sat in the tent with him, and he didn't want to hear their questions about what he was taking.

"No, sir. When I saw Muti earlier, he said nothing to indicate he might be freed. In fact, the man was silent. In his weakened state, I find it difficult to believe he had the strength to crawl out of the tent."

"Unless he faked his near death to fool us." Ben cursed. "And now we're the fools, because he's gone. When I find the man who helped him escape, I'll slit his throat." He started to say more, but David was there. A sideways glance revealed a stoic expression on his son's face. Ben swallowed more curses and reached out to touch David's arm. "I've got to get you back to your mother. Muti is capable of bringing down an army upon us."

"Father, I want to stay with you." His voice cracked. "Boys younger than me fight."

"If you were five or six years older, I'd hand you a rifle. But you're too young, and your mother would never forgive me." Ben shook his head. "I'd never forgive myself if I put you in danger. You'll be grown soon enough." Ben turned to Okuk. "You're the only man I can trust with my son. Take one of the trucks and deliver him to his mother. I wish Santino were here, then I'd send him in your place."

Commander Okuk rose from his chair. "I'll leave right away. Like you, I sense Muti may bring down a firefight on us."

Ben stood, and David reluctantly joined him.

"Will you return to us soon?" David asked.

"Yes, as quickly as I can get the situation here resolved." *I'd take you back myself, but it's impossible.* Ben pulled his son into a hug. "I love you. Take care of your mother for me."

He never knew when this might be his last glimpse of David. A father could not be more proud of a son than what he felt for the young man beside him. Each time he was with his son or thought about him, Ben understood why men with families rushed into battle and sacrificed their lives. He'd do anything for David. Anything. Since marrying Daruka and establishing a relationship with his son, Ben had resigned himself to do the good and noble thing for as long as he lived.

Ben watched Okuk and David leave. His pain-racked

body longed to call his son back. Such a strange mixture of sweetness and bitter reality. He wanted what he could not regain: time and an opportunity to recapture the past.

Cancer. He silently cursed the disease that strangled the life out of him. He didn't want to die in front of Daruka and David. If there were a God, he'd plead for Him to spare his family the image of a diseased man in a broken body.

At his tent, he swallowed a pill and snatched up his phone.

"Paul, got some bad news here."

"More fighting?"

"Worse. Somebody cut Muti loose."

"How did that happen?"

Paul's critical response raked at Ben's pride, and he didn't like it. "If I knew how he escaped, then I'd have the jackal."

"I'm sorry. Didn't mean to sound like your men weren't doing their job. What happened?"

"The tent was slashed, and he crawled out the back."

"I have no doubt you'll find him."

"Look, Paul, I called because I'm worried about you and Larson."

"I appreciate that. Santino is due back to Warkou today. But if he's not there yet, she needs to get out of the village."

"You're not with her?"

"I'm with Bishop Malou, and we're heading back to Warkou shortly. I'd say we're about six hours from here. I'll call her right away."

"Okay. I doubt if Muti stays in hiding long. Be careful. Tell her to get into that Hummer and stay hidden until Santino arrives." Ben slipped the phone into his pants pocket. Suddenly friends meant more to him than ever before.

The thought of Larson being hurt unnerved him. His thoughts ventured her way far too often, as they always had. At his and Daruka's wedding, he'd avoided eye contact with Larson for fear she'd see the truth. Who was he trying to fool? But for the first time, he wanted to love Daruka more than Larson. Maybe it would happen before he died.

He turned and stepped back into the camp. A fire of sorts had spread through his soldiers—one of suspicion and distrust. And although the flames lapped at him too, survival meant trusting the man carrying a rifle next to him. Trust was more important than the caliber of weapon or the number of men for or against you. Without it, the man and the cause died.

Ben would spend the rest of the day interviewing each soldier again. He'd find the mole and execute him in front of the others.

"All of you but the guards in front of my tent." Ben allowed his voice and presence to fill those around him. "One at a time, we'll go through this again. No one leaves. No one is to speak to another man unless we're attacked. Be aware that Muti may be gearing up for a firefight."

❖ ❖ ❖

Paul felt like throwing his phone. Why wasn't Larson answering? Four times he'd dialed her number, and it continued to ring, then roll over to voice mail. She didn't place the same value on keeping up with her phone as he did. Some days it was frustrating. Today it frightened him.

He listened to Bishop Malou explain to the villagers what it meant to live a life that mirrored Jesus. To trust not in men but in the God who controlled His creation with a perfect plan.

That's what I lack right now. Trust that Muti doesn't come after Larson with no one there to guard her. More so, Paul had to believe God would protect his family.

Once the service ended, Bishop Malou made his way to Paul's side. "I see the anxiousness on your face, my friend. And I saw you talking on your phone. Is there trouble?"

"Colonel Alier informed me that Muti has escaped." Paul pushed aside his dread of the bishop's truck not starting. "I'm afraid for Larson, and she's not answering her phone. I shouldn't have left before Santino returned."

"We shall drive to Warkou at once. But let us pray first."

Paul much preferred to pray along the way.

"My friend, the enemy plaguing your life is not too big for God."

Anger threatened to surface. "God expects me to take care of my family. And standing—"

A small family made their way to them before Paul could finish—a good thing, since the words on his lips were those of mounting fury.

"Bishop Malou, my family would like to be baptized before you leave."

The bishop held out his hand to the man. "You became a Christian during my last visit."

"Yes, sir. Now we want to be obedient in baptism."

Paul cleared his throat. "Bishop Malou must leave. He can baptize you the next time he's here."

The bishop smiled, not once taking his eyes off the man. "I will be happy to baptize you and your loved ones today. What a fine family you have, and I praise you for your decision today."

"We need to leave now." Paul would have left him in the village if not for the fact that they were traveling in the bishop's battered truck.

The bishop swung a quick glance back at Paul. Tension sprang from the man's body. "The Lord's work first. Then we go."

Paul clenched his fists and nodded. If he opened his mouth, he'd say things he'd have to apologize for later. Instead he walked to the truck for privacy and again pulled out his phone from his pants pocket.

Larson. In moments she answered the phone.

"Are you all right? I've been trying to call."

"Yes, of course. I was napping while Thomas slept. What is it, Paul?"

"Muti escaped from Ben's camp."

"How?"

"Ben doesn't know. He's angry, just like I am. Who knows where Muti is headed."

"Santino should be here soon."

"But I should be protecting you. That's my job."

"Must you be so sharp?"

Paul took a deep breath. "I'm sorry." He rubbed his hand over his face, as if to change the man he'd become of late. "I'll be on my way home within the hour. Bishop Malou is going to baptize a family first."

"Then things have gone well?"

He couldn't remember when his head hadn't been filled with worry about so many things. Had God forgotten him? "Ah . . . yes. Many have decided to become Christians."

"Wonderful. Paul, I love you. You can't be everywhere to solve all of the world's problems. You can only be where God wants you to be at any given moment."

"Easy for you to say. You're not in my shoes."

"Excuse me?"

"Please, Larson, take Thomas and drive away from the village until Santino or I get home. Better yet, drive to Ben's camp. You should be able to get there in two hours or less. Don't tell anyone where you're going."

"I have my rifle and my pistol. I don't think it's necessary."

"I said get out of there."

"All right." He heard her moving. Was she hurrying to Thomas's cradle? "I'll call once I'm outside the village."

"Just drive. Muti is a dangerous man. He was after you once, and he could be on his way there now. Larson, I have to know you're safe."

226

Suddenly fear threatened to overtake Larson. With one hand holding Thomas, wrapped in a blanket, and the other holding a pistol and an insulated bag containing several formula bottles, she yanked open the Hummer door and dropped her keys. Quivering, she stooped and grabbed them. Thomas started to cry.

"Hush, sweetheart. We're going for a ride." She strapped him into his infant car seat and kissed him. A glance to the backseat revealed a change of clothes for both of them and several diapers.

Help me, Jesus. I'm scared.

Moments later, she headed down the single mud-rutted road leading away from the village and on toward Ben's camp.

Twice of late she'd danced with death and won. She was pregnant, recovering from a bullet wound, and now one of her abductors had escaped. Paul was afraid for her, and his love translated into a wide range of emotions.

Thomas cried louder. She snatched up a bottle and held it for him while driving. She hoped she didn't have to shift gears soon. Soon the sounds of sucking replaced his weeping. She leaned the bottle against the side of the car seat and pressed the numbers on her phone to call Paul.

"I'm on the way."

"Good. Do you want to see if Ben can send someone to meet you?"

"No. I'm fine. I imagine he's shorthanded anyway." Larson stared into the face of her tiny son. *What can I do besides pray?*

"All right. Please keep me posted. Don't stop for any reason."

"I won't. Right now I'm watching Thomas's bottle so it doesn't fall from his mouth, talking to you, and driving."

"What a woman. I'm sorry for yelling at you."

She blinked back a tear. Stupid hormones. "No problem. I

love you. I'll call every thirty minutes until I get to Ben's camp."

The phone clicked, and she dropped it beside her. The truth shook her until she feared she might be sick. Paul would get himself killed if he wasn't careful. In fretting over her, he'd ignore his own safety, and one of his many enemies might get lucky. Larson refused to have her beloved husband's blood on her hands. What should she do? Make arrangements to leave Sudan and tell him about it later? But that meant deserting her beloved husband and the commitment they'd made to Sudan. Would he understand she only wanted to keep him from harm?

Dear God, I don't know what to do.

TWENTY-THREE

❧

*P*aul wound around the path to the edge of the river, where Bishop Malou stood in waist-deep water to baptize the small family. A crowd had gathered, and their hymn singing rose beyond the treetops. The bishop always preached at a baptism, which grounded Paul's dismay. With his luck, more people would want to embrace the waters, and he and the bishop might not get started back to Warkou until evening. Paul frowned while frustration snaked through his veins. Judging from the number of people streaming through the area, another village had been summoned to the event. That meant more decisions and more baptisms.

He should be glad—thrilled that so many people were becoming believers. Instead, a cloud of frustration settled upon him. What had happened to his joy?

Gazing out over the murky water, he searched for snakes or crocs. About a year ago, a croc had taken out after Bishop Malou in the middle of a baptism. If it hadn't been for one of the men shouting a warning, he would have been dead. Ever since, Paul had kept a watchful eye out for anything in those waters that resembled death.

Paul sucked in a breath. A young woman limped up to his side. She had an advanced stage of Guinea worm and carried a stick to wind the worm around it as it exited her leg. He hoped she didn't have any plans to step into the murky mess. She'd gotten the parasite from dirty water, and here the bishop was baptizing in it. Paul would need to bring Larson here to administer antibiotics and medications to ease the pain. If this woman had contracted the parasite, others would too.

The sad part about it was that the woman could get it again, and unless she and others like her learned to stay out of filthy water, the problem would continue. Between this disease and a host of others, he wondered how the people survived. Here lay his passion and Larson's. They were destined to help the people in any way possible. Would they abandon southern Sudan if the situation grew hot? He thought so. He believed so. But taking in all the needs of his surroundings, he was no longer certain.

Larson. He'd treated her shamefully, but at least he'd apologized. She'd be calling him in the next few minutes. The Hummer was an armored tank; she'd be safe until she got to Ben's camp. He sighed. His treatment of Bishop Malou had been just as rude. What was wrong with him? Glancing about at the spiritual and physical needs of these people, he realized fear had coiled around his heart—fear for Larson and his new little family's safety, fear for their health, and a tremendous fear that he could not protect them from any of it.

Bishop Malou waved from the water. "A few more people are requesting baptism."

Paul nodded, fighting the annoyance and disappointment building inside him again. "I'll call Larson and tell her we'll be late leaving." He forced a smile. But he couldn't guarantee that the rage wouldn't explode at any given provocation. Something had taken root in his heart, something he didn't like.

Leaving the group at the riverbank, he walked back to the truck. With the things he had to say to Larson, a little privacy was in order. He had to believe she and Thomas were all right. A nudging at his spirit urged him to start the truck. It had hesitated earlier today, and he figured the battery was about gone. If it needed a little attention, he'd rather do it now and not lose his temper about it later. Strange. His temper had not plagued him before, but now he felt it like a boil wanting to fester and spread its infection.

Paul inserted the key into the ignition. Nothing. Not even a turn of the engine. Larson used to pour Coke over the battery terminals of the old piece of junk she used to drive before the Hummer. She'd made a comment about what the drink probably did to a person's stomach lining. Ever since, he'd carried a can of Coke for that purpose. He opened the creaky door and slammed it so hard that he looked back to make sure it hadn't taken flight. Lifting the hood, he splashed the brown, fizzing liquid over the battery terminals and waited. With the hood still up, he tried starting the engine again. Nothing. He banged his palm against the steering wheel. Now what? Could things get any worse?

Lord, what is happening here? Everything I touch faces destruction.

Only a formidable silence met him. Paul rubbed his face and tried to listen to the small voice of God. But all he heard was the buzz of insects. Clenching his fists, he fought the overwhelming urge to unleash his anger. He had to conquer the fury raging through his soul before it controlled him. He knew he was in danger of pushing himself even further away from God, but Paul was angry with Him. Why were those who served God the ones being preyed upon? What was the purpose in all of this? He closed his eyes and attempted to pray. He despised his tormented soul and longed for the peace that came only from God.

His phone rang, and Paul knew instinctively that it was Larson. Although she was supposed to check in with him, he should have called her before wrestling with the dead battery.

"Hey, I'm sorry for being so short lately." He took a deep breath, wanting to sound like the caring husband who had everything under control.

"It's all right. I understand you're under a lot of pressure."

"I think you're under more than I am." Paul closed his eyes and envisioned her in the Hummer. "Is Thomas asleep?"

"Yes. Do you anticipate being home late tonight, or are you going to have Bishop Malou drop you off at the Rhino Battalion's camp?"

"Not sure. The truck's battery is dead."

"Isn't there a new one behind the driver's seat? I thought I saw one there when you and the bishop packed the truck."

"Let me check." He flung open the creaky door and searched behind the driver's seat. The moment his fingers touched on the square metal box, he belted out a loud whoop. "Wonderful. Now when the bishop is finished, we can hit the road."

"Well, I have a suggestion that may make your life easier."

"What's that?"

"I'm the source of your stress. I can move to Nairobi and fly back and forth to Warkou or other areas where medical attention is needed. You can't work when you're worrying about me and Thomas. You found suitable living quarters for us in Nairobi when you flew Santino to the university. I think the time's come for us to make the move."

Her offer gave him some degree of comfort, but the defeat in her voice bothered him too. "I am worried about you. But it seems like one problem leads to another. Living in Kenya and working here would be an adjustment for both of us."

"But I'm ready. The danger is not going away. My pregnancy brings another set of problems. This way you can rest easier, and all of us will be safe. Santino will be with us only a little while longer."

Paul took a long look around him at the beautiful paradise filled with lush green vegetation and the sounds of nature. It all contrasted with a government that didn't care about its people—a government that longed to kill him. "When I get home, let's plan a trip to Nairobi. We can look for a new home there."

"Good. I'll be at the camp in about an hour. This lady will be well protected."

He combed his fingers through his hair. "I wanted to leave two hours ago. But as long as there are people who want to hear Bishop Malou's message and wade into these disease-infested waters for baptism, he'll want to stay."

"That's how it should be, Paul."

"My *habibi*, I—"

"You've lost your joy." She wept softly. "I see it. I feel it. We've been in terrible circumstances lately, but it's not God's fault."

"He could protect us." The instant the words flew from his mouth, he regretted them.

"We're not here for a picnic. We're here to make a difference. No matter where we are in the world, there will be those who ridicule and persecute us because of our faith."

"How many of the people in those places will try to kill us?" Paul stared down at the torn seat. He yanked up a loose thread, and the rip grew longer. Did he dare reveal his thoughts of returning to California and contributing his money to various organizations that helped the Sudanese? There they'd all be safe. "I'm tired, Larson. Tired and frustrated. I feel like all I need is one little shove, and I'll burst into something ugly."

❖ ❖ ❖

When Larson was within thirty minutes of the Rhino Battalion, she phoned Ben.

"Where are you?" Impatience edged his words.

"I'm west of your camp. Should be there in a little while."

"Did you run into any trouble?"

"No. I'm sure this is nothing, but I feel better knowing I

don't have to defend myself against Muti."

"When I find him, he'll wish he was dead."

She didn't answer. Ben could be horrible to deal with when he was in a mood like this. Even if she did agree with him.

Within the half hour, Larson pulled into the camp. Hard men rose with rifles in hand to greet her in the evening shadows. Among them was Ben. He met her at the Hummer and opened the door. She saw the old look on his face, the one that spoke of love and regret.

"I'm sorry to inconvenience you," she said. "Any word about Muti?"

"No. Okuk has a few men trailing him. Not so sure this is a safe place for you if he decides to bring a firefight down on us. But better here than in Warkou with no one else there to handle a gun." He peered over her. "I'll get Thomas on the other side. Do I take the whole contraption he's in?"

She laughed lightly to ease the tension between them— the tension that spoke of the many years she'd failed to speak of his love for her. "I'll unfasten the carrier. He'll sleep in it."

"You can stay in my tent until Paul arrives."

She wanted to protest that being alone with him made her nervous. No doubt he felt the same. Once inside the tent, he lit an oil lamp and set Thomas's carrier in a corner. He was such a good baby, sleeping through all the turmoil around him. The yellow-gold shadows bouncing off the tent walls reminded her of the many late nights talking with Ben before Paul had entered the picture.

"I can make coffee," she said. "I see you have a fire going strong." *Just like it used to be.*

"We could argue about my tactics in battling the GOS."

She laughed. "Or the prospect of peace in the near future."

"Or my need to confiscate some grain from you to feed my men."

"And I could threaten to blow a hole through you if you cause my villagers to go hungry."

She finished measuring the coffee into an old percolator that looked like it had never been washed, and he set it outside over the fire. The moments ticked by. She felt his gaze boring through her, could almost read his thoughts.

"It never would have worked, Ben."

"Did you really give it a chance?"

"If I could have forced myself to love you, I would have." She turned to face him. They should have talked a long time ago.

"I used to think the problem was race." He chuckled, but the sound crackled in the air instead of making her laugh. "But you proved me wrong."

"I don't know what to say. We're both married, Ben, and I can tell Daruka loves you very much."

"She's a good woman. A good mother to a fine son."

"Give her a chance to make you happy."

"I'm trying."

She took a step toward him, then wrapped her arms around her shoulders. In the past she'd have hugged him for friendship's sake, but those days were gone.

"I respect you and Paul too much to interfere in your lives. But that doesn't mean the desire is gone."

"I know." Larson gazed into his dark eyes, and she shivered with the intense longing she saw there.

"I should have said all this before you two married, but I kept hoping you'd change your mind. Guess you must really love him."

"I do."

"I'll always love you, Larson. Nothing will ever change my feelings. Just promise me that if you ever need anything, you'll let me help."

❖ ❖ ❖

Paul and Bishop Malou were unable to leave for Warkou until the following morning. A storm had blown in with brilliant lightning that flashed its jagged swords across the sky and rain that fell in blinding sheets. Turmoil twisted inside Paul; a pounding headache and the roar of the storm kept him tossing most of the night. The what-ifs of his and Larson's life stacked up in his mind like a deck of cards. He wanted to pray, but the words refused to form. He read through many of the psalms and attempted to use Scripture as prayer, but he couldn't concentrate. Larson needed protection, and he wasn't there to provide it. She was Paul's responsibility, not Ben's.

What would he do if he came upon Larson and Thomas in a death heap? He'd be tempted to pull the trigger on himself without a second thought. At times he didn't think he could ever breathe again without her.

God, where are You in all of this? Used to be I knew exactly what should be done. I understood my work for You and knew the difference between right and wrong. Now all I see is gray. I'm miserable, but You already know that. When do the doubts end and I find direction?

The truck bounced along, and with no shocks, Bishop Malou and Paul often hit the truck roof. The jostling didn't help Paul's mood, and he was already operating on a sleep deficit.

"I can drive." Paul closed his Bible. Nothing made sense anyway.

"Maybe later. Right now I'm all right. Paul, how can I pray for you?"

He expelled a heavy sigh. "If I knew the answer to that, I'd pray for myself."

"Talk to me. I know Muti's escape is eating at you, but I sensed a problem before that."

"You remind me of your father. I miss Abraham. He had a way of peering into my wretched soul and loving me anyway."

The bishop smiled. "My father was the closest thing to

Jesus that I've ever seen. He had his faults, but he lived and breathed Scripture, always inching his way closer to the Lord."

Paul nodded. "Honestly, I feel like I need a spiritual doctor. I hate what this life is doing to Larson. Twice in the past month, she's nearly been killed by whoever is trying to kill me. She's agreed to leave the country and travel back and forth with her practice, but is that what God wants? To make matters worse, one of my brothers claims to be interested in Christianity. He wants to meet with me, but is his request a trap or a God-given opportunity? I feel like I should be doing more for the people in Darfur." He took a big breath. "I don't know how to be a father. God knows, mine had his own agenda." He rubbed his face. "I sound like a spoiled kid who can't have his own way."

"No, you sound like a man whose life is out of control. God is your spiritual doctor. He—"

"Don't waste your breath. God isn't listening or answering. Everything is quiet, like when the skies are darkening and everything is strangely calm before the lightning flashes and the thunder roars."

"What do you want Him to say?" Bishop Malou's soft tone reminded Paul so much of Abraham—so much that he shivered in the 120-degree temperature.

Paul shrugged. "To point me in the right direction. To show me what's right and what's wrong. Larson says I'm a color person—everything is either black or white—and gray disorients me. And I guess that's true. Am I supposed to live in Sudan and risk the lives of my family? Most of all, I want God to touch me with His Spirit. I've never felt so far away from Him."

The silence between him and Bishop Malou was strangely deafening. He'd spilled his guts like a kid caught stealing candy, and now guilt consumed him.

"All I can say is that the Bible has the answers to all of our

237

problems. I hesitate to give you such a pat response because too many people say the same thing. They don't have any idea how to help, and I'm not so sure I am any better. But I will pray for your peace and for answers to your questions. I will search the Scriptures for those passages that I believe will help." He swung a glance at Paul. "Do you want to know what I do see?"

"I'm not sure. You're as blunt as your father."

Bishop Malou laughed. "I'll take that as a compliment."

Paul moistened his lips. "It will probably make me mad, but go ahead."

"I see a man who is struggling to be godly, but his past keeps getting in the way. He wants to do it all, and the job had better be done right, or he's upset. Right now you view your life as worthless because it's moving in a direction that makes you unhappy. But God has it all under His control. Take the time to renew your relationship with Him, and then you'll hear His voice."

Paul winced. "Are you saying I'm trying to play God?"

"I don't know. Are you?"

The implication of the bishop's question angered him. "I can't expect God to take on Paul Farid as His pet project."

"Why not? Because of who you once were?"

Paul clenched his fists and stared out of the open truck window. The landscape swept by him. A flock of birds rose into a cloudy sky. A giraffe nibbled at the leaves of a treetop and stared at the intruders. To the left of them, a few zebras grazed, mixing with the comical warthogs and a single male impala. Up ahead, vultures picked at a carcass of something.

Who was he, anyway? What made him think he had any right to help the same people he'd persecuted? What gave him the right to expect God to answer his questions?

TWENTY-FOUR

———————— ❧ ————————

Larson expected Paul and Bishop Malou long before the noon hour. Her husband hadn't called for the last two hours, and the memory of their conversations yesterday haunted her. She wanted to see him and look deep into his eyes. *The windows of the soul.* Paul needed release from trying to save the world. She'd detected the anger that was eating at him like a parasite, growing until it threatened to destroy his faith. In the wee hours of the morning—when she should have been trying to sleep, since Ben had given her the tent— she'd thought of Paul and how much she loved him. How could she make him see that Jesus had faced ridicule and per-secution because He loved those who were lost and hurting? She and Paul could do no less. She wanted to tell him what rested in her heart, but she was afraid, afraid to stay in Sudan and afraid to leave.

Larson heard the sound first, the rumbling of a truck without a muffler. She scooted herself back from the small table in Ben's tent.

"Daddy's here," she said to Thomas and lifted him from his carrier. The rains had diminished for now. Perhaps she'd see a rainbow, a sign from God that she and her husband might find peace in their souls.

She sought his eyes, the dark pools of love and anguish—

the dark pools that held too much of a burden. If not for Ben and his men watching, she'd have run to Paul like a silly schoolgirl who needed the comfort of her man's arms. Instead, her heart hastened and her legs carried her onward.

He smiled and pulled her into his embrace. She gazed into his eyes and saw what she feared the most.

"Let's go home, my *habibi*," he said. "Some days I sense I will never see you again."

❖ ❖ ❖

Two days later, Ben came to a decision. He needed to see the doctor in Nairobi. He'd planned to make an appointment when he took Daruka and David there in August, but John Garang's death had halted those plans. The aggressiveness of the cancer had stepped up the pain, and the medication no longer managed it. Perhaps Larson could help him, but that meant telling her the truth. The last thing he needed was pity, especially after his admittance of love for her the other night. If this was how his life measured out, then he'd rather die now.

He found it increasingly difficult to go through the motions of living. Daruka no longer questioned him about his failing health, even when he couldn't eat and his face pinched with pain. She must have talked to David about it, because he didn't speak of it either. Ben hadn't seen his wife or his son for the past three days. Muti's escape had garnered all of his extra time, and the man still evaded them.

Before dawn, he bit back the agony and stumbled from his tent to talk to Commander Okuk. The man would need to be in charge while Ben made his way to see his family and then while he was in Nairobi. All traces of Muti had disappeared, but that didn't mean any of the Rhino Battalion had given up.

Ben needed to tell his country's leaders something about

his absence. But first he had to tell Paul the truth. The thought of confessing the cancer to a man he'd once hated scraped at his stubborn pride, but he had no choice. Time was running out, and the fervent pain weakened him, almost hour by hour.

Once he'd made arrangements with Okuk, Ben took one of the trucks and headed for Yar. With his life teetering on the edge, he needed to spend a day with his family. *His family.* All that those two words represented sounded good to him, for however brief the time. Soon he'd have to tell them about his health, but not until he had talked to the doctor. Maybe a new drug had been invented that would make all of this torment vanish. Euthanasia held a strong running.

With the sun moving up from the east, he decided not to put off the call to Paul any longer. He inhaled deeply and roused the courage to acknowledge what he could not change.

"Good morning. How is everyone in Warkou?"

Paul chuckled. "I hope this means you've found Muti."

"Not yet. But we have a few leads from one of the moles in Yar."

"Anything I should know about?"

"Not sure. Two of my men are holding the prisoners in the village. I plan to do a little questioning of my own while I'm there. One of them has a family, and I intend to do my finest work."

"You already know how I feel about killing family members to extract information."

"This is war, my friend. What if there is another plan to abduct Larson?" When Paul didn't answer, Ben changed the topic of conversation. "Is Santino doing his job?"

"I think Larson would adopt him along with Thomas. He's a good man."

"I agree." Ben chuckled. "Imagine that. You and I agree on something."

"A real miracle, my friend. If Santino intended to be

around longer, I'd have him investigate a problem. I wish I knew who had given my phone number to Muti and Nizam. It makes me angry, apprehensive."

"Makes me wonder if one of my men has sold us out. Whoever the traitor is has done a good job of keeping his cover. I'm looking forward to slitting his and Muti's throats. Have you heard from your brother?"

"No. I don't know what he's thinking."

Ben considered backing out of his real reason for the call, but a struggle for life also meant casting aside his pride. "I need a favor."

"You know I'll do whatever I can for you."

"First of all, I need your word that you'll not tell Larson any of what I'm about to say."

"I suppose. I don't like keeping things from her."

"There's a good reason."

"All right. What do you need?"

"A ride to the Nairobi hospital. When I was there for the bullet wound, the doctors found something else." Ben hesitated. "Cancer. It's in my back. They gave me around six months."

Paul gasped.

Ben hated this. "Say something, will you?"

"I'm really sor—"

"No." Ben cursed. "I don't want to hear all that. I need to see the doctor. The pain medicine is not strong enough."

"When do you want to go?"

"I'm heading to see Daruka and David, and then I'll drive on to Warkou. Say two days."

"Do they know?"

"No one but you."

"Okay. I'll keep it to myself. But sooner or later you'll have to tell everyone. Larson and I were planning a trip to Nairobi too, but I'll find an excuse to put ours off for a few days."

"I appreciate this."

"Did the doctors recommend any treatment?"

"The typical chemo and radiation. I said no thanks. I'll talk to you once I'm heading your way. Remember, if you value our friendship, no one is to learn about this."

"I understand."

Ben laid the phone on the seat. Had he entrusted too much information to Paul when his friend already carried the burden of his family's seeking to kill him?

❖ ❖ ❖

Larson stared at the blank screen on the computer in hope that the words would come to send an e-mail to her parents. Paul had stepped outside the clinic with his phone, and she guessed it was Ben from what she'd heard of the conversation. She hadn't been able to deal with Ben's confession the other night, and she still couldn't figure out how to tell Paul. The idea of keeping it to herself had crossed her mind, but that was wrong. She felt guilty, as though she'd betrayed Paul's love.

I haven't done anything wrong. I simply listened to Ben say how he felt.

Santino had arrived shortly after they had the other night. He and Paul had talked for over two hours about Muti's escape. She'd supplied food and coffee and tried to listen, but sleep had dulled her senses.

"What's wrong?" Santino sorted the latest paperwork from FTW and filed it into a drawer for Paul. "You're crying."

She hadn't been aware of the tears. But there they were, dripping down her cheeks and over her lips. She licked the saltiness and reached for a tissue, one of the few treasures of civilization that she kept in the clinic.

"Bad news?" Santino asked.

"I'm fine." She blew her nose. "I don't ever cry. No time for it."

"Is Paul in trouble?"

"He will be if I don't make life easier for him."

"How can I help?" Santino walked across the room and bent down beside her.

She glanced into his young face. "I'm being a woman. I'm tired and worried about Paul, Muti's escape, and a whole lot of other things that I can't talk about. Paul is so concerned about my safety, and I fear he won't take the necessary precautions to protect himself."

"He loves you and wants to make sure you're safe."

She nodded. "I can't have him stressed because of me. I'm afraid for him." She attempted a faint smile. "I'm afraid for me."

He smiled. "But I'm your bodyguard, remember? And today you have both of us. As far as Muti is concerned, let him try something. I'm ready to fill that jackal full of holes."

"You don't think I should leave Sudan?"

"Not at all. Your skill is needed here. Without you, many will suffer and die."

Maybe Santino was right. "When do you leave for school?"

"A few weeks, but I'm sure Colonel Alier would supply as many soldiers as you'd need. Besides, Muti will be found before he can cause any trouble."

"I wish I could be sure of that."

"Trust me, Dr. Farid. All of the problems you are having will end by the time I leave for school. The peace treaty is intact, and the leaders of southern Sudan are working with the government."

"I trust God." She took a deep breath. Her stomach twisted with unsettling emotions.

"I know you do, just like Paul, Aunt Sarah, and many others." His words were soft, caring. "So trust your God for your safety and for those you love."

She studied him. "You will be a great asset for Sudan. I'm not sure what you believe in, but I pray God touches your heart very soon."

He laughed. "With all of you praying for me, how can I resist?"

Larson nodded and blinked back the tears. A young mother with two children entered the clinic. Larson had a job to do, and fretting over her husband wasn't part of it. But she wanted his arms around her, and their world free from those who wanted them dead.

Was that so wrong?

Long after sundown that night, Larson sat with Paul outside their *tukul* with a lighted torch between them. The mosquitoes were worse than usual, but she and Paul kept themselves sprayed with repellent. She didn't want to think of what the stuff did to their lungs.

They weren't talking. Not that she considered exchanging words the only means of communication. Paul was miserable. She felt it and didn't have a solution.

"We have a saying back in the States that fits us tonight," she said.

He smiled but didn't look her way. "What's that?"

"Are we going to talk about the elephant in the living room or continue to ignore it?"

"I can't carry out the beast. It's too heavy."

She fought for words. What he didn't say meant more than what he did say. "We can't go on pretending it isn't there, either."

With his gaze fixed upon the darkness, he sighed deeply. "What do you want me to say?"

"Paul, you're depressed, and I don't know how to help you. Life hasn't been good for us lately. I'm willing to move to wherever you want. I was serious about that."

"I have to fly Ben to Nairobi in a few days."

"Can Thomas and I come with you, or do you have work to do?" He was close enough to touch, but she hesitated.

"Ben has some people to see. He's not sure how long it will take." He turned to look at her. "I love you. I'd do anything to protect you and Thomas."

Her eyes moistened. "And I love you. I want to see you

245

laugh and enjoy our life, but all I can do is pray."

"My upbringing keeps getting in the way of how I should think and what I should do as a Christian. My Arabic culture isn't something I can easily toss aside."

"And I wouldn't ask you to ignore your heritage. You should be proud of who you are."

"Not everything, Larson. I'm confused about my feelings toward my family in Khartoum. A little voice inside keeps telling me I deserve to die because I deserted them. Then I realize that's the voice of the Evil One and not of God. I can't figure out Nizam or Muti or what they're trying to accomplish. I've always prided myself on being a smart man, but this is a tough one. If Muti is working with Nizam, then why doesn't my brother show up here, and we'll battle it out? Or is the situation two separate issues? I feel like I'm a missing piece in a puzzle. And with all of our problems, I can't help but think God is punishing me for once believing in Allah. For some reason, God has forsaken me. Why else is He silent?"

She reached for his hand. "I hope you know those ugly thoughts are lies. You belong to God. He loves you. He may be quiet, but you are in His heart."

"I do believe that. Then I don't. One minute I want to step into Khartoum and knock on my father's door to tell everyone in his house about Jesus, and the next minute I want to hide because I'm afraid to die."

"We're all afraid to die at the hands of those who want us dead."

"But I'm a Christian. I should be ready to step over the line for Him."

"You're supposed to be willing, but you don't have to step barefoot into a snake's pit."

He reached over and kissed her cheek. "So we're back to the martyr's syndrome?"

"Possibly. Only you know the answer to that."

Together they listened to the insects, staring into the night as black as the fear that stalked them.

"And Nizam?" Larson asked. "What do you want to do about him?"

He squeezed her hand. "I love my brother."

"All I ask is for you to meet him where it's safe."

"You understand I have to do this."

"I do, even though I remember begging you not to see him." She hesitated. "I have a request. When you are in Nairobi, will you take the time to search out a home for us?"

"I can, and then we'll fly back there to choose the perfect one—if that is what God is leading us to do." He stood from the plastic chair and pulled her to her feet. "And you need a doctor for our baby."

And our children need a father.

TWENTY-FIVE

---

*B*en drove into Yar in the late afternoon. Tired and hurting, he wanted only to crawl onto a pallet and sleep. But he had a part to play—that of a husband and father. How long could he continue at this pace? His clothes hung on him as though he were an emaciated refugee from a missionary magazine, and his once-ravenous appetite had vanished with his extra flesh. He found Okuk studying him as if he'd had a private consultation with Ben's doctor. And Daruka and David. They had to see the difference. Maybe he should tell them all and be done with it. But he couldn't. That admitted defeat, and Col. Ben Alier never backed down from a fight. Even when he saw the odds were against him.

He opened the truck door but couldn't muster the strength to step out. Instead, he sat inside and took a few deep breaths before making his way to Daruka and David. Before he went to bed, he'd visit the prisoners. A slim figure made its way toward him. *Daruka.* He didn't deserve her. A searing pain torched his back and momentarily paralyzed him. *Leave me alone. Not now. She needs me.*

Ben smiled at his own revelation. He did care for Daruka. He was her hero, and he refused to disappoint her. He swallowed hard.

"You can't sneak up on me." She laughed. "I could hear

the door squeak from the next village."

"That's so you'll have food ready for me."

She laughed again and wrapped her arms around his neck. "I missed you."

"And what did you miss about me?"

She stood on her toes and kissed him lightly. "Everything, of course."

"You crazy woman." He kissed her, and she tasted sweet. Before cancer, he'd have picked her up and carried her into the *tukul*. But those days were nothing but memories. Would she forgive him once he was gone?

"David will want to see you." She caressed his cheek.

"Where is he?"

"With his goats. He reminds me of my father with his cows."

"Those cows are what bought your mother, and let me remind you that you cost me one hundred of them."

"And my father is grateful. He has more cows than anyone else in the cattle camp. But I'm worth it."

Yes, you are. "I'd have paid twice that amount." He meant it. "I'll go find David. Is he east of the village?"

She nodded. "I'll prepare food for you while you're gone."

The walk through the tall grass reminded Ben of when he'd searched out David to convince him that marrying his mother was a good idea. Ben had lied to his son then and lied to all those present when he took his marriage vows, but his heart had softened since then. As time passed, Daruka meant more and more to him.

Perhaps life might settle down here in the South. He watched the new government for signs of treachery—Arab Muslims were as trustworthy as a pit of snakes. He was skeptical and argued against cooperating with the new Government of National Unity, or GNU, but peace of sorts had come to his people. As expected, fighting still broke out here and there, but not like before. He'd referred to Khartoum as the

GOS for so long that the new name sounded foreign. The concept of southern Sudan voting to be a separate nation in six years sounded optimistic, and much work needed to be done before the election. Self-rule for his people offered a fragile optimism, and then there was the issue of the South's being paid for its oil according to its population. Not everyone on both sides agreed with the peace treaty. Even so, Ben chose to honor the agreement until someone else broke it—or until someone he loved or respected was in trouble. He'd been a warlord for too many years to just sit back and watch things happen.

All of his greatest aspirations had gone up in smoke when John Garang was killed in the helicopter accident. And the uncertain future clung to Ben like the smell of cow dung.

Once his men found Muti and whoever had fed him information and helped him escape, the battalion could relax. But was Muti a matter of southern security or a personal vendetta between Paul and his family?

Ben heard the sounds of angry men. He bent down in the grass and moved closer. His fingers wrapped around his pistol while the pain in his back nearly blinded him. Slowly he drew his weapon from his belt and listened again.

"These goats are ours. You stole them," a man said.

"No, I didn't. My uncle gave them to me in payment of work."

David. Ben had seen these kind of men before—steal what wasn't theirs and kill anyone who got in their way. His son would not be a victim.

He made his way through the grass, allowing his eyes and ears to guide him until he saw two men in a clearing. One had David's arms pulled behind his back, and another stood in front of him.

"We've had enough." The man in front of David shoved him to his knees and held a rifle to his head.

"My father will hunt you down for this." David's voice

sounded amazingly confident. Could it be his son wasn't afraid to die?

"We'll do the same to him as we will to you."

Ben stood and fired repeatedly. Blood spurted from the men's chests, and they fell. David fell facedown into the grass. With his senses pounding in his brain, Ben raced toward the scene. His son had to be all right. He had to.

"David. David, are you okay?"

His son rolled over onto his back, clearly shaken. "Yes. Father, I prayed you would come."

Trembling, the boy moved away from the bodies, and Ben helped him to his feet. Tears rolled down Ben's face, the first in years. He made certain the men were dead and pulled his son into his arms. Blood dripped from David's mouth, and the left side of his face would carry a few bruises.

"I didn't steal those goats." David pulled himself from Ben. "Uncle Reuben gave them in payment for work I'd done for him."

"I know, son. This world is full of men just like these. They don't deserve to live. Were there any more?"

"No, sir." David stared at the dead men, then shook his head. "They would have killed me if not for you. God sent you here."

"I'm sure He did." The thought of God using him to rescue David was a joke. Too soon his son would learn the truth about God, but Ben didn't intend to start that lesson now. "Let's get your goats and go home."

David called each one by name and herded them toward Yar. He walked alongside Ben.

"David, I'm getting you a rifle, and I'll show you how to use it and keep it clean. There are two things a man needs to learn. You protect those you love, and you fight to keep what is yours."

"I'll remember. I've seen fighting before. People killed. Women and girls raped. I wanted to be a soldier, but Mother said she'd die of a broken heart if I left her." David shrugged. "So I stayed. What good is peace if men like these try to hurt us?"

"In every country there are men and women who care only about themselves. They are motivated by selfishness and misguided reasoning. Best you learn that now. There is no perfect place in the world. Beware of who you trust." Ben recalled the man or men among his soldiers who had sold out to Muti. "Make sure those you call friend are worthy of your loyalty."

David walked a few feet more. "I miss you when you're gone. I'm glad you're my father, and I'm sorry for the things I said to you before you married my mother. I can tell you love her and me."

At that moment, Ben hated all he'd done to deceive his wife and son. More so, he despised his worthless soul. If he believed in God, he'd pray that they never discover the truth.

Ben couldn't seem to shake his anger after the attack upon David. He itched to slit the throats of the two prisoners whom he believed had betrayed him to Muti. He'd ordered his men to take the prisoners and any family members outside of Yar. The villagers would find out what happened to traitors, but they didn't need to listen to the screams of the tortured.

Leaving David with Daruka, Ben approached the tent where the prisoners were held. First he wanted to interrogate a man who had four children to raise by himself.

"Why did you spy on my men and report to Muti?"

The man shook so that he had to swallow several times before he could speak. He glanced at his young children. "He promised me money, but I never got it."

"Did you help him escape from my camp?"

"No. No, sir. I did not. All I did was tell him when you were in the village."

Ben pointed to his children. They were frightened, crying. The oldest boy looked to be around ten years old. "You're lying to me. I want some answers, or I'll kill your children one at a time, beginning with the oldest."

Tears streamed down the man's face. "Please, I know nothing. Kill me, but let my children live."

"What else did you tell Muti?"

The man's eyes widened. "I did not know him long enough to tell him anything other than what I said. He approached me after the first time you came to the village some weeks ago."

Ben doubted if the man could read or write. "How were you to tell him?"

"I was to make a mark on a tree outside of the village near the river. He took me to the tree so I'd know for sure. I can show you where."

Ben believed him, but he had to be sure. "Knowing Muti was a part of the North, you sold out your people for money?"

"I know I was wrong. I didn't think about it. All I wanted was money to feed my children."

"Are you Muslim?"

"I'm Christian. And I should have trusted God to provide, but my children are hungry."

Ben had already learned the man was poor, and his men had found nothing of value in searching his meager belongings.

"Please, Colonel Alier. Let my children go."

Ben ordered the oldest son brought to him. "Where is the money that Muti gave your father?"

"I haven't seen any money." The boy's arms and legs were the size of sticks.

"When did you last eat?" Ben took a glance at the other three children and saw they were all too thin.

"Two days ago," the boy said. "Your wife gave us some bread."

Ben glanced at the prisoner. Not so long ago, he'd have killed the man for what he'd done. But David . . . the hungry children . . . cancer . . . "Take these children back to the village and make sure someone gives them something to eat."

"Thank you." Tears rolled down the man's face. "Kill me now. I'm ready."

Ben studied him. *Pathetic.* "Once your children have eaten, you find someone to care for them. Then leave Yar. Don't ever show your face here again."

The man nodded but said nothing.

"Bring me the other prisoner." Ben didn't like the arrogant look on the second man's face. "Where is his family?"

One of the soldiers stepped forward. "He has none, sir."

Ben narrowed his gaze on the man. "What did Muti ask you to do?"

"To serve Allah."

One of the soldiers slammed his rifle into the prisoner's stomach.

"I asked, what did Muti ask you to do?"

"I have nothing to say to you. Do what you want to me."

Ben laughed. "You sound so brave, but we have ways to make you talk." He turned to the soldier in charge of guarding the prisoners. "Build a fire for me. I'll be back in a little while to interrogate this man. If he does not cooperate, then we'll kill him."

The prisoner said nothing, but he might change his mind.

❖ ❖ ❖

Paul stood outside the Warkou clinic and waved at Ben exiting his truck. He looked even thinner than the last time, his face gaunt and pale. The man held the record for stubbornness. Why had Ben found it so important to keep his health a secret? Didn't he understand his friends would want to help? Now Paul comprehended Dr. Khamati's evasiveness. Ben had most likely told his doctor to keep his records a secret. And why had Ben married if he knew he was dying?

255

Paul didn't plan to ask him that question. Some men's motives were best kept to themselves.

As soon as the plane was in the air, Paul glanced over at his friend.

"Do I tear into you now or later about keeping your medical condition a secret?"

"Later. I plan to sleep."

"Un-plan it. I want to help, Ben. There are all kinds of cancer treatments out there."

Ben leaned back against the seat. "I can't afford it."

"Now that makes me mad enough to land this baby and fight it out with you."

Ben laughed. "I'd have you flat in thirty seconds, with one hand behind my back."

"No arguments there. But I'm going with you to see your doctor, and we're going to see about treatment—the best we can find."

"The treatments will kill me."

"I thought you were an old fighting machine."

"I am, but I'm not stupid."

"Let me look into it. If it means flying you somewhere else in this crazy world, then I'll take care of it."

"Why?"

"Why not?"

Ben cursed, his normal manner of handling matters out of his warlord dominion. "I remember nearly choking you to death once."

"Kid stuff."

"Three years ago does not constitute kid stuff."

Paul sobered. All of the demons plaguing his mind seemed to surface at once. "Look at what I'd done before meeting up with you. We're friends, and I want—no, I need—to do what I can to help you lick this thing. Larson would never forgive me if I didn't do all I could to make you more comfortable or lead you to a cure."

"And how do you expect me to pay you back?"

"By doing all you can to help southern Sudan—or by protecting me from my family so my wife doesn't end up a widow."

"You know where to hit hard."

"Good. Glad that's settled. I figure the doctors will want to run some tests. I have things to do, so it works out just fine."

"If I'm gone too long, Daruka and David will worry."

"How long do you plan to keep this from them?"

Ben chuckled. "If you find a cure, then they'll never know."

"I love a bright outlook."

"Are you looking to move Larson and the baby to Nairobi?" Ben's question came so softly that Paul thought the man was drifting off to sleep. But the sad look on his face told it all.

"I think it's the safest thing to do with Muti and my family after me. We haven't made a definite decision, but we do plan to look for housing in Nairobi."

"I don't blame you. Larson and your children need to be safe."

Ben spoke her name reverently. *Larson.* Pity washed over Paul. His friend was dying. He was in love with a married woman, and she was pregnant. His entire life had been put on hold for too many years while he fought for Sudan's freedom. Worst of all, Ben did not want a relationship with the Lord. What could Paul do for the man besides pray for his soul?

TWENTY-SIX

"We need to have a celebration before you leave." Larson handed Santino a bottle of water. Unlike her and Paul, he didn't drink coffee. "We'll invite the whole village and the men from the Rhino Battalion. Have a soccer match and maybe play baseball."

Santino laughed. "All for me? What have I done to deserve this?"

Larson wagged a finger in his face. "You're heading off to college, which means another university-trained leader for southern Sudan. You're Sarah's nephew. You're my bodyguard. And we all love you."

"Okay, a party. But under one condition."

"What's that?" Larson eyed him skeptically.

"I want to help with everything, even the cooking."

Sarah broke into laughter. "Not even my Santino will help with cooking. That is all women's work."

Larson didn't agree with Sarah's statement. But some things about culture took longer than others to change. "Okay, Santino, you can organize the games. Paul and I will come up with some prizes. And Sarah and I will handle the food."

"I think I'd appreciate a celebration very much." Santino took a long drink of his water. "Today has been easy at the clinic. Tomorrow we'll probably be swarming with people."

He peered at Larson's bowl. "What is that?"

"Macaroni and cheese with a dash of hot sauce. I hated this stuff until I got pregnant. Do you want to try some?"

Santino shook his head and dipped his fingers like a spoon into his cornmeal mush. "No, thanks. I'll stick with *ugali*. What exactly is hot sauce?"

"Just what it says. Here, try some. You'll probably like it since you like spicy food." She picked up a saltine cracker and sprinkled a drop of Tabasco sauce on it, then handed him the cracker.

Santino stuck the entire cracker into his mouth. Before he had time to breathe, he reached for his bottle of water. "I get it. Hot sauce. I would have preferred knowing ahead of time what you meant."

She laughed. "Paul feels the same way."

"I think I might do well to stay single."

"At least until you've finished your education," Sarah said. "I've seen the way you look at the girls."

"Looking is not the same as getting married." Santino reached for another cracker, minus the hot sauce, and popped it into his mouth.

"And you could not afford the bride price," Sarah said.

Larson's phone rang, and she quickly answered without taking a look at the caller ID. She expected a call from Paul. His trip to Nairobi had turned into four days—something about Ben needing to do a few things. She hoped Ben was switching from the SPLA to politics.

"Good morning, Dr. Farid."

A chill rose inside her. The accent frightened her. "Who's calling?"

"Nizam Farid. Your brother-in-law."

"How did you get this number?"

He chuckled, a deep-throated laugh that stirred apprehension in the pit of her stomach. "I have my ways."

She took a deep breath to steady her frenzied nerves.

"What can I do for you?"

"I want to meet with my brother, but he's hesitant. Abdullah doesn't believe my interest in Christianity is sincere."

"I'm aware of your conversations." She willed her heart to cease its hammering against her chest. "He has to make the decision to see you."

"That is where I need your help."

"You want me to help you? I don't think there is anything I can do, especially since you sent Muti after me and had him pursue my husband."

"I know nothing about that. If you were put in danger, then I am truly sorry."

She really had no reason to believe him, but why argue? "What do you want me to do?"

"Oh yes. Tell my brother I called, and I want to hear more about Jesus from him. I've been reading a Bible, and I'm beginning to understand why he chose to become a Christian."

Larson's heart started to soften. "Are you ready to make a decision for Jesus?"

"I think so, but talking with my brother about it is very important to me. Surely you understand. We have the same upbringing. My decision for this Jesus means our family will want me dead too. I would then be forced to leave the country for fear of my life."

"Paul could help you."

"And I would need his guidance." He chuckled again, but this time it did not sound as menacing. "I've even been thinking of a name to take when I am baptized."

Larson smiled, trying to envision what Nizam looked like and if he and Paul shared features. Surely he meant what he said. "And what name appeals to you?"

"Barnabas."

"That means 'encourager.'"

"Wonderful. You think my brother will be pleased?"

"I'm sure of it. I'll tell him about our conversation. Is

there a number I can have him call?"

"Oh no. Too dangerous. I'll call him in a few days. You and I shall know each other too, right?"

"Our meeting depends on Paul." She hesitated, wanting to believe Nizam and yet needing to be cautious. "I'll pray for you."

"Thank you."

Larson stared at the phone long after the call ended. Now she fully understood Paul's dilemma, for now she faced the same problem.

❖ ❖ ❖

"What's the verdict?" Paul stepped away from the window at the Nairobi hospital.

"The doctor wants me to stay another week." Ben spat the words as though they were venom. "As if I haven't been poked enough. I'm beginning to feel like they're selling my blood on the open market."

"Maybe they are." Paul lifted a brow.

"Very funny. Daruka is going to think I deserted her."

"When I get back, I'll send Santino to tell her you've been detained."

"And call Okuk too. Just don't tell them where I am. I need to contact the SPLA and tell them I'm taking treatments for a medical condition. They don't need to know anything else, and I'll ask them to keep the information private. You have my satellite phone, right?"

"Yes, sir." Paul couldn't disguise his smile. He slipped Ben's phone into his nightstand.

Ben frowned. "What has you in such a great mood?"

"You. You're sitting there in a hospital gown barking orders like you're on the field."

"Clothes don't make a man."

Paul laughed. "Okay, I'll do your bidding and be back to

pick you up in a week. Seriously, has the doctor said anything to give you hope?"

Ben shrugged. "There's a possible treatment. Of course, he may be telling me that to keep me here."

"It's probably the first time in years you've had a good diet."

"Right. The food here reminds me of the tasteless glue served in refugee camps."

"When you get out of here, I'll treat you and Daruka to a steak dinner."

A wave of sadness swept over his face. "My wife has never been out of her village. Can you imagine the look on her face the first time she sees Nairobi?"

"I could bring her here. Your son too."

"I don't want them to know yet. If things change, then we'll talk about it."

"As in staying here in Nairobi for treatment?"

"Yeah. Or if the diagnosis is worse."

Paul nodded. "I'm praying for remission. How's the pain?"

"Whatever they are putting in the IV has taken care of it. I think it's a morphine drip. I'm actually sleeping, and I appreciate the private room." Ben gestured around him. "TV, phone, and my very own mosquito net."

"I never had any idea you felt so bad. Glad the meds are working. I'm flying home today. And I found some homes for Larson to look at."

"You don't sound excited about living here."

"I want this move to be what God wants for us."

"You're a better authority on that than I am. If I were a believing man, I'd say you and Larson have a direct line to God. Have you considered Juba?"

"It's crossed my mind. I imagine the influx of refugees returning over the next several months will be very large. They'll need medical care, but then again, NGOs from all over the world will camp there." Paul hesitated. "I've never been a man who wavered back and forth on decisions, but I can't seem to make one this time. Other than to get my family out of the snake pit in Warkou."

"With the South's capital in Juba, modernization will occur."

Paul reached out to shake Ben's IV-connected hand. "I'll talk to Larson. Guess I'll see you in a week. Rest up and take your medicine."

Ben saluted and laughed. "As if I had a choice."

❖ ❖ ❖

Two more days in the hospital, and Ben was ready to toss his gown into the trash and leave. But Dr. Khamati had given him a little hope—just enough to keep Ben from marching out the front door.

"The tests are providing necessary information for your treatment plan," Dr. Khamati had said.

"I have the same question I had before. How long can you extend my life?"

"Possibly five years."

"Quality?"

"I'm not sure. We've changed your pain medication, which appears to be managing the discomfort."

"What about the cancer spreading to other parts of my body?"

"I won't lie to you. That is always a consideration."

The conversation continued to repeat in his mind. For five more years of life, he'd endure the chemo, radiation, and whatever else his doctors might want to try. David would be seventeen then, and Daruka . . . well, Ben could have her prepared. She wanted another child, and the many times he'd been with her made him nervous. Daruka had raised one child without him, and he didn't want to leave her alone to raise another one. He hoped his physical condition and the medication kept him sterile. The doctor would have the answer to that question too.

"Colonel Alier?"

Ben glanced toward the doorway to an Arab man dressed in a dark silk suit and tie. He didn't look like a doctor. As before, Ben was not registered at the hospital under his real name, and he'd been placed on the VIP wing. "You're mistaken, sir. I suggest you check with the visitation office."

The man smiled. "My name is Nizam Farid. I believe you are familiar with my brother?"

"I have no idea who you are talking about."

Nizam pulled a chair alongside Ben's bed and seated himself. Ben recognized Paul's facial structure and penetrating eyes.

"I believe you're lying to me."

"Believe what you want." Ben picked up a newspaper, shook it, and feigned interest. It lay over the nurse call button beneath his fingertips.

"I'd like for you to get a message to him."

Ben pushed the call button. "You have five minutes to get out of here."

"Colonel, my intentions are honorable." Nizam smiled.

Ben trusted a hungry hyena more than this man.

"Sir, do you need assistance?" a nurse asked.

Ben despised the woman. She'd taken care of him before and seemed to have all the answers, but today she looked quite appealing. "Yes, I need a security guard to escort this man from my room."

Nizam stood. "No need. I'm leaving. My brother does choose a strange assortment of friends. You can tell him I'm looking forward to our meeting and discussion." He nodded. "I was simply in the city and thought I might catch him here with you. His wife is quite pleasant."

Larson? Has he been to see her? After Nizam left, Ben

phoned security and informed them that their safeguards had failed. He added a few of his own words to describe their inefficiency. Nizam now knew his room number. What had the man wanted? What would stop him from returning? If he really wanted Paul, he could find him in Warkou. Concern for Larson made Ben angrier. She did need to get out of Sudan.

Nizam had phoned Paul on more than one occasion, all on the pretense of learning more about Christianity. The man looked about as trustworthy as the northern government. Today's visit made no sense, unless it was to prove a point: that Nizam could locate anyone he wished.

Ben should have asked him about Muti. He opened the drawer in his nightstand and dug under his personal belongings for his satellite phone. He needed to put a call through to his friend.

"Paul, are you alone?"

"Yes, just me and Thomas. Are you being released early?"

"No. This is something else. I had a visitor this morning. Nizam."

"Are you kidding? What did he want? How did he find you? Never mind. He has his ways."

"I should have kept him here longer, but instead I called hospital security. I denied who I am and knowing you. What bothers me is why he came. And he mentioned Larson."

"He called her while I was in Nairobi this last time. What did he say about her?"

"Said she was pleasant. I have no idea what this is all about, but it doesn't sound good. Is Santino still there?"

"Yes. Do you think Okuk can spare any more men?"

"I'll tell him to send a couple of his best. They don't have much to do since the peace treaty."

"Larson wasn't alarmed with anything Nizam said."

"Think Eve and the snake," Ben said. "Someone is reporting your every move, as though this is some sort of cat-and-mouse game. Not only does our mole have access to your phone but also to Larson's and your goings-on. I learned that the mole in Yar was reporting to Muti and someone else, but the traitor died before I could learn more."

"Who could it be, Ben? Makes me wonder if they have a bugging device."

"Look through everything you own."

"I already have. I think I'll call Nizam myself and demand a few answers. Hopefully he'll answer one of the many numbers he calls from."

TWENTY-SEVEN

---

*P*aul scanned his morning e-mail. Lately he'd received mostly junk. Very frustrating, even with a "junk" folder in his Microsoft Outlook. He scrolled down through his in-box until he found the message he was looking for. FTW had a short assignment for him. A mission-oriented organization in Juba had requested food, school supplies, and Arabic Bibles to transport to remote villages. An easy trip, but it would take a few days, and he hated to be separated from Larson for any length of time.

"Just make the arrangements and go."

Paul turned to find his wife peering over his shoulder. "Are you spying on me?"

"I heard you moan and decided to see for myself what ailed you. You can't shelter me forever, and there are two soldiers plus Santino here to protect me." She bent and kissed his cheek. "You do your job, and I'll do mine."

He studied the screen. "If I leave this afternoon, I can load up in Nairobi, pick up Ben, then fly home after unloading the supplies in Juba. But that postpones our house-hunting venture."

"A few more days won't make a difference." She smiled. "Besides, I'm planning a party for Santino. Between the clinic,

Thomas, and the special celebration, I don't have time to fly to Nairobi."

"This event will be after Ben returns?"

She nodded. "I hope Daruka and David will come."

"I agree. I'll see what I can do to make that happen. Are you sure this is not our going-away party too?"

A melancholy look touched her lovely features. "Possibly. All our friends will be here. I asked Commander Okuk—"

"That man despises me."

"He wouldn't if he took the time to get to know you. But he likes Santino. I think the party will be more for Sarah's benefit than her nephew's. She's been down a bit lately, and I'm sure it has to do with his leaving."

"Have you asked her if she'd live with us in Nairobi if we left Sudan?"

"Yes. I added that Santino could visit often, and she could help me with the babies. She seemed pleased."

"Good. Ben wanted me to consider Juba."

"Oh?" Larson folded her arms and walked to the door of the clinic. Her wound had healed rapidly from the gunshot—a miracle for a woman who insisted upon doing everything all by herself. "I'd be fine there too. With the southern government headquarters there, we'd be safe." She tilted her head. "I'm sure the NGOs will move into Juba by the swarms. But it's whatever you choose."

Paul laughed and stood from his chair. "You are becoming entirely too easy to please. Where is my opinionated wife?"

"I do have my moments of . . . shall I say, hormonal overload? Seriously, I love you so much. I wouldn't trade our life together for anything under God's skies. When I thought Muti was . . . putting an end to all of this, I questioned our commitment here. But I don't want anything to separate us."

He walked to the doorway. Sunshine streamed through the treetops much like the light she put in his life. Taking Larson's hand, he led her outside. "There isn't a poem written

270

that speaks enough of my love for you. There isn't a diamond large enough that symbolizes my devotion. There isn't a flower on this side of heaven that is more fragrant or lovely. Our life is a journey to God together. There is no one else I'd rather walk the road with than you."

Tears filled her eyes. "What a beautiful poem. What is it from?"

"It's not a poem. It's my heart's song for you."

She leaned against his shoulder. "I look forward to the adventure of our lives together. Believe me, wherever you want us to live, I won't argue."

"You have too much faith in me."

"Not at all. I have faith in the God who leads you."

He kissed her forehead. Oh, if he could only trust as he used to. "We sound like two kids with grandiose dreams about tomorrow."

"Are those aspirations so futile? Next summer we'll have two babies, and I'm so very excited. Too many times I become depressed with our circumstances and wonder if my work does any good at all. I need my dreams so I can keep putting one foot in front of the other. I hope the new government in Juba and those men who also dream of a better tomorrow will make strides toward a better Sudan."

"I hope so, and I wish I had answers."

❖ ❖ ❖

Larson wiped the perspiration from her face. She could use the generator to run the fan, but she hated to waste it on herself. Saving it for a patient who needed a source of comfort made more sense. But since pregnancy had invaded her body, good sense often escaped her. Not a single patient needed her attention. It was well past noon, and the heat seemed to suck the life out of her. She whirled around and turned on the fan.

Santino smiled above a stack of patient files and another

mound of papers. "Missing your husband?"

"Always. He'll be home in a few days, and he calls often. Still, it's not the same as his being here."

"Is he bringing Colonel Alier with him?"

"Ah . . . yes. I didn't remember telling you about Ben's stay in Nairobi. I imagine he's talking with leaders of the South."

"That sounds safer than what he's done over the past twenty years."

"I agree. And with a wife and son, he needs to settle down." She wiped off the locked cabinet containing her precious medicines. "How's the project going over there?"

He blew out a heavy sigh. "I'm trying to find a reason for this mess."

She laughed. "My perfectionism mandates I keep some order to what I do."

"While the rest of us suffer?"

She reached inside the generator-operated refrigerator and pulled out two bottles of water. "Suffering is what you did for the SPLA. This should be a piece of cake."

"Piece of cake?"

"Easy." She handed him a bottle of water.

"Some of your sayings are strange to me."

She twisted the cap from the bottle and drank deeply. "Imagine how I feel as the rare white person among a sea of dark faces."

"And Christian at that." He sat on the floor of the clinic and spread out the files. "Now, how do I organize these?"

"Put them in alphabetical order by their last name, unless all you have is a first name. Start a separate file for those who are listed only by the date on which they received care." She pointed to the filing cabinet. "The ones in there are labeled but not filed correctly."

He groaned. "The university will be easier than this— more of a piece of cake. And I'm sure my job at the Hilton will not involve straining my eyesight because your writing is so bad. This doesn't look anything like the English I learned."

"Such complaints. Hey, I have a question for you."

He lifted his gaze, and she felt sure he'd welcome anything to keep from filing.

"Why do you think it's strange that I'm Christian? Nearly 25 percent of the South are believers as a result of the war."

"I heard you weren't when you first came here."

"I certainly had a lot of learning to do about who God is, but I'm a believer now. What about you? You told me that one day you'd explain your beliefs."

"My religion is similar to yours."

"Is it tribal?"

"I guess you could say that. From what I can tell, our views of the afterlife are similar. The difference is the way we get there."

Larson studied his face. "Why are you so reluctant to explain your faith to me?"

"Because you believe in telling the world about Christianity, and I want to understand it on my own without help." He gave her a smile, the one that reminded her of a little boy. "I do believe in God, and I'm pursuing my faith."

"I guess I can't ask for more."

Santino pointed to the files spread before him. "But you can ask me to do the impossible."

"Okay, I'll help until Thomas wakes up or a patient arrives." She took another drink of water. "You'll wish you had my filing to do when a professor asks you to write a term paper."

She opened the file cabinet. "I'll begin with these."

A shadow passed across the door, and a man entered carrying a young girl. A quick glance told Larson the child teetered on the brink of death.

"Please, doctor, my daughter is very sick."

Larson lifted the girl from his arms and noted her fever

and jaundice. "Do you live near a forest?"

"Yes. Others have been sick too. Most are getting better, but not my daughter. Can you give her medicine and make her better?" The man looked feverish.

"What did she complain of before she became so sick?"

"First she said her head hurt, then her back. She is very hot, and sometimes she seems to be cold."

Yellow fever. "Sir, how are you feeling?"

The tall man's frame reminded her of a brittle limb. "Not so good. I've walked here for three days."

Larson threw a cautious glance at Santino. "Would you find food and water for this man? Then I'd like to have his vitals taken, and I'll need to draw blood." She reached for the man's hand. "What is your name?"

"Matthew Bol, and my daughter's name is Lydia." His knees buckled, and Santino grasped his waist before he fell.

"I'll do my best for Lydia. She is very ill."

"Did the mosquitoes cause this?" Matthew leaned on Santino, who helped him to a chair.

"I imagine so. Once we have your daughter feeling better, I'll come to your village with medicine to help the others."

"Thank you. Most of the sick are children."

The man and his daughter had the symptoms of yellow fever, but Larson needed to be sure. They'd been fortunate to get through the rainy season with few outbreaks of the disease. She needed to get to the village before more people became sick. Usually the children were the ones who suffered most, because they played near the forests where the mosquitoes bred.

❖ ❖ ❖

Ben squirmed in the hospital bed. What was taking Paul so long to pick him up? He should have arrived hours ago. Ben had been in this godforsaken hole too long. Everything about it was depressing, but he had learned a bit of good news. Dr. Khamati wanted him to take chemotherapy medication along with another drug that had achieved some success in treating his type of cancer. The downside was he needed to return to the hospital every four weeks for three days of treatment. What kind of excuse could he give Daruka and his men? Ben had told so many lies that he feared he'd catch himself in one of his own. The thought should have been funny, but it sounded pathetic to him.

He rubbed his hands across his head. The chemo he'd taken in the hospital had already begun to thin his hair. Something else to explain to people. Larson would probably take one look at him and diagnose the big "C." In her next breath, she'd tear into him for not coming to her in the first place. Hard enough loving a woman he couldn't have. Why have her feel sorry for him too?

Ben missed his home—the open land, the wildlife, the birds that awakened him each morning, and the simplicity of life his people had known for centuries. And he wanted to head back. Right now. So where was Paul?

Ben closed his eyes. He dreamed of a peaceful village with laughing children playing beside gardens that weren't filled with land mines, and water wells free of contamination. He was a warlord, once hungry for the next firefight, now ready to live out the remainder of his days in the land he'd fought so hard to keep free. Impending death gave a man a new perspective. The doctor may offer a little hope, but truth was truth. It would take a miracle to prolong his pain-filled days.

"Ready to get out of here?"

At the sound of Paul's voice, Ben opened his eyes. "Ready and packed. Let's go."

"I've already picked up your prescriptions and talked to the doctor."

Ben scowled. "I'm not in need of a daddy."

"But you do need a keeper. You're not going to like this,

but Dr. Khamati insists upon seeing you tomorrow afternoon."

Ben swung his legs to the floor. "You can be a real pain in the rear."

"Let us reminisce about the times you not only were a pain in the rear but you also kicked mine."

Ben lifted a brow. "I'm so glad to get out of here that I'm not going to argue about tomorrow."

Paul picked up a small bag holding Ben's personal belongings, and the two headed for the elevator.

"Tomorrow is supposed to be a clear day for flying."

The elevator door opened, and the two men stepped inside with two nurses.

"Wonderful." Ben took a deep breath. "If it storms, we're flying anyway. Oh, what did you tell Daruka about my absence?"

"That you were in special meetings in Nairobi. The same story I told Okuk. I said you'd arrive in Yar in two days. I'm now officially a liar."

"I've got to tell her something. I now have four different bottles of pills." Ben watched the floor numbers descend to the lobby. "You kept this to yourself?"

"I gave you my word. But I don't like keeping anything from Larson. Look, Ben, one of us has to tell her. I'm thinking she could administer some of these treatments without your coming back to Nairobi."

"No." Ben's voice bounced off the elevator walls, and the nurses startled. "I can't. Not yet. Maybe never."

"She's already talked to me about how bad you look."

"I'll wear makeup."

The door opened. "You're a stubborn fool."

"I'm in good company. Now do you want to know every detail about your brother's visit?"

"Absolutely. He's coming to Warkou five days after Santino's party. He said he was flying in, and he'd be by himself.

We'd talked about California, but if he has plans to kill me, it doesn't matter where I am."

"I'll be there—with the entire Rhino Battalion."

"Good. I'll have Larson and Thomas at a hotel here in Nairobi. Since I'm going through with seeing my brother, I don't need to worry about my family."

TWENTY-EIGHT

———— ✦ ————

On the third morning after Matthew and Lydia Bol had first entered the clinic, Larson decided to visit their remote village. They were progressing well, and Sarah could administer their medicine. Larson loaded the yellow fever vaccine into the backseat of the Hummer along with mosquito netting, antibiotics, and miscellaneous medications to help treat the headaches and chills of the disease. Into another box, she tucked medicine to treat malaria. She'd strongly supported a humanitarian organization from the States that shipped boxes of mosquito netting to combat the many diseases caused by the insect. Where there were mosquitoes, diseases multiplied.

Larson drove west with Santino, passing a herd of graceful gazelles and moving on through tall grass. The twisted trunk of an umbrella acacia tree, a symbol of Africa, seemed to summon all those who sought relief from the scorching temperatures. As they neared the tree, a leopard stretched out on one of its branches—a rare sighting since the animal preferred the night. Remembering the gazelles behind her, she realized the leopard was checking out its next meal. How she loved this country and all of its inhabitants.

And how thankful she was for the Hummer's air-conditioning.

"How long will it take to get to the village?" Impatience edged Santino's words. "And how long do you think we'll be there?"

"I know where it's located, but I'm not sure of the name—if the village has one. It'll take us about five hours. I want to examine those who are sick, administer the vaccine, and see anyone who is ill. I'd like to give a training class for the women too."

"Health and hygiene?"

"Yeah. It's designed so the women can use what they have to keep their families healthy. If you could search out their water supply for me, that would be helpful. Providing there is a need for a well, I could talk to Paul about contacting Living Water to drill one for them. The organization makes regular trips to Sudan. So, in answer to your question, we'll be here possibly three days if we work hard."

By late afternoon, the Hummer had arrived at an area where she counted eight *tukuls*. In the near distance, a forest caught her attention. Lydia Bol must have gotten too close to the forest and the disease-infected insects. Larson would treat the children first.

She and Santino eased from the truck. The people were curious but stayed their distance.

"I am Dr. Farid, and this man is Santino Deng," she said in Dinka. "Matthew Bol brought his daughter Lydia to me. Both were sick, but they are doing much better. Matthew told me about others here who are sick with a disease caused by the mosquito. I have medicine to help you."

Her announcement initially brought suspicion, but when she mentioned Matthew again, a woman stepped forward and said her two sons were ill.

"Take me to them." Larson grabbed her medicine bag. "Santino, please bring the vaccines."

He nodded, and she followed the tall woman, just as she'd followed concerned mothers so many times over the past nearly eleven years. The remainder of the afternoon was spent treating those infected with various diseases. So many children were ill. Santino distributed the food supplies and aided her with injections. She saw the village's source of water, a murky river containing everything but clean, pure water. It all reminded her of why she'd stayed in Sudan and why she hated to leave.

"Help me spread the news about a class for these women." Larson counted the number of vials left for yellow fever. Wonderful. She had plenty. "Tell them it will be in the morning by the river."

"I don't think they're smart enough to grasp what they need to know."

Shocked, she bit back a retort. "Never underestimate what grassroots education can accomplish. These women don't want their families sick, and neither do I. Good health and hygiene start here among those who can make a difference."

The next morning on the riverbank, Larson stood with her backpack beside her. About a dozen women of all ages sat to listen. She'd given this talk a hundred times, and its simplicity saved lives.

"Thank you for coming this morning," she began. "I want to tell you how to keep you and your family from getting sick. My friend Santino said there is good water about an hour from here. Make sure you put it in a clean container. When you bring it back to your village, boil it. That destroys the things in the water that make people sick. If you are caring for someone who has diarrhea, make sure they drink lots of the boiled water and eat food. The sick person also needs some salt and sugar in the boiled water." Larson reached into her backpack and pulled out an oral rehydration solution spoon. "This is called an ORS spoon. The smaller scoop is to measure salt, and the larger one is for sugar. I have plenty of these for all of you. Make sure you use no more salt than the small scoop, or it could be very bad for the sick person."

She stared into their faces. Oh, how she respected their determination to understand what she was telling them. Blinking back the tears, she realized how very hard it would be not to live among these treasured people.

Santino waved to her, and she waved back.

"I'll be right there as soon as I pass out these ORS spoons and answer their questions."

He frowned. Santino needed to learn patience. Odd that she hadn't seen this side of him before. He desperately needed that trait to lead his people.

❖ ❖ ❖

Paul taxied down the runway at Wilson Airport with Ben beside him. It would be late evening when they arrived in Warkou, but he could help Sarah with the yellow fever patients and care for Thomas. Going home without Larson there saddened him, but she'd return the same day he took Ben back to Yar. Maybe that aspect of the situation was good. Ben preferred to avoid her, and the sooner he dealt with his feelings for Larson and gave them to Daruka, the better.

Soon the two men were soaring through a clear blue sky. Paul loved the thrill of flying, the sense of weightlessness, as though his craft and the countless birds of the earth had a secret. Today he flew lower than usual.

"Hey, take a look to your right." Paul pointed to a small parade of elephants.

Ben chuckled. "Since the peace treaty, the wildlife has been moving back into Sudan." He shrugged. "I read in a Kenyan newspaper the drought has drawn them into our borders. Whatever the reason, the idea of our animals no longer facing extinction or a mass exodus is good."

"I'd like to see the South set aside some national parks for the wildlife like President Museveni did in Uganda, possibly large safari camps like Kenya's Masai Mara or like those in Tanzania."

"We will. I'd much rather see a tourist trade instead of the influx of missionaries."

Paul laughed. "I sure hope the peace lasts. Seems like I can feel the pressure lifting."

"An old fighting machine like me lives for war. We don't know anything else. But I don't want Daruka and David to live through any more of it."

"Ben, you'd be a great asset to the government in Juba."

"I've heard that before, but my days are limited."

"We'll see."

Ben leaned forward. "Look at those wildebeests. Must be fifty thousand of them."

Paul peered down at the strange-looking creatures. "I wouldn't want to get in the way of them running."

"Me either. I had a round with a few hippos once. Tried to overturn a boat." Ben laughed long and hard.

"I haven't heard you laugh that much in a long time."

"Life gave me a bad hand."

"Not for long. You can draw again."

"Hard for me to believe you aren't preaching." Ben watched the wildebeests. Maybe he was envious of their freedom.

"I could, but I'd rather live it."

"I'm taking a nap." He crossed his arms over his chest and stared out his side of the plane. No doubt Ben felt Paul had a sermon in him.

He couldn't remember Ben ever talking this freely and easily. But he liked it. Cancer had given the man a unique perspective. "I'd like to fund David's education."

Ben sighed. "I appreciate what you did for Rachel, finding a place for her to live in California and getting her settled into college."

"I'll continue to take care of her."

"That's not what I meant. I'm thanking you for something already done, not something I'm asking or expecting for the future."

Paul cringed. "You're welcome. I'm glad to do whatever I can for you and your family."

"Thanks. Now I'm getting some sleep before we land."

❖ ❖ ❖

Ben had a strange feeling about bringing Daruka and David to Warkou for Santino's celebration, but it was important for Larson to include everyone who knew the young man, and Ben didn't want to come alone. He thought he could handle seeing her until he caught sight of the balanite trees that stood sentinel outside Warkou. He slowed the truck. Memories of Larson flew to the front of his mind, and he despised himself for it.

"I sense coming here makes you uncomfortable." Daruka's whispered words cut through to his soul.

"I'm sorry." He grasped her hand at his side. What else could he say? He'd been touched by this woman beside him, but he feared she'd realize he loved Larson or learn about his health before he was ready to tell her. David sat on the passenger side, or Ben might have been tempted to tell her the truth about his health.

Daruka had never ventured outside of Yar, but she was not ignorant. Ben marveled at her insight and wisdom. He saw how quickly she caught on to English, and she had taught herself arithmetic. He instinctively knew that if he took her to a huge contemporary city, she'd soon fit in. Daruka was much too smart for her husband. Even though she never mentioned his pills, he was certain she had put the pieces together.

"This Dr. Farid, would she have time to see me today?" Daruka asked.

Ben sensed panic needling his composure. "I imagine you could ask her. Are you ill?"

She smiled. "No. Not at all."

He relaxed. For a moment he'd feared Daruka knew the truth—all of the dark, ugly things about him. Most times he believed his past had brought on the cancer. Retribution.

All of Warkou celebrated with Santino. The village women had prepared plenty of food and set it on long tables in the clinic. A cow had been roasted, and there were huge kettles of *ugali*, tomatoes, cabbage, green beans, and many fruits. The rains attempted to spoil the soccer and racing games, but the men and boys played anyway—even Paul. Ben watched David compete with the other young men, proud to call the boy his son.

Ben glanced around and saw that Daruka had slipped away. Her wanting to see Larson had agitated him all afternoon. His gaze swept around him. Larson was not around either. Once the soccer game ended, he went in search of his wife, dreading what she might have learned.

Then he saw the two together talking in the corner of the clinic. Too many scenarios pounded in his brain. When he walked closer, he saw the women were smiling. Ben still wasn't relieved.

"There he is." Larson laughed. "We were just talking about you."

Daruka covered her mouth and giggled. "I have an announcement."

"What is it?" Ben feigned excitement.

"We are going to have a baby. I thought it might be too soon to tell, but the test is positive."

Ben thought he'd stepped on a land mine. That would have felt better than knowing he'd fathered another child. A child he might possibly never see.

"Are you happy?" Daruka asked.

"Of course." He forced a smile and wrapped his arm

around her waist. That gesture was the answer to all of his unsure responses.

Paul ambled to Larson's side. Sweat from the soccer game streamed from his body. He had two bottles of water—one to drink and one to pour over his face. After cooling himself inside and out, he kissed his wife on the cheek. Ben glanced at Daruka. Some things were simply too painful to bear.

"Ben and Daruka have good news," Larson said.

"Another reason to celebrate." Paul pulled another bottle of water from his pocket and handed it to his wife.

"We're going to have a baby," Daruka said.

Paul extended his hand to Ben and smiled. "Congratulations, old man. Our children will be less than a year apart."

Ben met Paul's gaze and forced another smile. "Thanks." *If I live that long.*

TWENTY-NINE

---

*E*xhausted, Larson lay on the pallet she shared with
Paul and let all the wonderful memories of Santino's celebration fill her mind. Except one. Ben looked worse
every time she saw him. Suspicion crept across her mind. Her
old friend was dying—his gray complexion and loss of weight
confirmed her fears. And Paul probably knew it. What else
had the two been doing in Nairobi? Why hadn't she the guts
to confront either of them? And why wouldn't Ben allow her
to help?

She wished sleep would carry her away before Thomas
awoke or daylight reminded her of the work ahead. Glancing
at Paul, she realized he was awake too.

"Daruka told me that Ben is taking four different kinds of
pills."

"Oh."

"Paul Farid, don't you 'oh' me. You've taken him back and
forth from Nairobi and evaded every conversation about his
health."

"I can't, *habibi*."

"Can't or won't?"

"Can't. I gave my word."

"I've been watching him, what little I've seen. At first I

thought it was simply a slow recovery from his gunshot. Then I feared infection. The thought of heart problems crossed my mind. But after today I think it's cancer."

"Don't you think he'd tell us if something were wrong?"

"Remind me when you're due to have your next yellow fever vaccination to use a dull needle."

He chuckled.

"It's not funny. He's asked you not to tell me, and you're being all noble about it." When he didn't respond, a sick feeling crept through her. It had nothing to do with her pregnancy. "Oh, honey. This is horrible. Maybe . . ."

"What?"

"Remember the night I drove to his camp when Muti escaped? I told you he admitted his feelings hadn't changed, but he respected you and me. Now I'm wondering if he was simply tying up loose ends."

Again silence.

"You don't have to respond. I expect you to keep your word. I just hope he's getting the best possible medical care, and he doesn't purposely stand in front of a bullet." She snuggled up next to Paul. "I could help him. Provide treatments closer to home. I hope you realize your silence confirms my suspicions."

He kissed her forehead. "You are going to be very sleepy in the morning, and I've got another flight to Nairobi as soon as the sun comes up. I'll be back tomorrow evening. Do you want to ride along tomorrow? Makes no difference to me, because either way I'll be making another flight day after tomorrow—to take you and Thomas to Nairobi before Nizam arrives."

"The second flight is better for me. I have too many patients. Paul, I'd almost forgotten about your meeting. This scares me."

"I understand. What is important to me is to have you far from here when my brother arrives. The people at the Mayfield House will take good care of you."

"I pray I still have a husband when it's over."

❖ ❖ ❖

Paul figured as long as he had to spend an hour in Nairobi
for FTW, he'd make arrangements with the university to con-
tribute a sizeable donation to Santino's education fund. The
young man had served well under Ben's command and had
been a great asset to Larson. When Santino was in Warkou
with Larson and Sarah, Paul knew his family was in good
hands. Now he and Larson could repay the young man with
an investment in his future.

He pulled his phone from his backpack and made a call to
the university office. "I'd like to make financial arrangements
to help a registered student with his tuition."

"And what is the student's name?"

"Santino Deng. He's Sudanese."

"Just a moment, sir."

Paul waited in the airport coffee shop, enjoying the dark,
rich brew and munching on a sandwich. Moments ticked by,
but he was comfortable in the air-conditioned building. Two
planes took off—Air Kenya, with tourists headed for the
Masai Mara. When all of this settled, he'd take Larson there
for a vacation.

"Sir, did you say the student's name is Santino Deng?"

The voice shook him back to his business. "Yes, he's en-
rolled for the fall session."

"We do not have a student by that name."

"There has to be a mistake." Paul's mind raced to come up
with any other name that Santino could have used.

"I don't think so. Deng is a common name, but we do not
have a Santino as a first or second name with a surname of
Deng."

"Thank you." He disconnected the call and leaned against

the wall. *Santino said he'd gotten a job at the Hilton Hotel.*

He called the hotel. Moments later, the manager confirmed that Santino was neither an employee nor had he ever completed an application for employment.

Why had Santino lied to them about school registration and a job? What had he done during the time Paul brought him to Nairobi to take care of school matters and employment? Santino hadn't asked for a ride back to Warkou from Nairobi . . . Paul had assumed a member of the SPLA had arranged the transportation.

Paul pulled out his phone again and dialed Ben.

"Hey, do you know who brought Santino back from Nairobi when he registered for school?"

"I assumed you'd gone back to get him."

"No. He said he had a way. How long did he serve under you?"

"Almost three years. What's going on?"

"He's not registered at the university, and he's not an employee of the Hilton Hotel. I'm trying to figure out why he lied. Do you know where he came from?"

"Sarah told me she had a nephew who wanted to fight. That's all I know."

"Is he her blood nephew?"

"I have no idea, but now I wish I knew."

"Ben, I need to do some thinking about this. Nizam is planning to be in Warkou in three days, and now this. Can you have the two soldiers there alerted to a possible problem? One more time, I'm asking you to do what I should be handling."

"I'm on it. We need soldiers guarding the perimeter of the village for your meeting with Nizam. It's only a couple of days away, so I'll go on ahead myself. And this gives me a little leverage with the situation. If Santino is up to no good, I want to be the one to handle him." He cursed. "I'm really slipping to have missed the signs."

Paul checked his watch for his scheduled takeoff time.

"Am I jumping to conclusions here if I say Muti, Santino, and Nizam may be working together?"

"I'm right there with you."

"Nizam might change his mind about coming after me if he learns that Santino's been apprehended." Paul's stomach lurched. "I've got to call Larson now. Have to get her out of there until one of us arrives. I'll take her and Thomas to Nairobi until this is settled."

"I'm leaving now."

Once Paul disconnected the call, he dialed Larson's number. It rang seven times before it rolled over to her voice mail. Alarm grasped his senses. She could be busy with patients. She could be busy taking care of Thomas. She could be sleeping. A number of diversions could be vying for her attention. Why was it that every time he needed to get hold of her, she didn't have her phone? His suspicions of Santino's possible treachery began to take form.

Santino had supposedly been in Nairobi when Muti escaped. While living in Warkou, he could have easily accessed both Paul's and Larson's phones and given those numbers to Nizam or whoever wanted the information. For that matter, he could have learned the numbers even before moving to Warkou by gaining access to Ben's satellite phone. Paul recalled Santino's reluctance to talk about his religion. The pieces now began to fit.

His phone rang. It was Larson.

"Are you all right?" He hoped he sounded calm despite the near-panic raging through him.

"Sure, honey. What's wrong?"

"Are you alone?"

"Santino and Sarah are with me. Ben's men are somewhere watching the road."

"Can you walk outside and talk to me privately?"

He heard her footsteps on the concrete floor. "Okay, I'm outside."

"I've discovered some things about Santino that concern me."

She laughed. "He's been a godsend for us. I can't imagine him doing anything to upset us."

"I don't want you to repeat what I'm about to say. All I want you to do is listen."

"Paul, you're scaring me."

"Santino never registered for school, and he's not employed at the Hilton. He lied to us. And the more I think about the situation with my brother and the fact that someone gave him our phone numbers, the more I suspect Santino."

She gasped. "What else?"

"He was supposedly on his way back from Nairobi when Muti escaped. And think about his keeping his religion a secret."

"What do you want me to do?"

"Ben and his battalion are on their way there. See if you can casually find out if Sarah is Santino's birth aunt."

"I know the answer to that."

"I don't want you to give yourself away in this conversation. So is he or isn't he?"

"Isn't."

"I want you to take Thomas and get out of there. In fact, take Sarah with you. Call Ben and let him know where you are. But do not let Santino see that you're upset. If you meet up with Ben's men, do not come back to the village until this is over."

"I understand. When will you be here?"

"By nightfall."

"If I learn any additional information, I'll let you know."

Larson walked back into the clinic to find she was alone with Santino and Sarah. Her heart thudded against her chest. Paul wouldn't jump to conclusions without confirming the facts. He was much too logical. Santino's involvement made sense—too much sense.

"Santino, why don't you call it quits for the day? We don't have any patients, and all the work is caught up. Besides, we have to get used to working without you again."

He peered up from a newspaper that Paul had brought back on his last visit. "Are you sure you don't need me?"

She shook her head. "I'm tired, and I'd like to have some alone time with Thomas."

Sarah replaced the broom. "I can watch the clinic while you take the baby back to your *tukul*."

"Thank you, Sarah. I appreciate this."

Larson watched Santino leave. Questions. So many questions plagued her that she couldn't wrap her mind around any of them. She recalled Santino's criticism of the women in the village where she'd taught the health class. Now she knew he'd lied about his future in Nairobi.

She walked to Thomas's crib and smiled at him in his sleep. So peaceful. "Sarah, how long have you known Santino?"

"About ten years. His grandmother was a good friend until she died in a GOS raid. Then he came to live with me."

"So he lived with his grandmother?"

"No. He came to me with the news about her death, and I took him in."

"I see. I know you're going to miss him."

"He's a fine man, but . . ." Sarah's face saddened.

"But what?"

"I don't understand some of his ideas."

Larson made her way to the woman's side. "Do you want to talk about it?"

"No." Sarah gathered up the dirty rags. "I'll watch the clinic for you. It will be better when Santino leaves for school."

Shocked by Sarah's response, Larson could only stare at her friend. "Is there something you should tell me?"

"I . . . I can't."

Sarah knows. Fear grappled with every inch of her. "Don't

293

keep anything from me that I ought to know."

The older woman stiffened, turned, and left the clinic.

Larson clenched her fists to gain control. She swallowed the knot in her throat. Her vision blurred. Santino had lied, and Sarah knew about his deceit and maybe more. Why?

I need to get Thomas out of here. Adrenaline gushed through her veins. She reached into the refrigerator for four bottles and set them on the counter. A full case of water sat in a corner by Paul's computer. She needed diapers, wipes, formula, and something for her to eat. A change of clothes.

"Are you going someplace? I thought you wanted to spend some time with the baby."

Larson whirled around to see Sarah.

"Take me with you, Larson. Don't leave me here."

❖ ❖ ❖

Ben wondered if he dared to count how many times in the past three months Larson had been in danger. At least she would be safe in Nairobi. But what about now with Santino? She needed to stay in Kenya. Enough was enough.

Since the change in pain medication, he didn't feel the jostling in the truck as badly, which helped his otherwise dour mood. An elevation in his energy level convinced him the meds were working.

But Santino? *How stupid could I have been?* He'd cleverly deceived all of them with his charm and good manners. Had he changed, or had everything been a lie from the beginning? He'd followed Ben into battle and killed enemy soldiers— probably his own allies. Did he have no respect for life as long as the infidels were destroyed too?

Ben pounded his palm against the steering wheel. Fury soared at the man he'd trusted. Santino must have set Muti free. He was startled. Santino was with Ben the day Muti had abducted Larson, but the young man had not shot either of the two men killed in the rescue.

Could Santino's treachery be part of a strategy orchestrated by Paul's family or the government? Ben tried to shake off the feeling that before the night was over, they'd learn the truth—hopefully, not at the cost of Paul's and Larson's lives.

THIRTY

"You knew." Larson trembled. Sarah's betrayal cut deep.

Sarah wrung her hands. Her eyes filled with tears. "I didn't want to believe it was true. I hoped what I heard was a mistake." She glanced around the clinic. "I'm so sorry. I don't think he suspects me—I mean, of knowing he is so evil. Let me go with you, please."

Larson heard the fear and the remorse. In Dinka culture, it was an act of cowardice to apologize, and there wasn't a word in their language for *please*, but Sarah had said the words in English. "All right. We'll discuss this later. Take the phone and the keys. I'll be right behind you with Thomas."

Sarah snatched up the items and a packet of diapers and hurried out the door.

What has happened here? Those I loved and trusted have deceived me. Larson dropped Thomas's bottles into an insulated container, along with a change of clothes and four bottles of water. Hoisting the bag onto her shoulder, she lifted her baby into her arms.

She was finished with running. This was the last time she'd run with her baby. Tomorrow she'd leave Sudan. She and Paul had their problems of late—most of them had to do with their relationship to God—but later those things would be resolved. After this was over.

Suddenly an explosion ripped through the air and crowded out her thoughts. Larson gasped and rushed to the door. The Hummer had burst into a heap of flames.

"Sarah! Oh, God, no."

She hurried with Thomas toward the body of the woman she loved as much as her own mother. Sarah had been tossed several feet from the burning Hummer, into the side of a *tukul*. Blood coated her body. One arm had been severed, and half of her face had been blown away. A crowd gathered. Screams and cries pierced Larson's ears.

She bent down to the dear woman, holding Thomas to her heart. "I'm so sorry, Sarah. I love you." Her friend had died because of her. *This was meant for me.*

"Dr. Farid, can you help her?" a man asked.

She shook her head. "Sarah's with Jesus now."

Dear, sweet Sarah. The one woman who knew Larson better than she knew herself. The dear woman who had prayed for her until she'd found Jesus. The dear woman who had told her it was okay to marry Paul, and that Ben would find someone else. The dear woman who had held Larson's head when she vomited with the pregnancy. The dear woman who spent hours helping Larson at the clinic. The dear woman who had been betrayed—just as Larson, Paul, and Ben had been betrayed.

Oh, Jesus, I loved her so. I know You are holding her in Your arms now. Please tell her how very much she will be missed.

Only the death of her beloved husband or baby could be worse. Sobs tore through her body, and she buried her face in Thomas's chest. How close she'd come to handing her tiny son to Sarah.

Suddenly the reality of the situation pushed away the anguish, and survival took precedence. Sarah had the phone when the Hummer exploded. Larson could not contact Paul or Ben. She was on her own.

She lifted her face, conscious of someone's arms supporting her.

"I can't believe Aunt Sarah is gone." Santino's voice quivered. "I'll take care of her body. Perhaps we can find Bishop Malou to conduct her funeral."

Larson stiffened. *I can't let him know.*

Every inch of her wanted to lay Thomas on the ground and scratch out the eyes of this man who pretended comfort, but then she'd be dead too. Raw emotions clawed at her heart. She had to outwit Santino. She had to make him believe that Sarah had gone to her death with his secret.

"I loved her so much." Larson swallowed the bile rising in her throat over what she must do. She turned her head and sobbed into Santino's murderous chest.

"I'll find out who killed her." He gripped her shoulders. "Muti had a hand in this, I'm sure."

"Paul and Ben will make him pay."

"You need to call them. You're in a dangerous situation."

Larson paused. Dare she tell him the truth? "I can't call either of them. Sarah had the phone with her."

Santino moaned. "Come on. Let me get you back to the clinic. I wonder where Colonel Alier's other two men are?"

Larson feared they had met their fate too. Thomas began to cry, not a soft whimper but a wail, as though he sensed the danger.

"I must take care of him."

"Go ahead and let me remove Sarah's body. It will help my grief."

You liar. You filthy, lying murderer. Are you insane?

Insanity she could have handled, but the realization that Santino was acting upon a well-thought-out plan seized her with terror.

He reached for Thomas.

"No, Santino. I'll carry my son. I need him close to me."

"I understand."

"Your taking care of Sarah will help me." She drew in a sharp breath. "I need time alone."

He nodded, and she made her way to the clinic. Reality rooted in the pit of her stomach. Santino had failed in killing her, but he had succeeded in separating her from help. What did he plan next? She had no means of contacting Paul or Ben. No way to alert them. No transportation. Only her pistol in the medicine cabinet.

The moment she stepped inside the clinic, she laid Thomas in his cradle, propped a bottle in his mouth, and lifted the insulated bag from her shoulders to the concrete floor. She made her way to the drawer that contained the medicine cabinet keys. Her fingers reached to the back portion of the drawer under clean rags and touched them. Relieved, she drew them out. With trembling fingers she unlocked the cabinet.

Her pistol was gone, and so was Paul's hunting knife.

Larson took a deep breath to steady her wobbly knees. *I cannot panic.* Inside the medicine cabinet were her surgical instruments . . . sharp ones that she could use as weapons. In the next instant, she wrapped the instruments in a clean cloth and placed them inside the insulated bag.

Thomas broke into a cry, and she picked him up, along with the bottle that had slipped from his mouth. She sat on the concrete floor and cradled him. Would Santino be able to tolerate a crying baby? He hadn't said anything before. *Think. I have to think. Jesus, help us.*

Her greatest fear entered the clinic and bent down beside her. He had her rifle slung over his shoulder. He surely had her pistol and Paul's knife as well.

"It's as though he knows Sarah is gone."

Larson swallowed. "Yes, Santino. I think so."

"I need to get you out of Warkou. It's not safe. The soldiers are dead."

"Where would we go?"

"I have an idea—a place where Muti could not find you."

Santino leaned in closer. "If the villagers tried to hide you, Muti would kill them all. We must go quickly."

He was right. She had no choice. Enough people had died. Larson stood. "I need ten minutes to gather up a few things."

"Make it five, and I'll help."

"Thank you. I need to leave Paul a note."

"Only if you can hide it."

She nodded. What choice did she have?

❖ ❖ ❖

A mixture of anxiety and dread simmered inside Paul as though a demon stirred an evil concoction. He couldn't fly home fast enough, and yet he must maintain safety standards.

Finally he saw Warkou in the distance as evening shadows fell upon the familiar scenery. He envisioned holding Larson, capturing her blue gaze with unspoken words of his love. Loving little Thomas had been easy, and Paul looked forward to holding his son and kissing his little face.

A trail of smoke snagged his attention. He peered into the distance. A fire?

Paul flew in closer. Black smoke rose from where the Hummer normally sat. What had happened? None of the villagers were in sight. He willed his heart to stay inside his chest while his stomach twisted. Larson would be there to greet him. He had to believe Santino hadn't been part of a plot to hurt his wife and son.

Ben's truck was parked at the other end of the village. Surely he had answers. Had there been a firefight?

After landing the plane, Paul grabbed his pistol and raced toward the clinic. He smelled rubber burning. The wails of far too many people pierced his ears. Not Larson. Not Thomas. Panic thundered throughout his body. *Dear God, don't let it be them.*

301

"Larson. Where are you?"

A man stepped from a *tukul*, a man whom Paul knew well. "Larson and the baby are not here."

"Where are they, Gabriel?"

The elderly man placed a hand on Paul's shoulder. "Terrible explosion happened. Sarah was killed. Santino took your wife and child to safety."

Sarah gone? "Do you know where?"

"No. He said that to tell us meant we might be killed too."

Paul raced toward the clinic. Ben might know where to find his family. He found his friend alone and standing in the middle of an empty clinic.

"Do you know how to find Larson and Thomas?" Paul fought to control the terror snaking its way through his senses.

"I arrived just before I heard your plane circling in for a landing. All I know is the Hummer exploded, and Sarah was killed. One of the villagers said Santino took Larson and Thomas."

"Why would she leave with him?"

"Maybe she had no choice. My men are dead."

"She might have left a note." Paul opened the refrigerator and moved aside the various refrigerated medicines on the second shelf to locate a flat box containing a dozen small boxes of typhoid pills. If she'd left a message for him, it would be taped on the underside of that box. He felt the edges for a piece of paper and nearly shouted when he realized something was there for him. Carefully loosening the tape from the box, he unfolded the note.

Paul,

By now you know Sarah was killed when the Hummer exploded. I'm sure the bomb was meant for me. She had the phone with her when the Hummer went up in flames, so I have no way to contact you. Santino believes the villagers are in danger if I stay, so I'm taking Thomas and leaving with him for a place where he says we'll be safe. I have no idea where we are going.

I love you.

Larson

Paul handed the note to Ben. While his friend read it, Paul pulled the medicine cabinet keys from the cloth drawer. "The pistol and my knife are gone," Paul said. "I hope she has them. She kept the rifle locked in the Hummer."

Ben swore. "If Santino was smart enough to plan all this and deceive us in the process, do you think he'd overlook where the weapons are kept?"

Paul shook his head. "I'm scared, Ben. Santino and Muti must be working together, which means my brother is in on this too."

Ben headed for the doorway. "They had to leave a trail. Bring a couple of flashlights, and let's find them. One of the villagers found my men's bodies. So it's just you and me. I have more ammo and two rifles in the truck. On the way, I'll call Okuk for backup, but they'll be on foot. The other truck won't start."

"That is probably what Santino wants us to do."

Ben turned and frowned. "We're smarter than he is—or his comrades."

And we have God on our side.

❖ ❖ ❖

Ben knew he had more sense right now than Paul did. The man was thinking with his heart—not his head. And if Ben wasn't careful, he'd allow his own emotions to overrule his logic. Although night settled quickly around them, Santino and Larson's trail was easy to follow. Too easy.

Three different people had gotten the best of them: Santino, Muti, and most likely that snake named Nizam. Who else walked a crooked trail?

"We're walking into a trap," Paul said. "I can feel it."

"Me too. But I want to get a little closer before we divert our steps."

"Do you have any idea where Santino might have taken her?"

Ben wished he did know. "No. I thought I knew Santino. He did everything he was told. Got along with the rest of the men. I've seen him risk his neck when we were in tight situations. I feel like a stupid fool. The man never gave a hint of betrayal."

"Makes me wonder if there's a reason why he didn't enroll in school and lied about having a job. Do you think we've made a mistake, and he's really taking care of Larson and Thomas?"

"There's only one way to find out, and that is to find them."

Already Ben felt the strains of his illness and fatigue. But he'd help Paul find Larson if he died trying.

THIRTY-ONE

———— ✦ ————

Larson sat on a fallen log with Thomas in her arms. The thought of a snake crawling up beside her had crossed her mind more than once, but she already had one deadly reptile keeping her company. She had no idea where Santino had led them in the dark, but she thought it was northeast. The night sounds rising around her created a cacophony that pounded in her ears as though preying animals stalked closer. But she was not nearly as afraid of them as she was of Santino.

"I'm going to scout around." He adjusted the rifle slung over his shoulder—the one he'd stolen from her. "If someone is trailing us, then I want to know who. Please rest as much as you can."

"I need a weapon while you're gone."

"Yes, you do." He reached inside his shirt and pulled out her 9 mm and laid it beside her. "I wish all of this wasn't necessary, but I couldn't risk your life."

She wanted to ask him why he'd stolen her pistol, but angering him made no sense. Just when she wanted to believe he was not a traitor, something else happened. At the present, she was all right. Whatever his plans, surely she'd learn them soon.

"I'd like to think Paul followed us." She stared up into his face in hopes of seeing a hint of his true character. Truth meant more to her at this point than speculation. "He'll have learned what happened and hurried after us."

"Probably so, and a good reason for you to rest."

Were her husband and Ben walking into a trap?

"He might have been caught in a firefight. But we've walked several miles, and I haven't heard gunfire."

She hadn't either. That was good. Or was she lying to herself?

"If not for the animals, I'd douse the fire." Santino sighed. "I'm not sure what is worse, the two-legged or four-legged predators."

If only I could believe you. "How will I know if you find Paul?" She would not tell Santino that Ben might be with her husband.

"I'll shout out to you. Otherwise, get free of this clearing."

She nodded and glanced at her sleeping Thomas. The insulated bag held four full bottles and her surgical instruments. She wouldn't hesitate to defend herself and her son.

Moments later, Santino disappeared, and she seized the opportunity to check the pistol. Empty. No surprise. She was so tired, sick with worry, and in desperate need to relieve herself. She touched her slightly expanding stomach. Her clothes were starting to feel a little snug. Would she and her family live beyond the next few hours?

The small fire provided a little light and kept the lions and hyenas away. Santino had piled a few branches beside her to dry out and feed the flames. Why did he continue in his attentiveness? Did he enjoy his ruse? Again she wondered if Santino was insane.

Paul, I need you.

You only need Me.

The voice of God whispered, and for the first time since the whole ordeal had begun—the Hummer exploding, Sarah's death—she sensed an unexplainable peace. She rocked the sleeping Thomas in her arms. The brightly colored scarf that had held him to her back when they walked was now wrapped around his tiny body.

The evening had brought cooler temperatures, but the air around her seemed to stifle her breathing. Or perhaps her own emotions threatened to cut off her air supply. She heard a rustling in the trees and caught her breath. Wrapping her fingers tighter around the empty pistol and clutching Thomas close to her breast, she peered in the direction of the sound. The fire had dimmed, but it still cast enough light to silhouette her features. Then again, a lion or hyena didn't need light to find its prey.

The figure of a man slipped into her view on the left.

❖ ❖ ❖

Paul hesitated to call out to Larson until he was certain she and Thomas were alone. Why had Santino disappeared and deserted them? Paul shoved aside his fear of walking into a trap.

She aimed her pistol straight at him. "Don't move, or you're a dead man."

"*Habibi*, it's me and Ben."

Her arm fell limp at her side. She stood from a log with Thomas in her arms and made her way toward him. "Oh, Paul. I never thought I'd see you again."

He gathered her up into his arms. "I'm here now. How are you?" In the shadows he searched her face to make sure she wasn't hurt.

"I'm fine, and Thomas is sleeping." She inhaled deeply and leaned into his embrace. "We have to get away while Santino is out scouting around."

"Then he has betrayed us."

"Yes, I have proof. And Sarah knew too."

"Is he alone?"

"I haven't seen or heard anyone else."

"Has he indicated his intentions?"

"Only his commitment to our safety. Every word from his mouth, every breath, professes his concern for me."

"I don't understand him, but all indications prove his treachery."

Ben stepped into the clearing. "I hope we're wrong. But I think the truth is about to surface. What went on this afternoon with the Hummer—"

"And Sarah." She nearly choked on the words, and Paul tightened his hold on her.

"I'm sorry, Larson." Exhaustion tipped Ben's words. "I complained about her, but she was a strong woman who did have my respect."

"Someone went to a lot of trouble to blow up the Hummer with the idea that I'd be the one to open the door. Now that I've escaped, I doubt if they're finished with me—or us."

Paul fought the fury threading its way through his body. "Let's get you out of here."

"Home?" she asked.

"Not yet." Paul kissed her forehead, and she shivered. "Ben's men won't be here until sunrise. A skirmish has their attention." No doubt another diversion for Santino's benefit. He glanced at his friend. "Where do we go?"

"I have a truck hidden about a mile from the village." Ben turned to Paul. "You could take her to Yar to stay with Daruka and David. She'd be safe until this is over."

"That sounds like a good plan." Paul glanced toward the fire and spotted the insulated baby bag. He lifted it to his shoulders.

"I have a better one." Santino stepped into the clearing with a rifle aimed at them.

"What kind of a plan?" Ben moved toward the young man.

"Don't come any closer, Colonel Alier. You're surrounded."

Paul glanced about, making a thoughtful appraisal of the

situation. He sensed there were others behind them, but those suspicions could be his own fears.

"I think you're lying," Ben sneered. "That seems to be your strongest trait."

The brush crunched under the boots of several men with rifles as they emerged from the shadows. Definitely not SPLA.

"As I said, drop your guns." Santino waved his rifle. "I won't hesitate to shoot any of you—the baby first, then the good doctor."

Paul and Ben slowly bent and laid their weapons on the ground. One of Santino's men snatched up Larson's pistol from near the log where she'd sat.

"Is this what you really want?" Paul stood between Santino and Larson. "Is whatever you were promised worth betraying those who befriended and cared for you?"

Santino laughed. "I've done this before, and I'll do it again. Get walking."

"Where are we going?" Ben asked.

"Back to Warkou, where someone is waiting to see all of you."

"Muti or Nizam?" Paul clenched his fists. *Does Santino know Ben's men are on their way to the village?*

"Both." Santino motioned with the rifle. "I have done what I set out to do. I have all four of you to deliver to Nizam. I'm a rich man."

Paul felt Larson's body trembling against his. "You blew up the Hummer and killed Sarah?" she asked.

"She got in my way. But you already know that bomb was for you."

Paul took a step forward, but Larson stopped him. "Don't give him an excuse to shoot you," she whispered.

The sound of her voice helped, but he couldn't stop the throbbing desire to wrap his hands around Santino's murderous throat. They had trusted him, when all the while he'd been plotting their deaths.

"Let's go." Santino's voice edged above the night sounds. "And in case either of you men have any heroic thoughts, the baby and Larson will go ahead of you to ensure your good behavior."

Paul had no reason to doubt him. He'd already seen what Santino could do. One of the men grabbed Larson from Paul's grasp. It took all of his strength not to turn and fight. But Santino had meant what he said.

❖ ❖ ❖

Ben tromped over the narrow path that led back to Warkou. Santino kept them at a fast pace. Whatever awaited them must occur before the sun rose. No one was permitted to talk, but the silence provided an opportunity for him and Paul to figure out how to get out of this mess. Their captors needed to be delayed, but how? Familiar landscapes came and went, every step bringing them closer to the village.

He swung a glance to check on Paul. No sooner had his head turned than one of Santino's men knocked him to the ground and kicked his side. He moaned, not from the sharp jab to his ribs but from the pain in his back.

"Keep your eyes ahead," the man said in Arabic.

"Can I help him?" Paul asked.

A moment later Paul's hand reached down to pull him to his feet. A good friend was hard to find, and Ben realized that Paul would go to his grave helping others. He deserved Larson—tough as it was to admit.

Daruka and David. Suddenly Ben wanted to live for his wife and son. During the short while he'd been married to Daruka, a trace of love had started to grow in him. Lately he'd recognized the warmth that spread throughout him whenever he saw her or heard her voice. She loved him completely, and although guilt assaulted him for the way he couldn't return her love with the same fervor, he did care for her very much. She'd raised their son with the same enthusiasm and vitality for life with which she woke each morning and greeted the day. David had learned much from her guidance and gentle ways. He looked like Ben, but he possessed his mother's heart. And now she carried another child.

The desire for life filled Ben with the strength to fight off the pain and outthink the jackal who held them captive. More so, he was ready to give his life for those he loved. Cancer was gaining ground on his numbered days. Let him die a hero's death for things that had purpose: his family, his friends, his country.

Miles from the captives, Rhino Battalion battled more opposition. Once the firefight was over, they'd move toward Warkou. Okuk led them. His orders were to surround the village and be prepared in case Paul's meeting with Nizam turned out to be a trap. Santino had taken Ben's and Paul's phones and turned them off, making it impossible for Okuk to call for verification or an update. But Okuk was a smart man. Perhaps he'd figure it all out.

From the direction of voices and the rustlings around them, Ben had counted six men besides Santino. Even with their hands free, Paul and Ben had no weapons. If Larson hadn't been with them, Ben would have initiated a diversion so Paul could get away. But Santino had threatened to kill Larson and the baby first, and he'd keep his word.

THIRTY-TWO

Larson watched Santino transform into a man she had never seen. He issued orders and knew each of his men by name. Those beneath him did not hesitate to follow his leading. What had happened to the young man who'd professed his alliance to southern Sudan and wished to obtain a college education? This stranger before her had scrubbed the clinic and filed patient records. He'd even fed Thomas and affectionately treated Sarah as an aunt. Now he'd killed and was ready to kill again. Is this what money and power did to a man?

His treachery squeezed at her heart and burned in her throat. She'd loved Santino like a brother and thought he cared for her and others. An awareness of her naiveté washed over her and brewed a caldron of fury. Snippets of past conversations, laughter, and intense work in the clinic dripped into the boiling pot.

Santino had deceived them all in the name of his faith. How many times had she asked him to explain his beliefs, thinking he still held on to tribal gods? Instead he followed Muslim extremists who encouraged him to lie to the infidels for Allah's sake. And he'd done that quite well.

Each step she took in the darkness fueled her anger, yet fear for the lives of her dear ones kept her swallowing one retort after another. She would gladly sink a knife into Santino's blackened heart. He deserved a torturous death for all he'd done.

She gasped at the hate in her own thoughts. She'd sworn an oath to save lives, not to end them. More importantly, she had committed her life to God by acknowledging what Christ had done on the cross for her wretched soul. Who was she to judge and condemn Santino?

Larson recalled the Bible's instructions to pray for those who persecuted believers. If she died tonight, she'd be in the presence of Jesus. If Santino died this night, he'd never know the blessings of heaven. From that realization alone, pity crept into her heart for Santino and all those who followed false gods.

Stinging tears flowed from her eyes. Surely not all of the good she'd seen in Santino was false. God could still reach him. Couldn't He?

God, help me here. I'm afraid, but I'm trusting You to save us from these men. I don't want to meet You with a heart full of hate and revenge. I can't bring myself to forgive Santino. Yet I must.

She swallowed hard and fought for self-control. Up ahead a faint light indicated they were nearing Warkou. As she plodded onward, she saw that the light came from her clinic. Who was there? Could it be Ben's men ready to set them free? She prayed so.

❖ ❖ ❖

Paul recognized the familiar trail winding back to Warkou. Would Nizam have a plane waiting to take them to Khartoum? The thought sat like acid in his stomach, not for him but for those he loved. Memories of the ghost houses loomed over him. He'd do anything to prevent Larson and Ben's being tortured. A glimmer of hope led him to believe that Thomas's life would be spared, even if it meant he would be raised Muslim.

"Santino, will you tell me what is going on? I see we're nearly to Warkou."

The man swung around and laughed. "Does it matter? Did you and your wife think that the government would do nothing while you aided the South? Missionary teams come and go with their few days of good deeds, but you are a stench to your family. No, I will not tell you what's ahead."

"Take me and let the others go. I'm the one you want anyway."

"I have my orders. No more talking."

"These people are—"

Santino stopped and threw a punch into Paul's stomach. The impact doubled him over, and he stumbled to keep from losing his balance. Santino grabbed him by the neck and jerked him to his feet. Larson cried out.

"I said to keep quiet." Santino tightened his hold on Paul's throat. "One more word, and I'll slice up your wife and the baby."

Paul's breath came in short gasps. He nodded. What else could he do?

Father, deliver my wife and child. Keep Ben from the hands of these men. I confess that I have been angry with You. Please forgive me.

❖   ❖   ❖

Ben studied the area around him while the small band made its way into Warkou. Most likely the village guards had been killed along with his two men. Santino had considered every detail to this point. Now to figure out what lay ahead for the rest of the night.

Together Nizam, Muti, and Santino had plotted the course of events during the past several months. Why hadn't one of them killed Paul when he was alone instead of creating this elaborate scheme? Plenty of opportunities had arisen in which they actually had him in their clutches. Most of this situation didn't make sense, and Ben could not grasp their motivation. But he did know that he would try to overtake his captors at the first opportunity.

A pocketknife lay inside his right boot. In the dark, he could easily pull it out, but he needed one of the men to knock him down first. He should have thought to pull it out the first time he'd been knocked to the ground.

"This is a bunch of crap, Santino. Looks to me like you have no idea what you're doing."

The butt end of a rifle cracked across the back of his head. Ben fought the dizziness and allowed himself to sink into the soft earth. He yanked on the knife and slid it under his shirtsleeve. Fighting the pain in his skull, he forced himself to rise to his feet.

Ben battled the grinding pain in his back and head during the remaining trek into Warkou. The knife rested against his flesh, ready for him to use.

Santino's men shoved Paul, Larson, and Ben through the clinic door, and it closed behind them. Larson nearly fell with the baby, but Paul caught her. Nizam and Muti were seated on a bench in the waiting area. Ben immediately recognized Nizam from the time he'd visited the hospital.

"Santino, what a fine job you've done here." Nizam stood. "We have them all, just as you claimed. This is perfect, well worth the wait. Your loyalty to the government will make you a wealthy man." He nodded at the guards. "Make sure the men have their hands tied." As two men forced Ben's hands behind his back, they discovered his knife and seized it.

Nizam chuckled and turned toward Paul. "Brother, I don't hear a warm greeting from you."

"Why don't you tell me what this is all about?" Paul's low voice sounded amazingly calm. "How did you get here?"

"It's very simple. I flew in while Santino had you out looking for your wife. I have what I want: you, your lovely wife, Colonel Alier, and—" He gestured to one of the closed doors leading to the examining rooms. "Muti, bring out our other guests."

Muti grinned and opened the door, pushing Daruka and David into the room with the other captives. White-hot fury welled in Ben's body, and he struggled to free his arms. In the dim light, Ben saw dried blood on David's face and a bruise on Daruka's cheek that circled above her eye. Her gaze flew to his, and for the first time he knew for certain that he loved her.

"I'll kill you for this." Ben wrestled with the bindings on his hands, but one of the men jabbed a rifle into his chest. "You touch my wife and son again, and you will pay."

"How, Colonel? Looks like we have the weapons. I've wanted you for a long time. Your death will cripple the southern armies." Nizam faced Paul. "You are a fool and will die a fool's death, but not before you watch your friends and family die."

"My men are due here anytime," Ben said.

"Not before dawn, and we have a long time until then."

Ben stared silently into his wife's eyes, willing her to understand that he loved her. She'd die because he had tricked her into marrying him. And David . . . his son would face an agonizing death. Both would lose their lives because of his deceit.

THIRTY-THREE

Paul wanted to believe Nizam would not give in to the evil he'd planned. They'd been close as boys. Their relationship couldn't have changed so drastically that Nizam would refuse to listen to reason. Yet Paul understood the teachings of Islam.

"I'm the target here," Paul said. "Let's board your plane and get out of here."

"Oh, we will." Nizam walked to Larson and lifted her chin. "Such a pretty woman. Too bad."

Alarm seized every part of Paul. "She has nothing to do with you and me."

Nizam focused on him. "I have nothing to say to you." He nodded at Muti and Santino. "Take Mrs. Farid, the baby, and the colonel's family to Abdullah's *tukul*. Tie them up. I'll be there shortly."

Paul's pulse raced. "Please, I'm begging. Do not harm them."

"You'll do more than beg before I'm finished." Nizam looked down his nose. "You'll go to your grave listening to the sound of their screams and smelling their flesh burn."

"You animal." Ben struggled against the ropes binding him. "You'll pay for this."

Nizam laughed. "No, you will pay for every day you

ordered men to fight against the government."

Paul swallowed hard. He had to stall. "Nizam, the SPLA will not let this go without retaliation. You're planning the death of a respected officer, his family, and a world-renowned doctor because of what? Pride? Religion?"

"The international community will get over it. You and I both know Darfur has their attention. This will be nothing more than a CNN crawl."

The knowledge of his own idiocy ripped through Paul's mind. How could he have been so blind? He'd fought his doubts since Nizam had first suggested a meeting. Paul should have forced Larson to leave Sudan. He should have gone himself. He should have . . . Now he was helpless to stop whatever his brother had planned for all of them.

God, please. "Let's talk about this."

"I'm finished talking," Nizam said. "Take these two outside so they can watch."

Paul planted his feet firmly on the concrete floor as though his efforts would stop the inevitable, but he was powerless against those dragging him outside. "Don't do this. It solves nothing. I'm the one you want."

But Nizam kept on walking toward the *tukul*, behind a man with a fiery torch.

Paul whipped his attention to Ben. Huge tears flowed down his friend's face. "If you've ever thought about calling out to God, now is the time."

"God? Where is God in this?"

"He's all we have, Ben."

❖ ❖ ❖

Larson viewed Thomas's peaceful slumber on the floor beside her as a blessing. Perhaps God would take her baby soon, and he wouldn't suffer. She glanced down at her stomach: the child she'd see in heaven. She'd heard Nizam's order to set the hut on fire with her, Thomas, Daruka, and David inside. How unspeakable for Paul and Ben. Sickening dread crept over her at what this must be doing to them. She'd shut Paul out of her life so much over the past several weeks. Ever since she'd learned about Nizam's wanting to see him, she'd begun to build a wall around her heart. She might never have an opportunity to apologize. *Lord, forgive my selfish heart.*

Nizam walked in, shoulders erect, reminding her of a man ready to conduct a business meeting. Perhaps for him, this was all their murders meant. But she couldn't give up. As long as there was life in her, she had to believe they would not be killed.

She stared into Nizam's dark eyes and shuddered at the resemblance between him and Paul. "Tell me, how will you live with yourself once you've killed innocent women and children?"

"I will have my reward in paradise." He knelt in front of her as though he was interested in what she had to say. "This means nothing to me. My duty is to kill the infidel."

"And what if you are wrong, and Paul and I are right?"

"Muhammad says differently."

"What do you say, Nizam? What does your heart say?"

A flash of anger swept across his face. "There is no God but Allah."

"I think you're fighting the truth."

He swung around to a man who held the torch. "Leave us. I'll light the fire."

Larson studied the man before her. She was afraid of his power, but something stronger than fear told her to continue. "I know you've read parts of the Bible because you talked about Barnabas. And I think you have a better understanding of Jesus than what your faith avails you."

"Do you think your talking is going to change my mind?" He stood and paced in front of her.

Larson glanced at Daruka and David. They were praying;

she could feel it. "I think you know enough about Christianity to doubt what you are doing."

"What does a woman know?"

"Tell me you didn't read more of the Bible."

Nizam's cold stare bore into hers. "I read enough to know you're wrong."

"You read enough to know I'm right. Think about it. You and Paul grew up together. He became a Christian, forsaking his family and power to follow Jesus. You were curious enough to find out what had persuaded him. You—"

"Enough." Nizam touched the torch to the roof and sides of the *tukul*.

Larson watched him disappear into the night. The crackle of fire met her ears. In an instant, flames lapped at the small hut. The smoke from the burning thatch filled her nostrils. "Daruka, David, you know we will see Jesus soon."

Daruka's sobs met her ears. "Poor Ben. How terrible this is for him."

"I pray God will comfort Father and Paul." David nearly choked on his words.

Oh, Paul, please remember how very much I love you. She longed to touch the smooth skin of her precious son. *Dear God, I feel so forsaken.*

Heaven. Before dawn lit the sky, they'd all be with Jesus.

❖ ❖ ❖

"Nizam, how can you do this?" Paul screamed into the night. His jaw tightened. His body stiffened. Several yards away, Nizam swung the torch high in the air as a sign of victory. Paul twisted at the ropes around his wrists, but men on both sides held him tight.

The thatched roof ignited, flames lifting demonlike fingers into the sky.

"Nizam, I beg of you, don't murder innocent people."

Ben said something, but Paul couldn't bear to tear his eyes from the burning *tukul*. The memory of how he'd once served the crescent moon haunted him. Now he served the cross, but where was God while his family burned alive?

"Kill me now. Let me die with my wife and child." Paul's words lifted into the night air. How could he go on without them? *Please, God, I was wrong not to trust You to take care of us. Is it too late?*

A few villagers awakened by the fire stepped from their homes, but Nizam's men stopped them.

Paul's throat stung with his pleas. How could God allow this? Perhaps he'd never know why. He was a God of love, not hatred and evil. But even though Paul didn't understand why his family and friends were about to be killed, he had to believe God was in control—His purposes were good and right. "God, I do trust You now, no matter what happens," he whispered hoarsely. "Help us, please."

Suddenly Nizam threw down the torch and stepped into the inferno. Paul held his breath. *What's happening?* All he could hear was the roar of the flames.

A woman's figure appeared in the doorway, carrying an infant. *Larson!* Then another woman and David. They stumbled away from the fire just as the *tukul* collapsed.

"Daruka!" Ben's voice echoed above the hissing fire. "David!"

They were free, but for how long? Where was Nizam?

In the east, the faint glow of dawn spread across the sky. Shots rang out, and the men guarding Ben and Paul fell, their blood soaking the ground. With his hands tied behind his back, Ben reached down and retrieved his knife from one of the dead men.

"Cut my ropes." Paul's voice graveled, a foreign sound to him. The need to get to Larson and Thomas left him trembling. "Hurry, Ben. Then I'll get yours."

Ben deftly freed Paul's hands. As soon as the ropes fell,

Paul grabbed the knife and slit Ben's bindings. He could see Larson, Daruka, and David lying on the ground while bullets whizzed around them. Thomas's frantic cries rose above the gunfire. They were sprawled out in the open with no place to seek shelter. A stray bullet—no, he refused to think about it.

Wordlessly, Ben and Paul snatched up the dead men's guns and crept toward their families. Within moments the firing ceased, and the Rhino Battalion emerged from behind *tukuls* and trees. Not one of Ben's men had been wounded. Not one of Nizam's men had survived.

Paul held his trembling wife. He didn't want to think of ever letting her go. So much to say, but the words refused to come. Her hair and clothes were singed, her eyebrows and eyelashes gone. The stench of smoke surrounded her, and she coughed incessantly. Yet she was alive. Had Paul told Larson how deeply he loved her? Perhaps the need in his soul had sent the silent message.

He stole a glance at Ben, who had enveloped his wife and son in his lean arms. Again, the big man wept. *How little a man values love until it threatens to leave him empty of its worth.*

"We have much to talk about," he heard Ben say to Daruka. "There are things I need to tell you."

"I probably already know." She touched his cheek. "If it is your cancer, I found out weeks ago, after you returned from Nairobi with more pills."

"How?"

"I took the bottles to David's teacher and asked her to find out what they were for." She coughed. "Please don't be angry."

"I think it's time for you to be angry with me. I'm sorry. I didn't know how to tell you. The doctor has given me a little hope, and after today, that means a lot. I have three reasons to live, and they have all to do with my family."

David stared back at the remains of the burning *tukul*. "I

think I have an idea what hell is like, and I don't ever want to forget it."

Ben nodded. "Maybe you need to share some of your faith with me."

Paul turned his attention to Larson, his mind assaulting him with unanswered questions. Exhaustion etched her face. He lifted Thomas from her arms and kissed his cheek. The baby's coughs disturbed Paul, but Larson would know what to do. Someday he'd tell his son about how God had delivered them all from the snares of death.

"Can you tell me what happened with Nizam?" he whispered.

"I'm not sure." She sucked in a breath and coughed again. "Not sure if we ever will know. I talked to him before he torched the *tukul*. I asked him about reading the Bible. And what was his heart telling him about God. I . . . I knew he'd read the Bible from the conversation we had some time ago." Tears streamed down her face, and he kissed her cheek. "He was angry, and that's when he started the fire. The flames . . . they were so hot. Just when we had given up, he came back, cut our ropes, and pushed us toward the doorway. I asked him why, but he didn't answer. He was the last one in the *tukul* and never made it out."

"I guess we'll never understand what happened."

"Do you think God reached him?"

Paul shook his head. "I don't know. But it no longer matters, because it's over."

She laid her head against his chest. A fresh spasm of coughing brought him back to the present.

"Ben, we need to get them to the clinic."

Ben led Daruka and David toward the concrete building. Paul hoisted Thomas to his shoulder and wrapped his arm around Larson's waist. "Let's get away from this. You've seen enough."

"Do you mean we're leaving Warkou?" she asked.

"Not Warkou. Not Sudan. God took care of us when we faced certain death, and I believe He will continue to protect us. I want this to be our home until He leads us somewhere else."

They made their way toward the clinic, still lit by the power of the generator, but no longer a scene of hatred and revenge.

She lifted her dirt- and tearstained face to his. "When I believed the end had come, I realized I'd pushed my feelings aside and had never fully apologized to you for all the times my anger came between us. I tried to think I could handle life alone if you were killed. But inside I was so scared. I believed courage was for me to shut out my heart to you. I'm so sorry."

"My *habibi*, we serve a mighty God. I had forgotten how powerful He is. I failed to trust Him and thought I could manage our lives alone. I kept trying to earn His favor and failing miserably. And I hid from you too many things. My recklessness nearly got you and those we love killed." He pressed his lips together. "Bishop Malou once accused me of trying to play God. Never again."

"So much death. Will southern Sudan ever rise above the years of war?"

"I hope so. I pray for the day when a Christian can travel back and forth peaceably between the North and the South, when the people of Darfur are no longer persecuted. When outsiders are not cautioned against entering our country. What the enemy refuses to acknowledge is the increasing amount of people the war has driven to Christ. Those who envision a reconciliation of all the tribes are calling out for God's help."

"I want unity for our people," Larson said. "And for our children."

He kissed her forehead. "We have a great love for each other and for Sudan. With God going before us, it can only be a matter of time before true peace exists. Can you imagine trained teachers? The villagers tilling gardens? Disease diminished? Clean drinking water? So much work is ahead, but I'm ready for it."

"It seems like a dream."

"Dreams of hope and freedom are what keep a man alive."

DISCUSSION QUESTIONS

1. Could you trust a man who had once persecuted your people?

2. Larson followed her husband into Darfur because she was afraid he might attempt to meet up with his family. Do you think that was a foolish venture? Why or why not?

3. Ben didn't want anyone to know about his cancer. What do you think was the real reason he wanted the information kept secret?

4. Do you think Larson should have left Sudan once she learned of her pregnancy?

5. How far would you go to reach unsaved family members?

6. Ben desperately wanted a relationship with his son. Did Ben learn anything from his pursuit?

7. Nizam indicated a sincere desire to learn about Christianity. Did you believe him?

8. Sarah went to her death with a terrible secret. How did you feel about her actions?

9. Santino lived two lives. When the book ended, what were your thoughts about him?

10. Nizam died saving the lives of Larson, Thomas, Daruka, and David. Why do you think he went back inside the fire?

11. Paul and Larson had issues of trust when the world around them seemed to crumble. What about you? Where do you turn when your world spins out of control?

I hope this book has encouraged you to help ease the plight of the Sudanese people. The following organizations provide aid to the Sudanese around the world.

Across
Head Office
PO Box 21033
00505 - Ngong Road
Nairobi
KENYA
www.across-sudan.org

Aid Sudan
7561 FM 1960 East #301
Humble, TX 77346
www.aidsudan.org

Christian Solidarity International USA
870 Hampshire Road, Suite T
Westlake Village, CA 91361
www.csi-int.org

SEA Partners
PMB118
1221 Flower Mound Road, Suite 320
Flower Mound, TX 75028

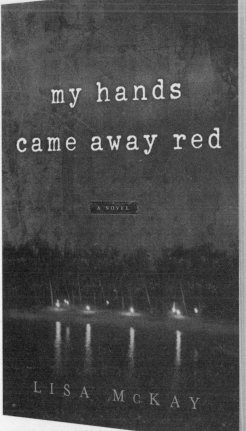

my hands
came away red

A NOVEL

LISA McKAY

ISBN-10: 0-8024-8982-6
ISBN-13: 978-0-8024-8982-1

"I thought you'd know on the day you died."
Unrealistic visions of a beach vacation compel teenaged Cori to leave her
complicated love-life behind to help build a church on a remote island in Indonesia.
Six weeks into the trip, a conflict that has been simmering for years flames to deadly
life on the nearby island of Ambon. Within days the church they helped build is a
smoldering pile of ashes, its pastor and many of the villagers dead, and the six
teenagers are forced to flee into the hazardous refuge of the mountains with only the
pastor's son to guide them.

by Lisa McKay

Find it now at your favorite local or online bookstore.

www.MoodyPublishers.com

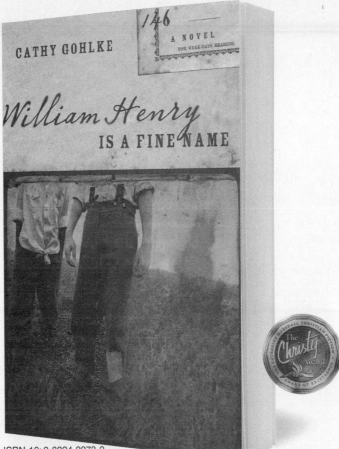

ISBN-10: 0-8024-9973-2
ISBN-13: 978-0-8024-9973-8

Colorblind.

They told him his best friend wasn't human. And the one thing he couldn't do was nothing at all. In the Pre-Civil War South, 13-year-old Robert's feelings of justice and loyalty have forced him to try and make sense of the surrounding chaos.

by Cathy Gohlke

Find it now at your favorite local or online bookstore.

www.MoodyPublishers.com